AN UNEXPECTED BETRAYAL

To Wolpert's surprise, a good portion of the anger in Burt's eyes faded away. He gazed wistfully at the stagecoaches, turned back to the men coming from the south and then looked at his gang. Some of them were struggling to get up, but most were crawling a few paces to dig in the dirt.

"You really mucked this up good for me, huh?"

"Yeah."

Burt squared his shoulders to Wolpert and took a few cautious steps back. "I ain't gonna run and I sure ain't gonna hand myself over to some double-crossin' backstabber like you."

"Didn't think so."

"Still, it's been good workin' with you."

Wolpert twitched at the earnestness in that remark. He hadn't seen it coming and didn't know what to say about it.

When Burt took his next step back, he dropped to one knee and drew his .44 in a smooth motion. . . .

Ralph Compton

Rusted Tin

A Ralph Compton Novel
by Marcus Galloway

A SIGNET BOOK

SIGNET
Published by New American Library, a division of
Penguin Group (USA) Inc., 375 Hudson Street,
New York, New York 10014, USA
Penguin Group (Canada), 90 Eglinton Avenue East, Suite 700, Toronto,
Ontario M4P 2Y3, Canada (a division of Pearson Penguin Canada Inc.)
Penguin Books Ltd., 80 Strand, London WC2R 0RL, England
Penguin Ireland, 25 St. Stephen's Green, Dublin 2,
Ireland (a division of Penguin Books Ltd.)
Penguin Group (Australia), 250 Camberwell Road, Camberwell, Victoria 3124,
Australia (a division of Pearson Australia Group Pty. Ltd.)
Penguin Books India Pvt. Ltd., 11 Community Centre, Panchsheel Park,
New Delhi - 110 017, India
Penguin Group (NZ), 67 Apollo Drive, Rosedale, North Shore 0632,
New Zealand (a division of Pearson New Zealand Ltd.)
Penguin Books (South Africa) (Pty.) Ltd., 24 Sturdee Avenue,
Rosebank, Johannesburg 2196, South Africa

Penguin Books Ltd., Registered Offices:
80 Strand, London WC2R 0RL, England

First published by Signet, an imprint of New American Library,
a division of Penguin Group (USA) Inc.

First Printing, September 2010
10 9 8 7 6 5 4 3 2 1

THE IMMORTAL COWBOY

This is respectfully dedicated to the "American Cowboy." His was the saga sparked by the turmoil that followed the Civil War, and the passing of more than a century has by no means diminished the flame.

True, the old days and the old ways are but treasured memories, and the old trails have grown dim with the ravages of time, but the spirit of the cowboy lives on.

In my travels—to Texas, Oklahoma, Kansas, Nebraska, Colorado, Wyoming, New Mexico, and Arizona—I always find something that reminds me of the Old West. While I am walking these plains and mountains for the first time, there is this feeling that a part of me is eternal, that I have known these old trails before. I believe it is the undying spirit of the frontier calling me, through the mind's eye, to step back into time. What is the appeal of the Old West of the American frontier?

It has been epitomized by some as the dark and bloody period in American history. Its heroes—Crockett, Bowie, Hickok, Earp—have been reviled and criticized. Yet the Old West lives on, larger than life.

It has become a symbol of freedom, when there was always another mountain to climb and another river to cross; when a dispute between two men was settled not with expensive lawyers, but with fists, knives, or guns. Barbaric? Maybe. But some things never change. When the cowboy rode into the pages of American history, he left behind a legacy that lives within the hearts of us all.

—*Ralph Compton*

Chapter 1

Sedley, Nebraska
1887

Some towns had long, proud histories. They sprouted up from gold rushes in distant hills or by the design of prosperous salesmen who'd banded together to fleece a particular stretch of an otherwise overlooked trail.

Some towns were carefully nurtured by a body of like-minded neighbors who simply admired the same view.

Sedley wasn't such a place. It was more of an afterthought populated by folks who didn't have the gumption needed to organize it into a proper community. Homes, a handful of saloons and a crop of various stores were clumped around a U-shaped street that didn't even have a name. One end was packed with shops ranging from a tailor's place to dry goods. From there, the street passed in front of some homes and curved to the east for a stretch before hooking north again, where it ended at a stable that rented its filthy stalls for a few cents more than they were worth and a livery that sold whatever horses its owners could find at something close to fair prices. At the middle of the street, like a bunch of slimy rocks that had settled to the bottom of a murky lake, was a pair of saloons. Both establishments had had names at one time, which had been painted onto signs that had become more appealing than a row of clay pigeons to the armed drunks who stumbled in and out of them at all hours of the day and night. With both signs shot to bits, the locals simply called the saloons "the First One" and "the Second One." Depending on which end of the street they lived on, folks switched the names as it suited them.

It was early winter, which meant the winds that ripped across the Nebraska terrain had acquired a steely edge that sliced through anything in its path. Buildings rattled and teeth chattered as the drafts made short work of whatever layers of clothing were wrapped around a body. Some might have complained about the harsh manner in which the elements pulled warm breath from a person's lungs, but such talk wouldn't come from those who made Sedley their home. They'd been stuck out in the prairies of western Nebraska for too long to think anyone would listen to their bellyaching.

Lucy Myles stood outside the livery her family had owned for the last year and a half. Dale and Matthew were nowhere to be found, but that wasn't unusual. Once the sun inched its way down instead of up, her two brothers were more likely to be spotted propped against a bar than lifting a finger to keep the Thrown Shoe Horse Sales and Livery in business. Although she was a pretty woman in her late twenties with a round face and long, dark hair, Lucy was no longer concerned with trying to appeal to any of the men in town. There were a few good apples in that batch, but the work of keeping her livery afloat, despite her brothers' willingness to let it sink, consumed too much of her day. It had been months since she'd put on the frilly blue dress she'd gotten a few birthdays ago. Tonight, like most every night, she covered herself with a thick shawl wrapped around her shoulders and heavy brown skirts that allowed dirt and manure to blend in to the hem. None of those garments stood up to the wind that stampeded in from the west.

Clutching her shawl a little tighter beneath her neck, she scowled in the direction of the First One Saloon. If she concentrated hard enough, she could just about pick out the sound of Dale's voice amid the chorus of bawdy laughter and off-key banjo plucking. This was his night to watch the place, but she didn't expect him to show his face where it belonged. If someone hadn't needed to be there to watch the new pair of spotted geldings that had arrived that afternoon, she would have left long ago.

"I swear to all above and below, I will skin you if you leave me here by myself," Lucy grumbled. Considering how often her brothers were absent and the selection of other companions that were available in Sedley, she'd become quite accustomed to talking to herself.

Someone staggered out through the saloon's batwing doors. Leaning forward as if that extra bit of closeness would help her pick out the details on the man's face, Lucy studied him for a few seconds and then leaned back again. "Damn it, Dale. Just buy the bottle and bring it here. All I need is a warm body to fill a chair. If there's one thing you can do right, it's sit."

She leaned against the post marking the corner of her lot. The saloons were still a ways off, but it was the best view she could get without leaving the livery unattended. Behind her was a patch of fenced-in ground that was just big enough for a team of horses to get some sun while they drank from a trough that was currently a quarter full of ice. The livery was bigger than the Myles homestead, which was at the back end of the cluster of nearby houses. While Lucy's eyes remained fixed on the saloon, her ears were alert for every little sound to come out of the structure behind her.

Hooves clomped against the floorboards.

Heavy, snuffing breaths were let out as the animals tried to keep warm.

Something creaked.

That last one caught her attention immediately. The wail of the hinge attached to the side door might as well have been a bell announcing the presence of a customer or lazy worker trying to sneak in and sneak back out again.

Twirling around while gathering her skirts, Lucy rushed around the fence line as quietly as she could. The leather of her boots was thin enough to make every step as subdued as if she were in bare feet. She knew right when to duck when passing a window and exactly when to hop to avoid getting tripped up by a rut or partially buried rock. By the time she'd circled around the livery, the side door's latch was just being eased into the bracket attached to the wall.

Lucy peeked in through the corner of a square window beside the door. Even though there was only one lantern in the livery casting its dull glow, she recognized the slender build and messy hair of her brother. He kept low as he approached the stalls along the opposite wall. Just past those stalls was the loose floorboard where the little iron strongbox was kept. Dale had probably forgotten to bring his money along for his drinking binge. The notion of other ways he might waste their small amount of income was enough to send her through the door and into the livery in a rush.

"Dale Abraham Myles," she bellowed while dropping a hand down onto the man's shoulder, "if you think you're sneaking back out just so you can go to that saloon, you're sorely mistaken!"

He straightened up and turned around as if trying to stay under her hand rather than shake it off. While his build and features were similar to her brother's, this man's face was different. Where Dale's mouth was all but covered by a scraggly mustache, this one's was a thin line drawn from one ear to another. Her brother had been fortunate enough to inherit his mother's little nose and took good care of it. This fellow's nose was slightly larger, but was crooked after having been broken on at least three separate occasions.

"Well, now," he sighed. "Ain't this a pleasant little surprise?"

Lucy pulled her hand away and stepped back. "Oh, excuse me. I mistook you for someone else."

Looking down at the spot where her hand had been, the man swiped his finger across his shoulder as if he was sampling icing from atop a cake. He passed his fingers under his nose and replied, "You can mistake me for anyone you like, darlin'."

"We're closing up," she said as she clasped her hands and placed her back against a post. "But if you need to rent a stall for the night, we can accommodate you."

"Don't need a stall."

"Then what brings you here?"

The man's narrow mouth hung open just enough to show the browned tips of his teeth. Light blue eyes flicked up and down her chest while his shoulders wriggled as if he was trying to get comfortable within his own skin. "Came for these horses."

She didn't need to take her eyes from him to know that the stall he'd approached was the one currently occupied by the two newly arrived geldings. "They're not for sale. We're holding those for someone else. Why don't you come back in the morning so I can show you some other ones?"

"These look plenty good to me," he said while staring directly at the curves of her breasts as if he could stare directly through all the layers of clothing encasing her. "How 'bout I take 'em off yer hands right now?"

"My brothers won't like that very much."

"Your brothers ain't here." Stepping toward her, he added, "Matt's losing his shirt in a card game over at the Second and Dale's getting his pole waxed at the First. If'n you take proper care of me with them pretty lips, I might be convinced to leave your stock alone."

The Myles brothers might not have been respected in town, but they were big enough to keep men like this one away from her. That is, if they were anywhere in sight. She kept a shotgun stashed near the front door, but that might as well have been at the saloon district as well.

"Take the horses if that's what you're after," she said.

"I already told you what I was after."

Inching toward the front door, she said, "My brothers will be back soon. That's why I thought you were one of them just a little bit ago."

"I suppose I'll just take my chances with that. Now get over here."

Lucy saw the gun at the man's side and summed up her odds of outrunning him or a bullet. Doing her best to stifle the tears burning at the corners of both eyes, she moved forward and clasped her hands even tighter in front of her.

"On yer knees."

Once she was close enough to smell the stink of the man's breath, she lowered her eyes, let her head hang low and even stooped her posture. Lucy gave every indication that she was following his command, without actually doing it. When she bent her knees slightly, the man assumed he was getting what he wanted and began unbuckling his belt. His eyes were partly closed in expectant contemplation, which allowed Lucy to get in the first punch.

Having grown up with two brothers, Lucy knew how to beat a man in a fight. Her fist thumped against the stranger's groin, doubling him over and forcing a pained, hacking breath up from the bottom of his gut. Before that breath was all the way out, she ran for the door.

Either this man was resistant to pain or was used to being rebuked by women, because he recovered from the blow quicker than Dale or Matt ever could. He grunted half an obscenity at her while forcing his body to move after her. Even though his legs were as wobbly as those of a newborn colt's, he managed to shamble fast enough to catch her with one flailing paw of a hand.

"Where you goin'?" he coughed.

It wasn't in Lucy's nature to scream. Instead, she kept her eyes set on her goal and tried to loosen the man's grip with a few quick backward kicks. The first couple only rustled her skirts, but the third drove her heel squarely into the man's shin.

He dropped to one knee, cursed some more, but held on. Tightening his grip around her arm, he looked up at her with a lurid grin and yanked her down to his level.

Lucy was only a few paces from the door, but turned away from it as if the escape route was ten miles away. She fell onto her side, caught herself with both hands and then rolled onto her back. The man stood over her and lowered himself to straddle her. The moment he reached to pull at the laces along the front of her dress, he was introduced to both heels of Lucy's well-worn boots. He winced as kicks landed on his chest and stomach, but he was wearing more than enough layers of clothing to absorb the impacts. Even so, her legs were just strong enough to keep him from getting much closer.

"All this fightin's got me worked up, darlin'. I can think of all kinds of ways for me to let off this kind of steam."

Waiting for him to come down a bit more, Lucy cocked back her right leg and put everything behind it to slam her heel into the man's face. She caught him just above the left eye, which snapped his head back and opened a nasty gash in his forehead. As soon as he staggered back, she pulled free and scrambled to her feet.

The man charged like a mad bull that was blinded by the blood that poured into his eye. He was blocking the way to the front door, so she pushed him into a post that ran all the way to the roof and tried to get by.

More foul language filled the livery. That, combined with the heavy sounds of struggle, caused the horses to shift uneasily in their stalls.

"You're only makin' this harder on yourself!" he snarled.

Lucy could make it to the side door in a quick series of running steps. It loomed in front of her like a gate to the Promised Land. If she could get to it, she'd be out of that livery.

Furiously wiping the blood from his face, the man rushed at her and spat. "There ain't no gettin' away from me!"

Even before those words were out, Lucy veered from the door. There was no salvation to be had through that passage. All that was on the other side of it was a cold night and a town full of drunks. She'd be either brought down before crossing her own fence or dragged to an alley somewhere a bit farther down the stretch. Either way, nobody would lift a finger on her behalf until it was too late. She grabbed on to the side of the closest stall and hauled herself up and over as quickly as her bulky clothing would allow.

Now that he was up and moving again, the man was quickly gaining steam. He remained hunkered over to protect his aching privates with as much of himself as he could. "That looks like a real good spot," he said. "Climb in and get settled. I'll be right there."

Lucy's fingers dug beneath the straw on the floor and scraped the boards beneath it. When the man pulled himself up over the low divider and into the stall, he found her huddled in the opposite corner.

That sight only widened his grin.

"Oh yeah," he grunted while using the back of his hand to wipe away the fresh layer of blood that coated his face like tribal war paint. "Ain't nothin' better than a little taste of sugar after all this hard work."

Lucy flopped onto her side and twisted around to lift the pitchfork she'd uncovered beneath all that straw. Gripping it with both hands, she jabbed the rusty tines straight out until she felt them catch in something solid. Even as the metal points stabbed him in the upper chest, the man didn't want to back off. Lucy pushed it in as deep as she could, but needed to lift the pitchfork up and out from her awkward position on the floor of the stall. She'd stuck him only a little, so she twisted the tool until she heard the man yelp.

He grabbed on to the pitchfork at the top of the wooden handle, forced it away and shredded a portion of his sleeve in the process. "It'll take more'n that to put me down, you stinkin' little—"

Before he could finish what was surely another unflattering comment, the man was taken down by a swift strike against his ankle. The instant she'd been able to pull the pitchfork away from him, Lucy used it to take his legs out from under him. On a clean floor, he might have been able to regain his footing. With all of the straw under him, however, it was a lost cause and his backside hit with a solid thump.

The man was chuckling to himself as he started to sit

up. When he tried to lift his head, he felt something sharp touch the middle of his throat.

"You'd best stay put, mister," Lucy warned him. "Or I may slip."

Keeping his head still, the man angled his eyes to get a look at what was holding him down. Even in the hands of a woman, the pitchfork was a threat. It wouldn't take much strength to push one of those sharpened tines through the skin of his neck. "All right," he said. "No need to get your feathers ruffled."

"My feathers ruffled? After what you did, that's all you have to say?"

"I didn't do nothin' more than chase you around this livery a bit. Ain't you up for a bit of fun?"

"That's not the sort of fun you were after," she said while pressing the pitchfork down a bit harder.

Squirming like a rodent with its tail caught under a cat's paw, he knocked the back of his head against the floor to give himself some breathing room. "I got carried away, is all. You wanna kill a man for that?"

"No. I'd rather kill a man for trying to force himself on a woman."

"You do and you'll swing for it," he told her with a knowing smirk. "Awful big price to pay for somethin' that didn't even happen."

Lucy stared down at him from the other end of that pitchfork as if she were sighting along the top of a rifle barrel. Things raced through her mind, ranging from the reasons she had to make good on her threat all the way to the possibility that his words held some water. She was no killer, but she wasn't a victim either. Whoever this man was, simply letting him go wasn't an option.

The side door rattled, announcing a set of footsteps that were almost loud enough to knock bits of dust from where they were lodged in the rafters. The boots making all that noise traded off between thumping against the floorboards and scraping the fallen straw into a pile in front of them as they moved farther into the livery.

"That you, Lucy?"

Without taking her eyes off the man on the floor, Lucy let out a breath. "Yes, Dale, it's me. Come over here right now."

"I just came for that fee we collected from that fellow from Omaha who put up them horses." More irregular steps drew closer to her and then stopped. "Why you standing in that stall, girl? Ain't it Matt's turn to clean 'em out?"

"Someone tried to steal our horses," she said, knowing that would be the quickest way to cut through the haze between her brother's ears.

Sure enough, Dale shook his head as if he'd been splashed with cold water and stomped to his sister's side. "Who the hell is that?"

"The man who . . ." Lucy stopped herself before telling him about the entire mess. Dale and Matt might have been lazy and irresponsible, but they still loved their sister. If either of them heard that someone had tried to force himself on her, they were likely to do something about it. Considering that Dale was drunk and the other fellow already had a pitchfork to his throat, the next course of action was bound to be harsh.

Both of the Myles brothers were known throughout town and not for anything particularly good. The last thing they needed was a man's death on his hands. On the other hand, if Dale was too foggy to jump at the chance to kill Lucy's would-be rapist, she would never be able to look at her brother the same way again.

"The man who what?" Dale grunted.

"The man who tried to steal our horses," she replied. "Weren't you listening?"

"Yeah, I just—"

"Get some rope. We can take care of him ourselves."

Chapter 2

Dale marched down the street with the other man on display in front of him. Several lengths of rope were wrapped around the horse thief's midsection, strapping his arms to his sides. Just for good measure, Dale had wrapped some more rope around the man's neck to be used as a leash. The more of his drinking companions who spotted him with his new pet, the giddier Dale became. By the time he'd passed both of the saloons, he was waving to the drunks in grand fashion.

Having traded in her pitchfork for a shotgun, Lucy followed the procession with her eyes dutifully affixed to the horse thief's back. She stood a bit to the side with her finger on both triggers so her brother wasn't blocking her shot. When Dale's friends shouted at the makeshift parade, she ignored them. Matt was nowhere to be found. That part wasn't much different from several other loud, aggravating nights in Sedley.

Compared to the homes built between the livery and the saloons, the houses clustered between the saloons and the shops at the opposite end of the street were smaller and more expensive. There were frilly curtains in most of those windows and brass knockers on a few of the doors. The homes at Lucy's end of town were generally larger because they'd been built by an entire family and expanded as that family grew. Shopkeepers, on the other hand, could afford to rent their homes, fill them with nicer things and move on.

One of the shopkeepers that had been in Sedley the longest was Dominick Moynihan. Not only was he an exceptional tailor, but he owned a shop named Fancy's Emporium that catered to men and women of refinement. At least, that was what his sign proclaimed. Apart from the saloons, Fancy's was one of the reasons Sedley hadn't dried up and been blown away by the harsh prairie winds a long time ago. Dominick's skill with a needle and thread brought customers from Dodge City and as far out as Montana or New Mexico. There had even been customers from New York City and Sacramento who'd ventured into town for a Fancy's dress or suit. Those customers also needed to drink, gamble and eat, so the wealth was passed along. It wasn't a system that could support a town with more than one street, but it suited Sedley well enough.

Once it had become clear that Fancy's wasn't going anywhere, other people took interest in the place. Some tried to rob Dominick and others tried to extort him for a slice of his profits. One man in particular approached the tailor with a proposition that suited them both nicely. He needed a place to conduct his own business and Dominick needed someone to watch out for his.

When they approached Fancy's, Lucy looked through the window to find the curtains drawn and no hint of light from within. She looked up at the sign to find another smaller shingle hanging from it that read SHER-IFF'S OFFICE AROUND THE SIDE with an arrow pointing toward the proper half of the building. Nudging the horse thief with the barrel of her shotgun, Lucy followed the two men along the perimeter of the shop and to a side door marked by another shingle with the words Sheriff Ezekiel Wolpert painted in a hasty scrawl.

"You think he's even in?" Dale asked.

The horse thief shrugged and said, "Probably not. Guess you might as well set me loose."

Lucy knocked on the door, thinking her chances were pretty slim that anyone would answer. Just casting an eye at the wild and untamed saloon district was enough to cast a disparaging light on any peace officers who took Sedley under their jurisdiction. After a few seconds, however, her slim odds actually paid off.

A set of slow, yet heavy footsteps from inside approached the entrance. After a short struggle with a door that must have been cut to fit a different frame, a man answered the summons and studied the trio outside. He stood just over six feet tall, had broad shoulders and a few extra layers of bulk under his waistcoat and trousers that came from too much town cooking. Long hair hung to his shoulders in a style that could have been reminiscent of Wild Bill's. On this man, it simply looked like a shoddy excuse to avoid paying a barber for a trim. A full beard covered a good portion of his face and intense, narrowed eyes stared at the bound prisoner as if through the glare of noonday sun. When his eyes angled toward Lucy, they took on a bit more of a sheen.

"What've we got here?" the bearded man asked.

"Horse thief, Sheriff," Dale replied. "Wanna take him off our hands?"

"Whose horses did he steal? Any from your livery?"

"No," Lucy said, "but not from lack of trying. I caught him red-handed in one of my stalls."

The sheriff's eyes remained on her as he asked, "You all right, ma'am?"

"Yes. For the most part."

He nodded slowly and shut the door.

Lucy blinked in silent disbelief. Just as she considered knocking the door open with her shotgun, it swung on its hinges once more. The sheriff, now wearing a long black coat and a weathered hat, stepped outside and shut his door behind him.

"Bit cold, ain't it?" Dale asked in a fumbling attempt to gain some common ground.

The sheriff's reply was only a shrug. Recognizing a different spokesman of the group, he looked at Lucy and asked, "What did you catch him doing, exactly?"

"He was trying to steal my horses," she said.

The thief rolled his head back as if it had suddenly lost its hold on his neck. "That's a bunch of—"

"Shut up, Frank," the sheriff snapped. "Ma'am, you say you caught him red-handed?"

"Yes. He even told me he meant to steal my horses."

"Is that all he did?"

Lucy's eyes fluttered open and shut and she glanced quickly over to her brother. Before she could decide how much more to say, the sheriff nodded and took the leash from Dale's hand.

"This isn't the first time Frank's pulled this kind of thing," the lawman said while walking down the street.

"Instead of bothering you any more than necessary, I'll toss him in the jail and sort the rest out in the morning."

Nodding enthusiastically, Dale said, "That'd be great! We really appreciate it, Sheriff . . . uh . . ."

"Wolpert."

"Right. Sheriff Wolpert. We really appreciate this. Don't we, Lucy?"

Following with her shotgun at the ready, she replied, "Yes, it's very good we were able to find the law, rouse him from his nap and bathe in the good fortune that he was ready to do his job."

Reflexively swatting her shoulder the way most brothers batted around their little sisters, Dale snapped, "That ain't no way to talk!"

"It's fine," Sheriff Wolpert said. "I'll take it from here. You might as well get back to whatever you were doing before."

"Really?" Dale said, reacting to the statement the way a hungry trout reacted to a worm dangling in front of its gaping mouth.

"Sure. I doubt this one will give me any trouble." Snapping the rope like a whip, Wolpert added, "Ain't that right, Frank?"

The horse thief grumbled a few unsavory sentiments, but didn't dispute the lawman's claim.

All too happy to split off from the group now that the saloons were in sight, Dale tossed a wave at the lawman and rubbed his sister's shoulder in the same spot he'd popped a few moments ago. "You need anything, you know where to find me," he hollered.

Lucy sighed.

Walking down the street, the trio roughly retraced

the steps that had brought the prisoner to the sheriff's attention. This time, however, the procession didn't garner half as much fanfare as before. When the locals caught the sheriff's eye, they nodded once and found something else to occupy their time. Even the respectful tips of hats were quick and not accompanied by so much as half a welcoming smile.

"The same goes for you, ma'am," Sheriff Wolpert said. "If you've got something else to do, you can get back to it."

"I'd rather make sure this piece of trash is where it belongs."

The horse thief licked his lips as he glanced back at her, nodding as if listening to a whisper intended for his ears only.

The sheriff clapped the back of Frank's neck, forcing him to keep his eyes facing front. "Suit yourself."

It was a short walk to the end of the row of shops. A few older structures marked the unofficial line dividing the saloons from the finer homes. For the most part, those were unused smokehouses or shacks with just enough bricks at their base to remain standing. Sheriff Wolpert went to one of the latter while fishing a key from an inner pocket of his coat. The walls of the squat cabin were made of dusty brick and capped with a roof constructed of beams that were nearly petrified. The single window in sight was bricked up, leaving nothing more than a vertical slot just over an inch wide. When Wolpert pulled the front door open, Lucy could see all the way through to a window on the rear wall that was obstructed by a set of thick, rusty bars.

"So what now?" she asked.

After positioning the thief in front of him, Wolpert

let go of the rope, placed his foot on the small of the other man's back and shoved him in. Frank was still scuttling and ranting in the dark when the door was shut and locked. Turning to Lucy, the lawman said, "He'll wait in there until I decide to have a word with him."

"If you remember he's there."

"Did I do wrong by you sometime that I forgot about?"

"Not directly," she replied. "But I've hardly even seen you about town doing your duties. I doubt you even know my name."

The sheriff extended a hand and said, "I know who you are, ma'am, but perhaps a proper introduction is in order. Zeke Wolpert. At your service."

Although she looked down at his hand, Lucy didn't shake it. "If you would have been at my service, I wouldn't have been attacked by that man in there. And if you were anything close to a proper sheriff, you wouldn't allow thieving friends of yours to work openly in a town that's small enough for you to stand at one end and toss a rock to hit the other."

"I can't be everywhere at once."

"No, but if you were anywhere other than that office of yours, the bad element might think twice before doing whatever they please to whomever they please."

The corner of one eye twitched. "Did he hurt you, ma'am?" Wolpert asked.

"Stop calling me 'ma'am.' My name is Lucy Myles."

"Sorry," he chuckled. "Does addressing you formally make you feel like a schoolteacher?"

"No. It reminds me that you're hardly more than a stranger in the town you're supposed to protect." Resisting the urge to put her shotgun to use after Frank pressed his face up against the window slot, Lucy turned and stomped away from the jail.

Sheriff Wolpert watched her go while flipping his keys in the air. He caught them a few more times until Lucy was out of his sight. Then, he leaned against the door and asked, "What did you do to her, Frank?"

"I didn't do nothin' to her," was the muffled reply.

"Did you attack her?"

"If I attacked her, she wouldn't be able to walk."

The sheriff's head turned so slowly that his bones nearly creaked in the cold air. He made eye contact with the thief for less than a second before Frank moved his face away from the window. "I know better than that," the lawman warned. "Speak up or I'll assume the worst."

"There may have been a scuffle."

"Anything like the scuffle when you and Burt robbed that cathouse across the state line?"

"Them were working girls. We didn't do nothin' more than what they're used to. After the lily-white customers that frequented that place, those girls were probably sad to see us go."

"Except for the one whose teeth were knocked out. Or the one that was put in the ground."

"Yeah," Frank grunted as he plopped to a seated position with his back against the wall. "Except for them two. So when the hell do I get these ropes off?"

"You heard what I told the lady."

"Mornin'? What kind of service is that?"

Sheriff Wolpert let his head hang as a tired smile drifted across his face. There wasn't the first trace of humor in his expression, but more of an amused sense of disbelief. After checking to make sure there was nobody close enough to see the front section of the jailhouse, he unlocked and opened the door once more. Keeping one hand on the gun holstered at his hip, he used the other to pull the door to within a fraction of an inch of being shut. "You got some nerve. You know that, Frank?"

The thief looked up at him and shrugged. Considering his current predicament inside all that rope, it was one of the few movements he could perform.

"You remember what I told you after that cathouse business?" Wolpert asked.

"Sure I do. You told it to all of us plenty of times."

Reaching down to grab the ropes crossing Frank's chest, the lawman hauled him to his feet and slammed him against the wall. "Seems like I should have told you one more time since you still didn't listen."

"We listened, Zeke. We just don't take orders from the likes of you."

"I don't approve of harming women. There's no cause for it."

"So you said before."

"Why would you muck about with that lady from the livery? And in my own town? What on God's green earth were you thinking about?"

"I was thinking about what any red-blooded man would think when he's got a fine lady in front of him. Now, are you gonna get me outta these ropes or not?"

"You're lucky I don't string you up with them," Wolpert growled.

"Now, what would Burt think about that when he came around again? He would take a cut out of yer pay—that's for certain."

The sheriff's mouth became a tight line. Although

Frank didn't wipe the grin off his face, he at least knew when to quiet down. Eventually, Wolpert reached into his pocket for a folding knife. Holding the little blade up to the thief's eye, he said, "I won't stand for any of that cathouse business anymore. You got that?"

"Oh, yes, sir, Sheriff."

"You're spending the night in this jail whether you like it or not."

"I got my corner all picked out. Just cut them ropes and I can stretch my legs proper."

As the lawman cut the rope strand by strand, he never took his eyes off Frank's face. The small blade lingered near the tender spot of Frank's stomach as if waiting for an excuse to turn and cut into something more vital than the binding. But like most rodents who lived longer than a day, this one knew when to keep to itself and not make any waves. When the rope was all cut and piled at his feet, Frank stepped away and rubbed his arms where the circulation had been cut off.

"What time are you gonna let me out tomorrow?"

"I'll bring you something to eat. After that, we'll have to wait and see what the judge says."

Frank had started to slide back down to have a seat upon the floor, but quickly reversed course and clambered back up to his full height. "Judge?" he snapped. "What judge?"

"The judge that makes his rounds through this county and the three neighboring ones. He should be along in a few days. No more than a week or two would be my outside guess."

"I ain't waitin' for no judge! Burt don't pay you to wait for any damn thing!"

When Frank moved closer to the lawman, he bumped against the barrel of a Cavalry model pistol. The gun had cleared its holster with a quick whisper of movement that had gone completely unnoticed by the fuming outlaw. The touch of the well-oiled iron brought Frank up short. The metallic click of the hammer being thumbed back sent a wary twitch through his entire face.

"Burt isn't here," Sheriff Wolpert said. "And neither is his money. Until that situation changes, you'll sit in the jail and stew. If you had any sense, you'd steer clear of this town."

"Them saloons are nice," Frank muttered.

"I warned you to keep your nose clean and stay away from any woman you didn't pay for. Are you trying to make a fool out of me, Frank? In my own town?"

The anger had run its course through Frank's system. The arrogance that had been there earlier had boiled off like water that had been left in an unattended kettle. "I, uh, didn't think about that, Zeke. Honest."

"I know you didn't think. You never think. That's your problem. If my arrangement with Burt is going to stand, I can't have mangy dogs like you sniffing around making things difficult for me."

"When I went into that livery, I just—"

"Shut up!"

When Wolpert said that, Frank jumped as if he'd heard the bark of the Cavalry pistol in the lawman's hand.

"You're going to sit in this jail until I come for you. Understand?"

Frank nodded.

"Burt should be coming through town before too

long and I'm sure he'll want to hear about what happened. He may even come up with enough money to spring you out of here before the judge comes along."

"You're really gonna put me in front of a judge?" the horse thief asked as his eyes grew wider than saucers.

"It's either that or try to explain to that nice lady why I cut you loose after what you did." Wolpert eased the hammer of his pistol down and holstered the weapon. "What do you say to that?"

Making his way to a corner far from the sheriff and the only door leading out of the shack, Frank grumbled, "I say you're a crooked, backstabbing son of a bitch."

"What was that?"

Although he had the sand to glare at Wolpert from his corner, Frank didn't have enough to make another sound.

The lawman nodded slowly and headed for the door. "Didn't think so."

Chapter 3

The first few hours of daylight were Lucy's favorite. Deep oranges and yellows filled the sky. Winds slowed into breezes that brushed the cold against her cheeks as opposed to stabbing it through her entire body. Most important, however, the entire town was quiet.

During her childhood years on a ranch in eastern Wyoming, quiet was easy to come by. It was so cheap that she never fully appreciated it. After coming to Sedley, she'd quickly learned to cherish any moment when the drunks weren't hollering, the saloon girls weren't cackling and her brothers weren't grousing about something or other while rattling about in the house or livery. After the previous night's events, Lucy needed some peace more than ever.

After tending to the horses, she straightened up the livery to get rid of any trace of the horse thief's presence. Her tasks included sweeping the straw so it covered the floor evenly, testing the latch on the doors to make sure they hadn't been weakened, arranging the stalls to the exact state they'd been in before the attempted robbery and making sure the pitchfork was somewhere she could get to with a minimum of fuss.

After all of that was done, she stepped outside to enjoy the last few moments of calm before more folks started wandering up and down the street or hollering their greetings back and forth at each other. Despite the fact that it was a bit cooler than the day before, Lucy wore a coat that was thinner than the shawl she'd wrapped around her yesterday. The breeze's icy fingers found her a little faster, which sharpened her senses and made the new day's scent that much more enjoyable.

Right on schedule, more people emerged from the houses and businesses on either side of the street. She watched them go through their daily motions, wondering if her own routine was so predictable. One figure broke from the pack and wandered up the street toward her end of town. She picked him out immediately and studied him even harder once it became clear that he was headed for the Thrown Shoe.

It was Sheriff Wolpert. Even with his black coat wrapped tightly around him, Lucy recognized the lawman from a distance. His narrowed eyes somehow seemed colder than anything the weather had to offer. By the time he came to a stop in front of her, Lucy was standing at attention and returning his gaze with one of her own.

"Good morning, Lucy."

His soft tone didn't match the harshness of his features. Hearing her name spoken by that voice went a long way to putting her at ease. Of course, she wasn't about to let him know that.

"Sheriff," she stiffly replied.

"I came by to see if you're all right."

"I'm fine."

Wolpert took a moment to look around at the livery and then took in the sight of her. Unlike the hungry looks she got from other men, this one was carefully subdued. "So you truly weren't hurt," he surmised.

"Why all the interest, Sheriff?"

"The man who tried to steal your horses . . . I know what he's capable of."

"I'm sure you do."

"You won't be bothered by him anymore." After one more look at her, the lawman tipped his hat and turned away.

"When's he getting set loose?" she asked.

Wolpert stopped. "I'm not sure yet. Maybe never. Depends on what the judge says."

Lucy didn't even try to stifle the little humorless chuckle that came up from the back of her throat like an unexpected burp.

Spinning around on his heel, Wolpert closed the distance between them in just two steps. "You don't believe me?"

"Most folks around here wouldn't believe that. The only difference between me and them is that I'm not in the mood to keep up appearances anymore."

"Appearances regarding what?"

"Being stuck with you," she replied with disgust tainting her words.

"Stuck with me? I was elected to this spot, in case you didn't know."

"Not by me and not by any of the other honest business owners around here. Word has it that you slid in behind your desk after Sheriff Vincent was killed. There's even been word that the ones who put that badge on your chest are the same ones who put Sheriff Tate in the ground."

The instant she said those things, Lucy wanted to take them back. No matter what she thought about the validity of her claim, she knew she'd crossed a line. She could feel it all the way down in the marrow of her bones in the same fashion that a cat knew when a bigger predator was getting ready to pounce. Lucy held her ground, since it was the only option left open to her.

The lawman ground his teeth together and eyed Lucy carefully. Nothing on his face betrayed whether he was watching to see what she would do or waiting for the chance to do something himself. Finally, he said, "Whatever you heard, I didn't have anything to do with what happened to you. When I tell you there's no need to worry about that horse thief in my jail, I mean it."

"Fine."

Sheriff Wolpert nodded to himself and took half a step away from the livery. Suddenly, he stopped and looked at her once again. "What did I do to make you so cross at me?" he asked.

"Nothing. You do nothing," Lucy replied. "Maybe that's my problem." Since she'd come this far, she didn't see a reason to hold back. "Until last night, I didn't even know where your office was. My brother knew, but that's only because he's been tossed out of both of those saloons more times than he can count."

"Yeah, but I've always treated both of your brothers fairly."

She drew in a lungful of cold air and let it out in a

burst of steam that drifted from between her lips. "This town doesn't even have a church and it sure doesn't have anyone interested in reading the Good Book, but that's got nothing to do with you. I suppose I should pack my things and find somewhere else to live. That way, nobody will have to listen to me complain anymore."

"If you have any problems with anyone, you come see me." Walking away slowly, he glanced back at the livery and added, "You can complain all you want when you stop by. I'm sure I've heard worse."

Lucy watched him amble down the street toward the saloons. Even though he strode into the growing number of people walking up and down the length of the town, he was never swallowed up by the group. Folks didn't acknowledge him outright, but they were careful not to get in his way. Even if Lucy didn't quite know what to make of him just yet, something told her that she truly wouldn't need to worry about that horse thief any longer.

Sheriff Wolpert walked directly to the Second Saloon and took his spot at the end of the bar facing the door. While some locals may have disagreed about which saloon was First and which was Second, he had no such difficulty. Whatever the place was called, his regular haunt was the only place whose whiskey didn't taste like sour piss in a dirty bottle.

"Howdy, Zeke," the bartender said as he set down a glass and filled it with firewater. "Heard there was some trouble at the Thrown Shoe the other night."

"Word travels fast."

"Sure does. Especially when it's got help."

After tossing back the drink, Sheriff Wolpert glanced toward the back of the room where the faro tables were set up. His eyes went directly to the seats behind the table flanking the dealer. As always, the three bruisers sat in those spots like birds on a telegraph wire. They were the source of more than just rumor in town and were also another reason why Wolpert frequented that establishment. Tom was a big fellow with long hair and a brushy mustache. Cade sat next to him and kept his own mustache trimmed down to a thick line on his upper lip. The third man was Juan and he was the cleanest of the three. There was almost always a woman on his knee, and this time was no exception. She played with the chain crossing Juan's belly, which was attached to a watch that had more than likely been stolen. All three of those men were armed. They made that clear enough as they rose from their seats and stalked across the room.

"Fill it again," Wolpert said.

The barkeep looked nervously between him and the three men closing in on him. "You might wanna keep an eye out, Sheriff."

"I see 'em."

"Looks like they want to have a word with you."

"Then fill it before they get here."

Pouring enough whiskey for it to flow over the top of the glass and splash onto the bar, the barkeep found somewhere else to be before his presence was requested again.

Wolpert listened to the approaching stomp of feet against warped floorboards as he sent the second gulp of liquor down to meet the first. While the tap of the glass against the bar was still rattling through the air, he pivoted on the balls of his feet and faced the trio of gunmen. "Your game's busier than ever," he said. "I must've done something right to pull all three of you away from it."

"Where's Frank?" Juan asked.

"He tried to steal some horses last night, so he's in my jail. Didn't you hear?"

Tom was several inches taller than the other two, so when he moved forward it was like a wave of poorly groomed beef rushing the bar. "Yeah, we heard. And we've been tellin' everyone that Frank won't go in front of no judge. He's a friend of ours and we don't let our friends get treated that way."

When he spotted Tom's hand wandering toward the holster slung over his shoulder, Wolpert slapped his hand against the butt of his Cavalry pistol.

Cade had a youthful face that seemed even more so when he grinned. "Ain't no need to pull that old gun of yours. I doubt it'll even shoot straight anymore."

"It'll do just fine," the sheriff warned.

"Be that as it may, we're not looking for a fight. We're just looking to get our friend out of his predicament."

"Let's take it outside," Wolpert said.

Once again, Tom started to lunge forward. This time he was stopped by the back of Cade's hand. "There's nothing to take outside," Tom said. "If you wanna start something, you can start it right here."

Since he couldn't push the larger man back with one hand, Cade stepped in front of him. "What's on your mind, Zeke?"

"Business," the sheriff replied. "And I don't conduct it in saloons."

After a second of consideration, Cade nodded and said, "All right. Lead the way."

As Wolpert turned to head for the door, he realized no less than half of the room was staring at him intently. The other half was trying their best to watch from the corner of their eyes.

Once they were outside, Wolpert went down the street. The other three men didn't try talking to him until they reached the jail. The sheriff stood in front of the only door leading into the barred shack, faced the three gunmen and held his ground. He knew he wouldn't have to wait long before one of the others sparked a conversation.

"Open that door," Tom said.

"Not until he pays for what he did."

Juan stepped forward, placing his hand under his jacket. Even as Wolpert reached for his gun, Juan pulled his hand out to reveal a bundle of money. With a flick of his wrist, he sent the cash sailing toward Wolpert. "There you go. Consider his debt paid."

When Wolpert ran his thumb along the edge of the bundle, Tom snarled, "It's all there."

He was a long way from taking any of those men at their word, but Wolpert could tell he was speaking the truth. He'd handled more than his share of similar bundles to recognize whether or not one was light. "Burt usually handles this sort of thing."

"Sure," Cade replied. "But he won't be in town for a few days, and like you said before, the faro game's been awfully crowded. What about that door?"

Wolpert kept the money where he could see it for a few more seconds before tucking it into a shirt pocket. Finally, he looked at all three men in turn and said,

"You mosey along and I'll see to it that Frank catches up."

Juan shook his head. "No. You got your money. Let him out."

"I want to have a word with him."

"You'll get it. Open the damn door."

Knowing that any further argument wouldn't have been well received, Wolpert fished the key from his pocket and unlocked the door. Not surprisingly, the prisoner wasn't quick to run for the exit after having been put in his place the night before.

"Come on out, Frank," Wolpert announced.

From the back of the single room, one shadow separated from the others. It shuffled toward the light and stopped just shy of the sheriff's reach. Squinting to get a look at what was behind the lawman, Frank asked, "Is that Juan and those other two card cheats?"

"That's us!" Tom announced happily. "We raised the money ourselves. Who needs Burt Sampil?"

When Frank strode outside, Wolpert placed his hand flat upon the horse thief's chest and stopped him in his tracks. "You won't go anywhere near that livery, you understand?" the lawman warned.

Basking in the knowledge that his three friends were there to back him up, Frank snarled, "You're bought and paid for, law dog. Get your hand off'a me and step aside. If'n we need anything else from you, we know where to find you. And if we decide to get us some of the fine horseflesh I saw at that livery, we'll help ourselves."

Narrowing his eyes to intense slits, Wolpert said, "You'd best think that over."

"Oh, I had all night to think."

"You take one step toward the livery or cast so much as a glance at that lady and I'll kill you."

All three of the men from the saloon backed up a step and put their hands upon their guns. Seeing his friends' reaction, Frank grinned and smugly said, "That's real tough talk from an armed man. Funny how it's directed at the only one of us that ain't heeled."

"It's directed at you," Wolpert replied. "And if it makes you feel better, go ahead and arm yourself. You're free to do whatever you please."

That put a dent in Frank's bravado, but Tom liked the sound of it well enough. The big fellow drew his pistol, flipped it around in his hand and extended it so the grip was pointed at the newly freed horse thief. "There you go, Frankie."

Wolpert's eyebrows flicked up as he said, "Right. There you go. Take it if that's what you need to listen to the advice I got to give." Since Frank was slow to reach for the gun, Wolpert stepped to one side and positioned himself so he was facing all four of the others. "What I got to say goes for the rest of you. The deal was for you to keep your noses clean while you're in my town. I got jurisdiction in plenty of other towns in this county, but this one is my home. I don't piss all over your homes, so don't piss on mine. Is that clear enough?"

Snatching the gun from Tom's hand, Frank kept it lowered. He even hopped back a step when Wolpert snapped the full brunt of his glare onto him. "Since when do you start laying down rules?" Frank asked. "We been payin' you to do worse than look the other way when some horses get stolen."

"That was before," the sheriff said. "I'm telling you now to take your dirty business elsewhere. Also, I won't be part of harm coming to women." He looked around to all the faces in the vicinity. All three of the men from the saloon nodded grudgingly.

"Maybe it's just one particular woman," Frank snapped. "One thing's certain. I don't take guff from some crooked lawman who thinks he's better'n me."

"You'll take it," Wolpert said. "Or you'll do something about it."

And there it was.

Hearing those words while carrying a loaded gun, Frank knew what was expected of him. He could either tuck the gun under his belt and his tail between his legs, or he could answer the challenge that had been laid down. With the other three standing right there as witnesses, the horse thief didn't have any other options.

For a second, Sheriff Wolpert thought Frank was going to throw a punch or spit some more foul language at him. Then, a grim resolve drifted onto the horse thief's face and his grip tightened around the borrowed pistol. Tom's gun was a newer model .45, but Wolpert's Cavalry pistol might as well have been a part of his own hand. When the .45 started moving to aim at him, Wolpert drew his weapon, thumbed back the hammer and pulled the trigger in a fluid motion.

Both guns fired nearly simultaneously. The .45 sent its round into the dirt several yards behind Wolpert and the Cavalry pistol's drilled a hole through the center of Frank's chest. After that, things took a turn for the worse.

The three men from the saloon weren't quick enough to save their friend. By the time Wolpert turned on them, however, all of their guns were clearing leather.

Rather than fire another three shots, Wolpert holstered his pistol and charged straight at the man closest to him. Juan was just about to pull his trigger when the sheriff took hold of his gun hand and forced him to aim at Cade. Even if Juan hadn't been fighting to regain control of his weapon, Wolpert wouldn't have allowed his next shot to draw any blood. If that's what he'd wanted, he would have just kept firing his own trusted pistol.

Juan's gun spat its rounds into the air well above Cade's head. Even though he could have returned fire, Cade chose to retreat to find cover behind a barrel near the corner of a neighboring building. That left Tom to contend with and that's where Wolpert directed his next few shots. One hissed through the air and punched into a wall several yards behind the big man and another ricocheted off one of the bars of the jailhouse's window. This gave Juan enough time to get his bearings and start pulling his wrist out of Wolpert's grasp. When he could feel Juan preparing for a powerful tug, Wolpert let his arm go so Juan's momentum sent him staggering backward. Before Juan could come back at him, Wolpert drew his pistol and cracked the side of the gun against the other man's temple.

Juan dropped and the lawman set his sights on Cade. Having dealt with all of these men plenty of times, he knew what they were made of. Wolpert took quick and careful aim as he fired three shots into the barrel that Cade was using as refuge. Sparks flew from the hoop toward the bottom of the barrel and splinters flew as holes were punched through the rounded barrier. Sure enough, the moment Wolpert let up, Cade scampered away from the barrel and bolted for the street.

"That leaves you and me, Tom," Wolpert said. "Frank dug his own grave, but that don't mean you have to lie in there with him."

The bigger man had his gun in hand, but didn't have the weapon raised. Judging by the look on his face, his temper was fighting with common sense as to what he should do from there. "Holster that shooting iron and I'll know you don't intend on killin' me."

"I'm the law in this town. You'll drop your weapon first and there won't be any trouble after that."

Scowling at Wolpert as if he were looking at a disease on two legs, Tom extended his arm and opened his hand. His gun slipped from between thick fingers and hit the dirt with a solid thump.

True to his word, Wolpert eased his Cavalry pistol back into the leather holster strapped around his waist. "There now. That wasn't—"

Tom's fist chopped through the air like a club and connected with Wolpert's jaw, snapping the sheriff's head to one side. Wolpert ran forward before his vision even had a chance to clear and wrapped Tom up in a bear hug while forcing him back. At least, he tried to force him back. Wolpert's boots ground against the dirt, digging uneven trenches and moving Tom back less than only an inch or two. The big man balled up a fist and dropped it onto the sheriff's spine. Wolpert's legs trembled on impact, but didn't allow him to drop. After shoving away from Tom, Wolpert took a stand and began punching.

The lawman's fists knocked against the solid meat of Tom's midsection without doing one bit of damage. Only when he delivered an uppercut straight to Tom's chin did he even catch the big fellow's attention. Spitting a wad of blood to the ground, Wolpert said, "Call a stop to this right now and I'll let it pass."

"Let it pass, huh?"

"That's right."

"Whatever you do now, there'll be hell to pay for killin' Frank. Burt's gonna hear about it."

"I'm sure he will," Wolpert replied. "If he doesn't hear the news from you or either of those other two, I'll tell him myself."

Confusion registered on Tom's face like a wince that had been brought about from a powerfully bad smell. "Why would I believe you'd do a fool thing like that?"

"I don't care if you believe it or not. You want to argue about it, fight some more or call an end to this mess?"

Tom considered that for a couple of seconds and looked over to Juan. He was rubbing the bloody wound on his temple and figuring out where he was. It looked as though it would be another few minutes before he arrived at an answer. Looking back to Wolpert, Tom said, "Hand back that money we gave you."

"That was to pay for Frank's release and I released him. What happened after that doesn't enter into it."

"Burt'll want it back when he hears about this."

"Then let him ask for it."

Finally, Tom let out a grunting laugh and shoved Wolpert aside. "Have it your way. Kill you now or kill you when Burt gets back. It don't matter to me. At least the other way might earn me a bonus." The big man ambled over to Juan and lifted his partner to his feet as if he were lifting a child by the back of his coveralls. The two left without another word and Wolpert let them go. If more bloodshed was what they were after, they wouldn't have to wait long for it.

Chapter 4

Sheriff Wolpert didn't have need of deputies. If he was bested in a town as small as Sedley, he intended to turn in his badge anyway. Most folks knew better than to cross him and the truly bad men paid him to move along without incident. Unfortunately, having no deputies meant not having anyone help bury a body. Wolpert set about the gruesome task, while taking the occasional break to tend to a few others, and had Frank planted by nightfall. When he was finished, he found his way back to a glass of some of the best whiskey in town.

"Rough business today, huh, Sheriff?" the barkeep said.

"Yeah."

"So ol' Frank Wellsley is dead and buried?"

"Yeah."

"You killed him?"

Wolpert looked up from his glass and showed the bartender a tired, flustered glare.

Throwing up his hands, the barkeep said, "Just making conversation."

"How about you make another one?"

"Them other three ain't been back to the faro table for a while. Word is they might be coming for you."

Wolpert shrugged and finished his whiskey. The comforting burn scorched all the way down his throat and warmed his body from the inside out. When the next wave hit, he welcomed the subtle dizziness. "They had their chance. Here," he said while slapping some of the money he'd been given onto the bar. "I'll take the bottle."

Pouncing on the sale, the barkeep had the bottle ready and in front of him in no time. "Burt Sampil's coming to town."

"You waited for me to drop some real money before telling me about that killer, huh?"

The barkeep's eyes widened and his jaw dropped. Some of the color drained from his cheeks as he sputtered, "I was going to tell you! The last thing I'd want is to see you gunned down in the street like some sort of—"

"It's all right," Wolpert chuckled. "I already knew about Burt."

"But I was still going to tell you before you left."

"I know. Take a breath. In fact," the lawman added as he lifted his bottle, "take a drink. This one's on me."

Even as the barkeep tried to say something else in his defense, his hands went through the motions of picking up a glass from behind the bar and filling it with the sheriff's whiskey. After he had his drink, the only sound he made was a long, contented sigh.

The saloon was busy, even without the main faro

game running. There were still cards being dealt and working girls making their rounds. Sheriff Wolpert glanced about the room and kept his ears open for signs of trouble, but wasn't expecting much with the three gunmen occupied elsewhere. When they made their move, they wouldn't be sneaky about it.

As if on cue, a hand dropped onto the back of his shoulder. Wolpert acted reflexively. He gripped the bottle around the neck, spun around and clamped his fist around the front of the other man's shirt. Holding the bottle up in preparation to strike, he watched the other fellow's expression shift from focused determination to stark terror.

The man stood just a hair above average height. His simple clothes were rumpled and dirty as if they'd been picked from the top of a pile and thrown on in a rush. His hair was tussled in a similar manner and his bloodshot eyes were surrounded by deep wrinkles that could have been put there by laughter just as easily as by age.

"I just wanted to shake your hand," the other man said. "You helped my sister by putting that scum where he belongs."

"Your sister?" After taking a second to let the whiskey burn from his senses, the sheriff nodded. "You're Matt Myles."

"That's right."

"You really shouldn't rush up on an armed man like that."

"I wanted to have a word with you before you left or—" Matt added while glancing at the bottle in Wolpert's hand, "Before you wouldn't remember what I said."

"How's your sister?"

"Fine. She's a strong one, you know. Still, it's good to know someone was able to look after her when me or Dale couldn't be there. Much obliged to you for that. Anything you need, just let me know."

The sheriff didn't even try to think about what he might be able to use Matt for. As far as he knew, all Matt did in town was keep the whores busy. Plastering on his most convincing smile, the lawman raised his bottle and said, "I'll keep that in mind. Care for a drink?"

"Oh no," replied a stout redheaded woman who'd appeared like a specter from the shadows to wrap her arms around Matt and drag him to the back rooms. "He'll need to be at his best if he's going to go another round."

Matt shrugged and draped an arm around her. "Whatever you say, Caroline."

As soon as Matt was out of earshot, Wolpert looked at the barkeep and muttered, "That was an easy sale."

"Yep," the bartender sighed. "She'll probably have him on the hook for more by the time they cross the room. That bottle's less than half-full now. Want me to set another aside for ya?"

"Sure. Why not?"

It was late by the time Lucy found her way to the side of Fancy's clothing store, but not too late for her to hear two different songs drifting from the saloons. Each was sung by a chorus of drunks and neither of them was anywhere close to being in the right key. Since the singers' voices were better than usual, Lucy counted herself lucky and enjoyed the night walk.

A dusting of snow covered the street and was stuck on the buildings like cobwebs. When another breeze kicked up, it brought along with it a swirl of snow from the rooftops. She clutched her shawl around her and knocked upon the door to the sheriff's office. There was no response, but a good amount of light seeped out from under the door.

"Sheriff Wolpert?" she said to the closed door.

After a few seconds, a voice replied, "Yeah?"

"It's Lucy Myles. Can I come in?"

"Door's open."

She tried the handle, but the door wouldn't budge. Trying once more just to be certain, she said, "No, it's not."

When she heard footsteps from inside, she stepped back and tucked her chin down to protect her face from a powerful gust of steely cold air. The latch was fumbled back and the door was opened a crack. Then, the steps headed away. On her next attempt, the door swung open.

Now that she didn't have a shotgun in her hands and a horse thief in her sights, Lucy had a moment to examine Wolpert's office. It looked every bit as cramped as what might be expected in the back room of a tailor shop. A small desk took up one half of the room. It looked to have been a rolltop model, but the top section was busted to leave only a flat writing surface. Not that it mattered, since there were only three pieces of paper stacked on top of it. A rifle rack hung on a wall next to a set of coat hooks and an old milking stool occupied another corner. Other than that, the only thing inside the space was Wolpert himself and a little metal pan containing a load of burning coals for heat.

The sleeves of his shirt were rolled partly up and one suspender hung off his shoulder. The Cavalry pistol was in his hand and the glint in his eye made Lucy unsure of whether or not he intended to put it to use.

Then, Lucy caught the scent of liquor in the air. She'd smelled that particular odor more than enough to recognize it as the source of Wolpert's current disheveled state. "Remember me, Sheriff?"

He squinted at her before snarling, "Course I remember you. Why wouldn't I?"

"Is this a bad time?"

Wolpert slid behind his desk and dropped onto his chair. Although he barely wobbled, Lucy recognized the unsteady way in which he moved. Between both of her brothers and memories of her father, she'd seen the telltale signs all too often.

"Good a time as any," he said. "What's on your mind?"

"I wanted to stop by and thank you."

"Thank me, huh? For shooting Frank Wellsley, I suppose?"

"Not as such. I wanted to thank you for seeing that whole situation through. It's a shame that it turned out the way it did, but honestly . . . I didn't think it would get resolved at all."

"Why not?"

She pulled in a deep breath and shut the door behind her. Feeling the need to sit down, she could find nothing but the milking stool. Rather than lower herself that close to the floor, she remained standing. "You don't get a lot of visitors here, do you?"

"Not as such," he replied, while only vaguely mocking her earlier tone. A few seconds after that, a twinge of regret drifted across his face. "I suppose most folks know they can find me out and about. Have you had any more trouble?"

"No. Today was fairly slow. What about you? Any . . . trouble?"

"Are you tryin' to say something, ma'am?"

"Actually, yes. I heard you accepted money from the same men who tried to break that horse thief free. Word is that you accept money for a lot of things. Do you recall that time when my brother Matt couldn't pay what he owed to one of those women at the Second Saloon?"

Wolpert smirked and said, "Yeah. Those girls put him into some hot water that night."

"Yes, they did and it only took ten more dollars to get him out. He said you took the money and looked the other way rather than toss him into jail."

"What would you have preferred?"

"I would have preferred the jail time," she quickly replied. "At least that would have taught him to handle his affairs properly instead of adding one more misstep to the ones he's already taken."

Pressing his fingertips against his forehead, Wolpert closed his eyes and asked, "Can this wait for some other time?"

"No," she snapped while approaching the desk. "You'll hear what I have to say and if it hurts, you've only got yourself to blame for drinking too much."

"Fair enough."

"Matt spends a lot of time in one saloon and Dale spends his time in the other. Between the two of them, they hear just about everything that goes on in this town and see just about all of the folks who pass through.

The gunmen who paid you to let Frank go aren't happy that he's dead."

"So I heard." Wolpert snapped his head up and rubbed a kink from his shoulder. "For a woman who didn't even know where my office was a little while ago, you're awfully concerned about my affairs."

"Matt hears what's going on and he told me he had a word with you. Then he told me you commenced to drinking right after you and he spoke. That's a good way to get yourself killed, Sheriff, and I'd hate to see that happen to you."

"Why? You never noticed me before, so why the hell would you care whether I live or die now?"

"I noticed you," she told him. "I just never noticed that you were a good man until you shot that horse thief."

In the span of a few seconds, several emotions made themselves known on his weathered features. Along with the initial confusion, there was also disbelief followed by varying shades of anger. "Killing another man makes me good? Either I'm drunker than I thought or you've got a mighty strange way of looking at things."

"People say you accepted money for letting Frank go," she explained. "You didn't look surprised when I mentioned it, so I assume it's true. If it is, there's no reason for you to have shot him unless something else happened."

Shifting his eyes before his guilt became too apparent, Wolpert said, "Maybe you shouldn't believe everything you hear. Rumors are wicked things."

"Considering what I heard from the Parkinson family that lives within a stone's throw of the jail, I'm inclined to believe this rumor more than the rest."

Wolpert cursed the nosy Mrs. Parkinson under his breath and rubbed his brow.

"Mrs. Parkinson says my name was brought up before the shooting," Lucy explained. "She didn't say anything else, but I think you were warning those men to stay away." She quickly raised a hand and added, "Whether it's true or not, just let me say what I came to say. I don't know why I believe you'd protect me, but somehow I do. Call it woman's intuition. Perhaps I've always seen something in your eyes whenever you look at me. Even if there wasn't, I suppose there is a part of me that's glad that horse thief is dead. I saw something in his eyes too and it wasn't good. You did your duty, Sheriff. I appreciate it. Since most folks don't have much to say to you, I thought I'd give you my thanks."

"Well, thank you, Lucy."

"It's late, so I'll be going. Please, just promise me you'll take care of yourself."

He nodded unconvincingly.

"I hope you do," she said sincerely. "I'll be thinking of you."

It was a simple sentiment, and surely spoken with innocent intent, but it had a profound impact on the man who heard it. Even after Lucy Myles had left his office and closed the door, Wolpert was still mulling those words over in his head.

She'd be thinking of him.

If they'd been spoken by anyone else, the lawman wouldn't have hung on to those words for more than a second. At best, he might have dismissed them with a wave or rattled off something else to put an end to an otherwise pointless conversation.

"How are you doing?" someone might ask.

The expected response was along the lines of "Good. And you?"

For some, the phrase "I love you" was reflexively followed by "I love you too." Sheriff Wolpert knew about that reflex all too well. After being married for several years past the point where it stopped being a good idea, he and his wife were both guilty of tossing those words about like pennies at a high-stakes card game. They didn't mean much under the circumstances and didn't make a dent in either player's outcome.

But for some reason, the possibility that Lucy might be thinking of him at some later date stuck with Sheriff Wolpert. Perhaps he liked the notion of someone in town associating his name with something other than a means to an end or a sham with a badge pinned to its chest.

Or perhaps he knew he'd be thinking of her too.

If he concentrated, he could still hear her saying those words. In the years that he'd been living in Sedley, he'd watched Lucy go about her business more times than he could count. He'd seen her at the livery, making her rounds to the stores, going to and from her home. For his first few months in town, he'd been living with Jane as husband and wife. After that fell apart, he had to conduct himself as if he were still a family man. When that disguise became too thin to maintain, he'd just wanted to distance himself from every soul in the world. From then on, approaching another woman, even one as fine as Lucy Myles, didn't make much sense.

He had jobs to do.

Everyone knew how he got them done.

The town tolerated him and the rest of the county

didn't give a damn if he lived or died. When those things created the sum of a man, what difference would one woman make?

That difference seemed a whole lot bigger when he knew that woman would be thinking of him. Suddenly, carrying on the way he had with no regard for himself or his duties seemed like a bigger crime than all the ones he'd let pass. If someone like Lucy thought highly enough of him, it seemed only fitting to be worthy of her notice.

"What the hell is wrong with me?" he snarled while hauling himself to his feet and stomping toward the door.

Lucy hadn't pulled it shut tightly enough and the night's chill was seeping in like water through the hull of an old boat. Upon reaching the door, Wolpert grabbed the handle, opened it and held it in place. The cold air washed over him, cutting all the way through his muscles to chill the blood coursing through his veins. He stood there until the innermost part of him was cold as a snake's skin. Pulling in a deep breath was akin to sticking his head into an icy lake. Wolpert's eyes snapped open and the fire that the whiskey had stoked inside him was promptly snuffed.

"That's better," he sighed.

Outside, all he could see was the snow-encrusted wall of the building next to Fancy's. Even as the wind started to hurt the unprotected skin of his face and hands, Wolpert lingered to savor it. Something about the stark cold made the world quieter. It gave the wind purpose and forced folks to leave the night to those who were equipped to handle it. If he closed his eyes, the sheriff thought he could hear a branch rustle from the trees growing alongside the road two miles outside town.

The headache caused by the liquor spiked from one side of his skull to another, and still the quiet was worth the pain. Wolpert savored the calm for as much as he could bear it because he knew it wouldn't last much longer.

Chapter 5

It was early evening the next day when a man rode into town on a light gray horse. His clothes were dirty from his time in the saddle, but he sat tall and surveyed the street with eyes that darted within an unmoving head. Besides the gun strapped around his waist, he carried two rifles that hung from boots on either side of his saddle. Folks took notice of him the way they would notice any stranger arriving into Sedley, but they held their tongues and averted their eyes until he'd passed. Even after that, they were reluctant to chatter.

It wasn't Burt Sampil's first time in Sedley. Normally, he arrived when there was less daylight falling upon his gaunt, clean-shaven face. The few times he'd arrived at an earlier hour, he'd circled around to the back of the saloons and entered that way. For a man with such a large price on his head, discretion outweighed convenience for nearly every aspect of his existence.

He reined his horse to a stop just shy of the hitching posts outside the First Saloon. One of the plainer houses between it and the livery had a rail in front of its porch and Burt snapped his reins around that within seconds after his boots hit the dirt. He flung his jacket open as if to welcome the biting cold and stomped up the short set of steps that led to the house's front door. Before he could knock, Cade pulled it open for him.

"You're a day early," Cade said.

"That a problem?"

"No, I just thought—"

"Where's Frank?"

Cade stopped short, seemingly unable to get his mouth to form another sentence. After taking a gulp of air, he said, "Frank's dead."

Burt peeled off his coat and threw it onto the chair just inside the front room where Tom was dozing. "I know that! I mean, where's he buried? He should have been carrying something."

"Oh, you mean the pouch from those saddlebags? I got it right here."

Rolling his eyes disparagingly, Burt gritted his teeth and had nearly ground them down to nubs by the time Cade returned with a pouch that looked just big enough to carry a boy's supply of marbles. "I went back for it while Frank was in jail. One of the livery owner's brothers was there and he's a lot easier to get past than—"

"Than what?" Burt snapped. "A woman?" Since Cade didn't have an answer to that, Burt snatched the pouch from his hand. He weighed it quickly and pressed it between his thumb and fingers. There was only one small item in the pouch, so he didn't feel the need to open it. "This was supposed to be done quietly."

Juan appeared from a back room, tucking his shirt into his trousers while a dark-skinned woman struggled to make herself presentable behind him. "It was quiet," he assured Burt. "Nobody but that one livery-man knows we went back."

"That's not what I'm talking about. With all the fuss made when Frank went, it don't matter what happened after." Burt removed his hat and ran the palm of his hand over the thinning section of hair on top of his head. When he made a second pass, he pressed hard enough to make a bald spot. "Where'd you find the pouch?"

"It was with the gear that came along with those horses from Omaha," Juan explained. "Cade arranged for us to slip in and I got it. The liveryman don't even know anything is missing."

"And it was just the one pouch?"

That question caused every other face to drop. The only one to maintain their calm was the woman. She seemed more anxious to get out of the little house than take part in whatever was going on inside of it.

Finally, one of the men spoke up before they caught hell for keeping their mouths shut. "Yeah, Burt," Cade said. "It was just one pouch. That's all Frank said he was after."

"How many horses were there?"

"Two."

Burt stalked forward, shoved Juan aside and grabbed the woman by the hair. Now that she was pulled out of the dark room and into the light, the golden color of her hair could be seen. Her cheeks were flushed and she grabbed on to Burt's wrist with both of her slender hands. Even when she dug her nails into his arm, she didn't come close to breaking his grip. When he spoke again, it was through a tightly clenched jaw. Suddenly, Burt seemed more like an animal when he snarled, "Who's this one, then?"

Although he knew better than to try and put his hand on Burt, Juan rushed forward to insinuate himself as much between the other man and the woman as possible. "Just some whore I brought in for the night."

"You know her any better than that?"

"Yeah, Burt. She's my regular girl. We go way back."

She hung on to his wrist loosely, trying more to alleviate some of the pressure than make a futile attempt at escape. "You know me," she said. "The last time you were here . . . we were together."

Burt's eyes narrowed and his lip curled back as if he was trying to display a set of fangs. "I remember you," he said. "Stayed with me the entire time, right?"

Her head moved up and down as much as his grip on her hair would allow.

"Kept your mouth shut that I was here. Otherwise, I would have heard about it."

She didn't say anything and didn't make a move in hopes that he'd let her go and forget she'd even been in the house. Instead, Burt drew the .44 Smith & Wesson from his holster and pressed the end of the barrel against her forehead. "Or maybe you said something to that barkeep," he snarled. "You know the one I mean?"

"N-no. There're lots of barkeeps. I—I don't . . ."

Juan placed a hand on Burt's shoulder, but stepped to one side so he wasn't an easy target. "She knows better than that," he assured him.

"Then she should've known better than to be here!"

"You weren't supposed to be here!" Juan said. He glanced back and forth between Burt and Cade. Tom had stood to watch the proceedings, but wasn't inclined to join them. "Isn't that right, Cade? Tell him!"

"No," Burt snapped. "I want her to tell me. Go on, honey. Tell me what I want to hear. Tell me the truth now and I can at least know whether or not your word is worth anything. If you did speak out of turn that other time, I need to know where I can show my face around here. *Comprende?*"

He let go of her hair, eased the side of that hand along her cheek and cinched his fingers around her throat, leaving just enough room for her to breathe. Sweat had begun trickling down her face and body, soaking into the wrinkled slip she wore. "This is important," Burt whispered while easing the gun away from her forehead. He lowered the weapon just long enough for her to draw breath and then jammed it against her chest directly over her heart.

"I didn't say anything to anyone!" she yelped. "I don't know how to prove it, but I didn't. I swear! Ask anyone and they'll—they won't tell you anything because I didn't—Oh God!"

And like a ray of sunlight cracking through an unexpected hole in the clouds, Burt's storm passed. He lowered the .44 and stroked her cheek with the back of his hand. "That's good enough for me, honey. If you're steady enough to keep lying through all of that, we wouldn't stand a chance against you anyway." Turning to Juan, he added, "You always did know how to pick 'em."

The woman didn't seem to know if she should be relieved yet or not. She inched her way back toward the room from which she'd come and hurried all the way in as soon as she was out of Burt's reach.

"So," Juan said, "you knew about Frank?"

"Word travels fast," Burt explained. "I heard that ol' Frank was put in the ground. Why don't you tell me the rest? Oh, and be thorough."

Glancing nervously toward the room and the woman who had just been terrorized by Burt's line of questioning, Juan got all his thoughts in a row so he could spool them out in proper order.

A few hours later, the wind had died down enough so that the only sounds were the restless shuffling of a few unlucky horses tied to posts along the street and the rapping of knuckles against a door. The knocking echoed down the street and along the trail leading away from town without stirring so much as a hint of a reply. It came from the front door of a small cabin in the cluster of nicer homes near the shops. The place faced out toward the rear end of town as if it had been exiled there so as not to detract from the dwellings nearby. The man who stood on the rickety porch could turn around, look out from the top step and see nothing but open prairie while the rest of Sedley was in the cabin's back lot.

Burt stood on the porch with his head down so his hat covered the upper portion of his face and cast a shadow from the moonlight to obscure the rest. With his long coat bundled and collar up, he could have been anyone that had wandered in from parts unknown. While his efforts would have been enough to fool just about anyone, they weren't enough to fool the man who owned the cabin.

"What the hell do you want, Burt?" Sheriff Wolpert

asked as he stepped around the cabin from the side that faced the shopping district.

Burt stuffed the hand he'd been using to knock into his coat pocket. The other hand had already slipped through a slit in the pocket to rest upon his holstered Smith & Wesson. "Damn, I wish I knew how you walk so softly. You must have cat's feet."

"Working with you has given me a lot of practice at sneaking around. State your business and be quick about it. My head's about to split apart."

"Surely you've been expecting me."

"Yeah, but not until tomorrow." Wolpert climbed onto the edge of his porch without using the steps. The warped boards groaned under his weight. If not for the uneven slope that led up to the cabin, he would have pulled up the porch completely. In deference to a few of the town's burrowing rodents, he left it in place.

"Are you gonna invite me in?"

"If you're here to pay me back for what happened to Frank, we might as well do it out here," Wolpert replied. "Shorter distance to drag the body."

"Mine?" Burt sneered. "Or yours?" After a few seconds passed, he grunted, "How about neither? If I came to kill you, I wouldn't have taken the chance of you sneakin' up on me."

"Then why are you here?"

Burt's response to that was an impatient motion toward the front door. Since he doubted he'd get much more than that until he opened it, Wolpert grabbed the handle and stepped inside.

Looking around at the sparse furnishings and clutter

strewn about the single room, Burt asked, "You don't even bother locking your door?"

"I'm the law in this town. Why would anyone rob me? Not that I got much worth stealin' anyhow."

"Considering how well I pay you, this takes me by surprise. Didn't you and that wife of yours have a nice place farther down the street?"

"She's not my wife no more. We went our separate ways."

Burt's eyebrows shot up as he unbuttoned his coat. "What happened? You two always seemed happy."

"Then you weren't looking closely. What would you know about it anyway? You only met Jane once."

"Still, sorry to hear it."

Wolpert studied the other man's face while he started a fire in the stove that sat in the middle of the cabin. In a strange sort of way, Burt truly did seem sorry to hear the news. Then again, Burt could shoot a preacher between the eyes and look genuinely surprised when nobody showed up to give that Sunday's sermon. "She and I never did see level on much."

"She always thought you should be a straight-arrow lawman?"

"No," Wolpert grunted. "She thought she should get most of the money I took in."

Burt let out a whistle and lowered himself onto an old chair that was missing its back. "And here I thought the weather was the coldest thing in these parts. Speaking of cold, I did hear about what happened to Frank."

"Those other three couldn't wait to tell the tale, huh?"

"Nope. Heard about it at my hotel in Elk's Bluff. It was the talk of the town."

"They never did have much to talk about over there."

"Some shopkeeper was trading with a caravan that came from here. He spread it all over town that Sheriff Wolpert was cracking down hard on horse thieves. The upside to it is that a few horse thieves I know blazed a trail for Wyoming quicker than a bunch of rabbits."

Smirking, Wolpert eased himself down onto the edge of the slanted wooden frame supporting a mattress that was thinner than the stack of blankets piled on top of it. "Least Frank did some good before I put him down."

"You gonna offer me a drink?"

"I would if I hadn't already drunk it all."

"Then how about you tell me what kind of burr got under your saddle to get you to shoot Frank Wellsley!"

Despite the steady rise of Burt's voice from a low rumble to a growl, the sheriff's face registered only some mild discomfort from the growing amount of noise within the enclosed space. "Frank wasn't abiding by the rules we laid down. I said your men could stay here if they behaved themselves. Stealing horses doesn't fit into that agreement."

"What if that was on my orders?"

Wolpert looked at Burt intently. "Was it?"

Burt nodded solemnly.

"And why weren't those orders put through me first?"

"You take orders," Burt said. "I don't give a rat's ass whether you approve of them or not. Besides, he was one of my men. If he does something that warrants him getting shot, I'll do the shooting."

"What about forcing himself on a woman? Is that enough?"

"Was she a town girl or one of the working variety?"

"Does it matter?"

For a second, Burt didn't seem to understand the difference. Then he shook his head and rubbed his eyes with the side of his hand. "Women will stab you in the back or shoot you in the front just as easy as a man will," he sighed. "When will you get that through your head? They ain't a bunch of angels just because they wear skirts and smell nice."

"She was a local girl who works at the livery," Wolpert explained. "She didn't pose a threat to a man like Frank and there was no reason for her to be in your sights."

After pulling in a deep breath, Burt let it out in a huff. "Frank was a wild one. You certain he harmed her?"

"Yeah, and he was about to do it again as soon as I set him free."

"How can you be so sure of that?" Burt asked.

"Because he told me so."

"Well, Frank always was a man of his word. Fine," Burt said as he clapped his hands together as if he were dusting the dead man off his conscience. "I'll let it slide because you did make it clear my boys were supposed to leave the angels of this fair town alone. But don't ever so much as scold my men again unless I know about it. Makes me look bad."

Wolpert nodded halfheartedly.

"Good. That's settled."

"Not quite," the lawman said. "Why would you order Frank to steal those horses? Aren't there enough animals roaming in other counties that you can pluck?"

Burt's grin was wide enough to display a set of narrow teeth that looked more like something belonging in a cat's mouth. Several of them were chipped or rotted away, leaving the remainders jagged and uneven. "That's what I meant to talk to you about in the first place."

"Good. Can we get it over with so I can sleep?"

"Or we can wait until morning," Burt said as he stood up and flapped his coat so it hung straight down to his ankles. "That'd give me some time to stretch my legs and see if the local cardsharps have gotten any better than the ones in Chimney Lake."

Chimney Lake was another town in Wolpert's jurisdiction. The last time Burt had gambled there, the only one to come out ahead was the undertaker. Cleaning up the mess wasn't half as tricky as finding a way for Burt to ride away from it without getting his neck stretched at the end of a noose. Rather than take a chance on that sort of event hitting Sedley, Wolpert braced himself and said, "Fine. Say what you came to say."

Settling in as though he'd been invited to stay for Sunday dinner, Burt said, "Them horses belong to men who work for several big shippers including Wells Fargo. They were riding through Omaha carrying a haul bigger than anything we've ever gotten before."

"Really? Those horses must have had some real good hiding places."

"Didn't need much space to hide this," Burt replied as he removed the pouch that had been given to him earlier that night.

"You want me to guess or—" Wolpert was cut short when the pouch was tossed to him. Any other time, he would have been able to snatch it easily. After all the whiskey he'd drunk, the lawman counted himself lucky that he deflected the pouch before it smacked him in the face. He grunted while bending down to scoop it up off the floor and then dumped its contents into the palm of his hand. "A key?"

"Yep. One of two keys. The other one's probably in the bridle or—"

Suddenly, Wolpert jumped to his feet. "Hold on, now. This means your men went back and stole them horses? Damn it, you're worried about you looking bad? How do you think this makes me look?"

The next thing Burt tossed hit Wolpert's chest. The sheriff held it there and immediately recognized the texture of the thin bundle of cash. "That's to smooth this over. There's more comin'."

"Enough to pay for those horses?"

"Enough for you to buy those horses, the livery they were taken from and every other thing in this godforsaken town."

The whiskey haze had soaked into his system and become swirling pain a while ago, but Wolpert had to wonder if some of it wasn't still hanging on. He checked the bundle of cash once more and guessed it was slightly smaller than the normal amount he received for looking the other way when a petty crime had been committed. "What's on your mind, Burt? I won't let you use this town for a refuge if you bring the federals in after whatever scheme you're planning."

"That ain't quite it."

"So enlighten me."

"You might want to sit down for this."

Burt Sampil's mood swayed faster and wider than the tip of a lasso. Instead of trying to get him to speak more succinctly, Wolpert played along. After sitting back on his cot, he held his hands out and gazed expectantly at the outlaw. "Good enough?"

"This is a big job," Burt replied. "So big that I need you to go along for the whole ride."

"Where?"

"Back to Omaha for one. That's where those horses came from and men will be looking for 'em if they don't show up wherever they're bound to go. They probably already organized some sort of search and I need someone with a badge to report back that everything's back on schedule. Can't have Wells Fargo getting wise that there's something amiss."

"Isn't Wells Fargo still after you for those stagecoach robberies outside of Tombstone last year?"

"Five thousand dollars on my head alone," Burt proudly replied. "After I took that shipment headed for the Dakotas, it doubled. I hear them boys at Wells Fargo have hired men who do nothin' more than hunt me down. Why do you think I need so much outside help with this job? To get these keys where they need to go, I'll need some particular men. You need to spring them out of Dog Creek Jail."

Wolpert's stomach fell as if the rest of him had been dumped off the side of a cliff. "You expect me to just waltz in and waltz out of Dog Creek with prisoners?"

"Throw your weight around. It's what you do, ain't it?"

"It's not as easy as all that."

"Well, you must've just spoiled me rotten over the last few years," Burt said, sneering. "Usually, all I need to do is tell you my troubles, throw some money at you and then wait for them troubles to disappear. It's been like that ever since your predecessor stepped aside."

Wolpert winced at the sound of that. He always winced when he thought about Sheriff Vincent and what had become of him.

"Besides," Burt added whether he took notice of the wince or not, "things will get real messy if you don't step up like I'm asking you to."

Relieved to feel his painful memories washed away by a wave of anger, Wolpert asked, "Is that a threat?"

"No, and it ain't fortune-telling either. Without you there to do things all official-like, my boys will have to go in there and bust them men out unofficially." After letting that sink in for a moment or two, Burt added, "And if they ain't up to the job, I'll go in and do it. Shouldn't take too long, but it could get a lot messier than if some crooked lawman just rode up and asked nicely."

A heaviness filled the air around Wolpert as though the weight he felt on his shoulders was taking physical form.

"Aww," Burt cooed. "You don't like being called that? I suppose I don't like being called a killer or a thief, even if that's what I am. So," he said in a tone that was a stark contrast to the previous one, "what's it going to be? You gonna help me and get rich or step aside and let things get messy?"

"If I'm to do this, I want to do it alone."

"No. You'll take my men along. Otherwise, them prisoners might be overly zealous when they get out."

"Then your men will follow my orders," Wolpert said, since he hadn't truly expected to be granted his first wish.

"Sounds agreeable."

"Whatever the final take of this job is, I want half."

"Ten percent."

"Thirty."

"Twenty. That's more than any of those three you butted heads with the other night will get, so don't ask for a penny more."

Since he would have settled for fifteen, Wolpert sealed the deal and said, "Now get out of my home so I can get some sleep."

Chapter 6

Sheriff Wolpert had to walk only a short way across town, but there was a whole lot of history separating him between his cabin and the little house he'd used to call home. It was midmorning when he made the trip and the street was filled with people tending their business or riding into Sedley for the first time. The lawman tipped his hat to all of them without getting a single response. He considered striking up a conversation with the owner of the general store, but that would have only delayed the inevitable. Wolpert had business to conduct and there was no getting around it.

Walking up the steps that led to an all-too-familiar front door, Wolpert removed his hat and knocked. Curtains were moved aside from a front window so someone inside could look out at him before quickly pulling them back into place.

A petite woman reluctantly opened the door. Her short black hair was tied back with a kerchief, but Wolpert knew well enough that the soft curls were normally bouncy as coils of ribbon. Her rounded cheeks were smeared with dirt and the front of her light brown dress was equally smudged. He could remember days when such a disheveled state would endear him to his wife even more. Now she just looked annoyed and dirty.

"What is it, Zeke?" she asked.

"Doing some cleaning?"

"Yes, and I'd like to get back to it."

"I just wanted to let you know I'd be away for a while. Just in case someone asked about me."

"Nobody asks," she snipped. "They know you well enough to figure out what you're doing and I'm always glad to see you go."

"I'm still living in that old cabin on the edge of town."

Standing in the doorway as if to block any hope of entry, she said, "If you think I'm letting you back into this house, you're mistaken. You're no more my husband than you are a real lawman."

In the time when he'd been courting her, those words might have cut him to the quick. Compared to some of the other beauts she'd thrown at him of late, they were fairly tame. "I'm not trying to stir anything up with you, Janie. I . . ." He had no problem spotting the flicker of disgust that drifted across her face. Lowering his head and holding his hat in both hands, he said, "Sorry. I meant Jane. All I meant to say was that I'm still living in that cabin, so there's no living expenses as such for me. If you need any money to get along, you're welcome to it."

Jane's anger lessened, but not by much. "I need to get some new windows to replace the ones blown out by that storm in the fall. And then there's food and such."

"Here," Wolpert said as he fished out one of the

bundles of cash he'd recently acquired. "Before you think of anything else, just take this. It should keep you going for a while."

She snatched the money from him quicker than a dog helping itself to table scraps. After flipping through the bundle and stuffing it into a pocket, she looked at the lawman even closer. "What have you been into lately?"

"You haven't heard?"

"All I heard is that you gunned down poor Frank Wellsley. Did someone pay you for that?"

"Poor Frank, huh? How is it that you take anyone's side, so long as it isn't mine?"

"After living with you, I learned that anyone else's side was worth taking."

Wolpert had to chuckle at her sense of drama. Of all the time they'd had together, he'd spent most of it on the trail while she spent whatever money he'd brought home after the previous ride. Jane wasn't exactly an evil woman, but she figured cooking his meals entitled her to most of what he'd earned no matter how much blood he'd spilt to get it. Back when they used to live in the bigger house, he'd been shot while collecting protection money from the pig farms out east. Jane complained just as much about tending to his bandages as she did about the money they'd missed from the part of the route he'd been forced to neglect because of his injury. When he'd gotten angry enough to say something, she'd kicked him out of her life and there was no sign of her disposition improving in the slightest.

"I'll be away for a while," he said. "Maybe a long time."

"Do you have a new job lined up?" Suddenly, Jane's

face brightened more than the day when he'd proposed. "Is it something big? Will we be rich?"

Wolpert couldn't help being disappointed with just how simply her mind worked. He thought she might get worked up if she caught a whiff of the money that Burt had offered, and here it was. Too bad that was the only thing he knew that would make her smile again. "No," he sighed. "We won't be rich."

"Oh," she huffed as every trace of joy disappeared from her. "Whatever you get, I want my share, you know."

"Yeah. Believe me, I know."

His next stop was the Thrown Shoe Livery. The large front doors were wide open and Matt sat in a chair with his feet propped up on the second rail of a fence encircling the small lot next to the stable. "Howdy, Sheriff," he said.

"Good day to you. Your sister about?"

"She's cleaning the stalls."

Once again, Wolpert wasn't surprised. By the time he'd walked past Matt and into the stable, the other man was stretched out and resuming his nap.

The first sign of Lucy Wolpert he found was a glimpse of her rump poking out from the corner stall. She was on all fours, vigorously scrubbing the floor with a brush in each hand. "I'd stand up to say hello, Sheriff, but I'm too busy. After all the trouble we both went through, those horses were still stolen."

That was the third nonsurprise that day. Wolpert braced himself and hoped he wouldn't hear anything unexpected when he asked, "Was anyone hurt?"

Continuing to scrub the floor as if she were trying to

dig all the way down to bedrock, Lucy replied, "No. The yellow dogs snuck in and out in the middle of the night. Lord only knows how that could have happened considering the fine job my brothers do of watching this place."

Wolpert tried to keep quiet, but had to chuckle when a loud snore erupted from Matt's open mouth. Looking up at him with a stern glare, Lucy eventually let her head hang. She swiped away the hair that had fallen to cover her face and said, "They didn't leave a mess, but I just want to be rid of everything to do with those thieves or the horses they stole."

"That stall looks plenty clean to me."

"It is. Still, I need something to keep my hands busy before I knock a hole through a wall or wring the necks of these good-for-nothing lazy fools I'm surrounded by. Sounds sort of crazy when I come out and say it like that."

"I don't know," Wolpert said while offering her a hand. "We've both had to deal with our fair share of idiots lately. You should try keeping the drunks in line day in and day out. That'd be sure to drive you out of your mind."

She took his hand and gripped it tightly while pulling herself to her feet. "More than likely, we both deal with the same drunks." Now that she was up, Lucy dusted herself off and took a moment to survey the stall. For a place meant to be used by horses, it was immaculate. "I guess I'm done here."

"This stall is cleaner than where I lay my head every night, so I'm inclined to agree. Why didn't you tell me about the horses being stolen?"

"It won't make any difference. Even if you found them, someone would just come by to steal them again. Some kinds of trouble will find you no matter what you do to avoid it. This way I'm rid of the whole mess."

As much as Wolpert wanted to commiserate with her, he held his tongue. While he could sympathize with what she'd said, he wasn't in the same boat. The trouble that found him was more like a current of water flowing along a ditch he'd dug with his own two hands. While it was tough to stanch the flow completely, there were times when it could be diverted at least for a while.

"Here," he said while handing her a bundle wrapped in an old newspaper. "I brought you something to make up for your trouble."

Her forehead wrinkled suspiciously as she took what he offered. After peeling back the paper, Lucy uncovered the money and then pushed the bundle toward him again. "What's this?"

"Something to make up for what happened. Or perhaps it'll go a little ways in making up for it."

"Where'd it come from?"

Wolpert blinked and sifted through those words a few times in his mind. After dealing with Jane not too long ago, he wasn't prepared to have to explain a stack of money so extensively. "It . . . There's a fund for this sort of thing."

"Is there?"

"Yes, and it's meant to pay restitution to those like yourself who—"

"Take it back," she snapped.

"Why?"

"Because you're lying. Folks who talk too much about

something they should already know are lying. Take the money back. It's too much anyhow."

"Fine. You caught me."

Still holding the money, Lucy tilted her head a bit as if that allowed her to see the lawman from a different perspective. "I did?"

"You're right. There's no fund. I got that money from Frank Wellsley and the other men responsible for those horses being stolen. I've done some digging into the matter and discovered a few things. Namely, there were men who paid Frank to get those animals from you. Since that job was carried out at your expense, it only seems fair that the money goes to you." When she still seemed hesitant to keep the money, he added, "It's either that or it goes to paying for a fancy headstone for Frank."

"Well," Lucy said as she reeled the money in, "since you put it that way, I suppose I might as well help myself to some restitution."

Wolpert nodded. "Good. I'm glad you see it that way."

She flipped through the cash, stopped just under halfway through the stack, peeled away most of the bills and handed the remainder to Wolpert. "That should cover what I would have gotten for those horses."

"And the gear?"

"Yes."

Seeing that he wasn't going to convince her otherwise, Wolpert accepted what was left of the money.

"Thank you, Sheriff. Maybe this'll be enough to take my mind off scrubbing these stalls from top to bottom. I've been thinking that maybe I should practice a little of what I'd been preaching."

"What do you mean?"

"You know, all that talk about you doing your duty.

Well, I was raised to repay one kindness with another. When was the last time you had a big home-cooked supper?"

"It's been a while." Even before he and Jane had parted ways, it had been a long while.

"Then come by our house tonight. What's your favorite?"

"No need to go through all that trouble."

"No trouble. Besides, I didn't say I'd cook whatever you told me to. If it's too much trouble, I'll let you know. Now what's your favorite?"

More than anything, Wolpert wanted to answer her question. It was a simple answer, really. Pork chops with mashed potatoes and pan-seared apple slices. He'd eaten that meal for the first time at a place in Chimney Lake during a time well before Burt made his mark there. The hotels or restaurants he'd visited were sloppy enough to mess up cold oatmeal and Jane never really cared what he wanted to eat.

In the few seconds it took for all of that to run through his head, Wolpert's thoughts took a turn. He studied Lucy's face, watched the way she stood and even recalled the tone of her voice when she'd last spoken. Perhaps she was trying to butter him up for some reason. Maybe she wanted to get him to let his guard down or say something that he'd wanted to stay hidden. Plenty of folks wanted to get on a lawman's good side, especially when they knew he was for sale. Lucy could just be another one of those.

The second he thought along those lines, Wolpert hated himself for it.

"How about steak?" Lucy offered. "You look like a steak sort of man. I can bake up a pie and—"

"No, thanks, ma'am," Wolpert cut in. "I've got business to tend to that'll take me out of town for a spell."

Lucy didn't try to hide her disappointment. "Oh. Well, you didn't seem like you were in a hurry. If you'd like something to eat before you go . . ."

"Thank you kindly, but no. I really just meant to make sure you got this restitution before I was on my way."

"All right, then." Lucy straightened her posture, wiped her hand on the front of her skirt and extended it to him. Looking him in the eyes, she remained rigid and expectant to make it clear she wouldn't move until she got what she was after. Rather than disappoint her again, Wolpert shook her hand.

Lucy's skin was soft, despite the calluses and rough texture created by years of hard work. More than that, she was the warmest thing he'd touched in recent memory.

"I appreciate all your help, Sheriff. And the restitution was a nice surprise. The offer for supper still stands, so feel free to drop by if you have time before you leave town."

"Thank you, ma'am."

Even though it was tough for him to let go of her, Wolpert couldn't get out of that stable quickly enough. Once she was behind him, he got his feet moving and didn't let them stop. After he stepped through the front doors and turned toward the street, he tossed the remaining money to Matt. "Here you go," he said. "That's to help get the livery cleaned up."

It took Matt several seconds to get his feet down from where they'd been resting on the fence rail and even longer for him to regain his balance. By the time he fumbled with the bundle to get a look inside, Wolpert was halfway down the street. "Anything I can do for ya, Sheriff, just say the word."

"Look after your sister!"

"Sure will!" Matt shouted back. Once the lawman had walked a bit farther down the street, Matt angled his chair toward the stable doors, propped his feet back upon the rail and closed his eyes.

Chapter 7

Wolpert wasn't partial to trains. He didn't have any-thing against them, but he simply preferred to have a horse beneath him that took him where he wanted to go. Even if he wound up riding alongside a set of train tracks for most of a journey, he liked knowing he could steer one way or another and even stop if the mood struck him. Sitting in a train, sealed up with all those folks in a rattling tin can with the cinders blowing in through the windows, Wolpert was trapped. Then again, he felt just as trapped while carrying out the orders handed down by Burt Sampil. Taking a train to save some travel time seemed much less of an ordeal in compar-ison.

Omaha was a prosperous town with a healthy wild side. For many, it had been the last bastion of civiliza-tion before heading farther west in covered wagons or less. In more recent years, it had retained the feel of a town built on a precipice. Folks of all shapes and colors roamed the streets. Saloons and brothels were easy to come by. The smell of stockyards was always in the air and nobody batted an eye at the sight of three strangers walking along the side of the street.

Wolpert, Tom and Cade had ridden into town, leaving Juan at the train station closest to Omaha's western border. They could have disembarked even closer to their destination, but decided it was best to take some time to get a feel for the town. This had been Wolpert's idea and was a halfhearted attempt to give him an extra hour or so to think of how he would approach his current task. The fact that his attempt had worked so handily opened up several more possibilities where manipulating his overseers was concerned. The lawman had no delusions that every one of his moves was being scrutinized. With Burt giving them their orders, the other three men could be ready to do just about anything.

"That's the place," Cade said as he pointed to a wide building on Pierce Street. "That's where them horses came from."

"So you've been here before?" Wolpert asked.

"Juan and two of the fellas that're in jail scouted it out to steer 'em to your neck of the woods."

"Were you or Tom ever seen here?"

After considering that for a few seconds, Cade replied, "Yeah, but not doing anything against the law."

"Nothing against the law, huh? So all of your noses were completely clean and nobody here in Omaha could possibly have a bone to pick with you?"

Both of the other men glanced at each other for just long enough to bring a pair of guilty consciences to the surface.

"Right," Wolpert snapped. "I'm going in there on my own. The whole reason I was brought in on this job is to try and do it without a fuss. You boys have a problem with that?"

If Cade or Juan did have a problem, they lacked the gumption to say a word about it. Instead, they clenched their jaws and allowed Wolpert to walk ahead. When the lawman crossed the street, they took positions down a ways from the long building beneath the sign that read UNGER'S HORSE TRADING.

As Wolpert approached the main entrance to the wide building, he tugged on the lapel of his coat to make sure his badge was still pinned to the shirt beneath it. When he was in the boundaries of his jurisdiction, it was rarely necessary to mark himself in such a fashion. Folks either knew who he was or found out the hard way. In Omaha, however, Wolpert was hoping a friendly demeanor and proper credentials would suffice.

"Afternoon," Wolpert said to a kid no more than eleven or twelve years old who swept the area around the front door. "I'm here to talk to the man who owns this place."

"That'd be Mr. Unger," the boy replied, twisting his dirty face into a mix of bewilderment and apprehension. "Who're you?"

"I'm Sheriff Zeke Wolpert from Keith County."

The bewilderment on the kid's face deepened. "Where's that?"

"How about you fetch Mr. Unger?" When the boy didn't move so much as a muscle, Wolpert added, "Now."

The sharp tone in the lawman's voice was better than a swat to the kid's backside in getting the boy moving. He scurried into the building, made a sharp turn toward what looked like a small office near the front of the place and disappeared through a door. Wolpert strode across a floor covered in straw and counted no fewer than two dozen stalls within the building. Some workers drifted between the stalls, tending to the horses in them and straightening the tools or supplies situated on the walls or in the corners. Before the sheriff got to within spitting distance of the door, the boy came running out. Hot on his heels was a short man with a large belly wearing a string tie and a gray vest over a wrinkled white shirt. Because of the amount of time he'd spent so close to a tailor, Wolpert could tell the fat man's pants were made from expensive material that had been poorly stitched together.

"I'm George Unger," the fat man said as he waddled toward the sheriff and stuck out his hand. He smiled widely, showing the yellowed section of teeth that more than likely were frequently clamped around a cigar. "What can I do for a fellow lawman on this fine day?"

"You're a lawman?" Wolpert asked.

"Formerly. I rode with Marshal Ben Stanford out in Platte City. Ever heard of him?"

"Sure," Wolpert said as he gripped the other man's clammy hand. "How long did you ride with him?"

"Just long enough to catch Jesse Farrell and the Reece Brothers after they robbed them two banks. Made all the papers!"

"Ahhh," Wolpert sighed, trying to feign some enthusiasm. George spoke with all the bluster of a man who'd gotten roped into riding on one posse and never stopped bragging about it.

"So," George said, "where were you from again?"

"I'm a sheriff from Keith County."

"Never heard of it."

"Not many folks have. It's a few days west of here. I came to have a word with you about those horses that were stolen."

George's face darkened and he hooked both thumbs under his belt. There wasn't a lot of room to spare in that vicinity, so his belly took on two distinct dents to accommodate them. "Which horses might that be?"

Wolpert came up short. With everything else that had been going through his mind, he'd let a few things slip to the wayside. At the moment, all he could dredge up was a vague picture of the animals that had been in Lucy's stall. Trying to describe that picture wouldn't have amounted to much more than "four legs, two ears and a long face." Sparing himself that indignity, Wolpert said, "They were two fine animals that must have come up missing within the last few weeks. Surely Wells Fargo knows the ones I'm talking about."

"Yeah, I think I do recall them now. Why don't you step into my office and tell me the rest?"

"That's really not necessary. I just wanted to come out here and let you know I've picked up the tracks of those thieves who stole your animals."

"I see," George replied with a minimum of emotion.

"You . . . um . . . did know they were missing, right?"

George yanked his thumbs from where they'd been wedged and propped both hands upon his hips. "Of course I knew they were missing!" he bellowed. "This is my business! I started this place when it wasn't anything more than a lot and a damn fence! I make it my business to know everything from what my stock eats to which ones have a loose shoe. What kind of question is that?"

"Didn't mean to ruffle your feathers. Normally, someone gets a little more upset when their property is taken." The instant those words came out of his mouth, Wolpert wanted them back. Sure enough, they weren't received well.

"Upset? You don't think I'm upset?"

The next few moments were a rush of heated swearing erupting from George's reddening face. Wolpert did his best to weather the storm without paying much attention to it. As a lawman, he'd become skilled in knowing when to respond to a threat and when to keep his head down and just let the other man blow off some steam. As he waited for George to lose some of his wind, Wolpert noticed that none of the other workers within earshot were paying their employer any mind whatsoever. These sorts of tantrums must have been commonplace, especially directly following the loss of those horses.

Eventually, the whirlwind of profanity from George's mouth abated. Wolpert started listening again to hear ". . . suggest that I'd let a thing like that pass is quite simply absurd."

"Have you taken any steps toward finding those horses?"

George allowed his mouth to remain open. His eyes rattled in their sockets as if they were about to pop out of his skull. "Weren't you listening to what I just told you?"

Rather than get another torrent started, Wolpert took the offensive. "Just answer my question, sir. I just got off a train for much longer than I prefer to extend you the courtesy of telling you about your stolen property, so the least I expect is some cooperation."

While the previous rant had gone all but unnoticed, the lawman's slightly upraised voice caught the attention of all the workers in the building. Wolpert could feel their eyes on him and didn't let his own gaze waver from where it was firmly locked.

George stewed for a couple of seconds before replying, "I suppose I may not have told you that there were some men I hired to go after my livestock."

"Can you call them off?"

"Why would I want to do such a thing?"

"Because," Wolpert said without a pause, "they could get underfoot in my own efforts. I've been tracking men across my county who are known horse thieves. They're probably taking your property to be sold within the next week or so and I want to nab the entire ring. Having more inexperienced gunmen fumbling about will only scare away the big fish."

"I assure you, the men I hired are not inexperienced."

Narrowing his eyes, Wolpert thought of something that would genuinely raise his ire. That way, his face reflected a convincing trace of anger when he said, "Whoever they are, they're not to interfere with official affairs in my jurisdiction. Is that clear?"

"Yes. Most definitely."

"Now, if you have any details as to their current whereabouts, I would appreciate that information. In return, I will be able to make arrangements with you in regards to where your horses are to be shipped once they are recovered."

George looked over to where some of his employees were standing and then nodded. "That sounds more than fair. Come with me into my office and I'll give you everything I have."

"What about those men you hired? Have they left Omaha yet?"

"They haven't figured out where to go just yet."

"Well, if you won't call them off, at least allow me to have a word with them. Perhaps we can come to an agreement to pool our resources."

Like most rampaging beasts, George wasn't so quick to get riled up again once he'd been allowed to run for a bit. He nodded meekly and said, "The information you want is in my office. Would you mind following me?"

"Not at all, sir."

As he followed George across the main floor, Wolpert glanced up to find a path of planks laid down between the overhead beams. It wasn't enough to be considered a second floor, but must have been a good method for a few skinny overseers to watch the horse stalls from one vantage point.

George's office was nothing less than a temple to his own perceived, and heavily overblown, greatness. Every picture on the wall had him in the forefront striking a pose that would befit a war memorial. Documents on the wall ranged from certificates and diplomas advertising the accomplishments of one George R. Unger. The desk was big enough to camp under. Even the pens looked expensive and since he didn't want to hear the story of how they were acquired, Wolpert didn't stare too long at them.

"Have a seat," George said as he waddled around to

the larger chair behind his desk. "I'll get that information."

"If it's a location, a general idea would be good enough. I've got men scattered throughout the state and I just need to know which ones to alert."

The sheriff's lie either didn't go over or simply didn't make a difference in George's decision, because he didn't stop sifting through the papers in his drawer. "No trouble at all," he said. "I feel bad about shouting before. Times have been hard lately, with the theft and all."

"I understand. Why don't I just find a room for the night and you can pass the word along to your men however you need to? I can come back tomorrow for whatever papers you find in your desk there."

"Please, Sheriff Wolpert. I insist. Have a seat."

The longer he left Cade and the others to their own devices, the more uncomfortable the lawman became. Since he knew correcting the other man's mispronunciation of his name would probably be ignored, Wolpert sat down and tried to think of a quick and easy way out of that office without raising any suspicion.

"So," George said, "it sounds like your men are pretty good at their jobs. When those horses came up missing, I couldn't find a trace of them or the men who took them."

"Yeah, I've got some good trackers."

"Maybe they could use some help. The men I hired would prove to be mighty valuable."

"No need for that. Just call them off."

Wolpert was getting an uneasy feeling. Part of that was because he'd wound up in the office despite his previous reservations. Another bad sign was the way that George kept searching through the same drawer without seeming to find anything.

"My security around here is pretty tight," George continued. "I've got guards patrolling the building at night and men watching over it during the day. A thief would have to be pretty good to slip anything by me."

"I suppose so. How about I leave you to go through your papers at your leisure?" Wolpert offered as he stood up. "There's other business for me to attend to and I'm sure you've got enough to keep you busy."

The office door was opened, allowing a fellow in a rumpled white shirt and black vest to step inside. His shirtsleeves were rolled up to show a pair of forearms that looked thicker than some of the beef being tended in the town's stockyards at that moment.

Ignoring Wolpert's last words, George continued along his own train of thought. "A thief would have to be really good, or more likely, he'd have to have connections inside my operation to get this job done. What've you got to say about that, Sheriff?"

Wolpert knew something was amiss even before the slab of beef in shirtsleeves had stepped inside. He tested the waters by trying to walk past the big fellow and was immediately stopped by a hamlike hand pressed against the center of his chest. "Best take that hand off'a me, son," Wolpert warned.

The big fellow smirked and shoved Wolpert with enough force to knock him against the front of George's desk. The lawman allowed himself to stumble just enough for his hip to catch upon the desk, which made it easier for him to lift his leg up and drive his boot into the big man's gut. Unlike George's, this man's ample stomach wasn't formed by lard. It was solid muscle and Wolpert's boot thumped against it without drawing much more than a twitch from his target.

As soon as he saw the big man lift his fist, Wolpert held on to the desk, swung both legs up off the floor and rolled to the side. The fist slammed into the desk hard enough to lift George's end off the floor. George hopped up as well, jumping from his chair and gleefully stabbing a finger at the fleeing lawman.

"You're not just some law dog trying to find my horses! You'd be the Sheriff Wolpert who works for Burt Sampil. Now, those are the sorts of connections that could get into my place and escape with my horses," George declared. "Tell me why you're really here and I may be able to call off Ricky here before he tears you in half!"

Even if Wolpert was inclined to answer, he didn't have time to form a single word before Rick took another swing at him. He ducked under the punch and drove a straight jab into Rick's belly. Wolpert's intention was to hit the other man in the same spot his previous kick had softened up. Unfortunately, Rick's torso was about as soft as the side of a mountain. Wolpert stepped back and when Rick moved in to get a hold of him, the lawman delivered a powerful uppercut to his jaw.

That one had an impact on the big fellow and sent Rick back a few steps.

"Whoever you are, mister," George said, "you'll be sorry you showed your face in my town."

Rick wasn't as slow as most men his size. Rather than rely on his bulk to do his fighting for him, he was quick enough to grab hold of Wolpert before he could get away. Once he closed his fist around the lawman's wrist, he reeled him straight into a punch that took Wolpert off his feet.

The punch landed so heavily that Wolpert barely even felt it. One second he was desperately trying to get away and the next, he was lying on his side. After a portion of the fog cleared from his head, Wolpert could tell he hadn't exactly fallen. He was dangling from Rick's grasp like a rag doll being carried by a very large child. This child didn't take very good care of his playthings and proved it by kicking his rag doll in the ribs.

Wolpert acted out of reflex when he drew the Cavalry pistol from its holster and pounded the side of its barrel against Rick's hand. When that didn't loosen the big man's hold on him, he tried again using the butt of the pistol's grip. A wet crunch mixed with the sound of Rick's pained grunt was quickly followed by the thump of Wolpert's body against the floor. No longer dangling like a broken toy, Wolpert scurried away from Rick and jumped to his feet.

"That's enough!" the lawman said. "Whoever you think I am, you're making a hell of a big mistake." Wolpert took a quick glance at the doorway. Standing just outside the office were no fewer than five men, each of them pointing either a shotgun or a pistol at the lawman.

Chapter 8

Tossing his gun and handing himself over to the firing squad hadn't been enough for George Unger. The businessman wasn't satisfied until his men had swarmed into his office, surrounded Wolpert and forced him to endure a few more clubbing blows from Rick. And just when the lawman had been about to keel over, George stepped in to deliver what he considered to be the final knock. His smooth, flabby fist slapped against Wolpert's face like a piece of wet liver. After that, the sheriff's other wounds piled up to force him into unconsciousness.

When he awoke, he was in a room without any windows and tied to a chair. The ropes keeping him in place had so little give in them that they might as well have been steel bands. Lifting his chin sent a rush of pain through his entire upper body. Even though his neck hadn't been broken by Rick's savage attacks, it had come dangerously close.

". . . think he's coming around," said a vaguely familiar voice. "Wake him up."

Before Wolpert could speak on his own behalf, a bucket of water was dumped on his head. The shock of the cold caused him to jump, which, in turn, caused another wave of pain to shoot all the way through every aching bone in his body.

"Glad to see you up and awake again," the hazy vision of George said through all the cobwebs that had collected within Wolpert's skull. After blinking some of the water from his eyes, the lawman caught sight of George perched on the edge of a chair directly in front of him. A grin filled the lower portion of George's chubby face and he clasped his hands between his knees. "Well, awake anyway."

"This is a hanging offense," Wolpert grunted.

"You sure about that?"

"If it isn't, I'll make it one!"

"You know, I was a bit worried about that," George explained. "But it didn't take much asking around to get the word on you. Apparently, even if you are the real Sheriff Zeke Wolpert, that don't mean much. Everyone in Keith County and even folks from neighboring ones know that there's no real law in that part of the state. Not since Sheriff Vincent was killed. Plenty of folks around here know Keith County's lawman is just a known crook wearing a badge, making his rounds and collecting blood money for killers and anyone else who'll pay his fee. Is that you, mister?"

Wolpert wasn't about to answer that question since everyone in the room already knew the answer.

George leaned forward and shuffled to within a few inches of Wolpert's chair. "I suppose you probably really are Sheriff Wolpert," he said. "That'd explain why you'd associate yourself with a bunch of known horse thieves."

"And what makes you think I didn't come all the way out here for the reason I told you?" Wolpert asked.

"Because I got word that you'd be coming to throw me off the scent." George shook his head and lowered himself back onto his own chair. "No, you're here for something else and I know what it is."

In the time that had passed since he'd opened his eyes, Wolpert could make out a few more details. The roar in his head had died down just enough for him to hear some of the same sounds he'd heard when he'd entered Unger's place of business. More than likely, he was still in that same building. It looked as though he was in an old storage room with bags of feed piled along every wall except for the one with the door. Two men armed with shotguns stood in front of that door. The largest figure in the corner had to be Rick. Either that or Wolpert was even unluckier than he'd thought and there were two grizzly bears on George's payroll.

Unable to stomach the smug grin on George's face any longer, Wolpert asked, "So, why do you think I'm really here?"

"You wanted to know where those horses were headed."

"If I was the one who stole them, wouldn't I already know that?"

After a quick nod from George, Rick lumbered out of the shadows and delivered a chopping right cross to Wolpert's face. Since he was tied to the chair and unable to roll with the punch, the lawman felt the impact all the way down to his toes.

"That's what you wanted to know," George snapped. "Don't pretend otherwise."

"Who's pretending?"

No sooner was the question past Wolpert's lips than Rick's fist was once more bashing into his face. That half of his head was still numb from the first blow, but the bigger man's knuckles opened a nasty gash that trickled blood onto the corner of Wolpert's mouth.

"It won't pay to try and fool me now," George said. "I've wasted enough time with you already. Where the hell are my damn horses?"

"You've got plenty more to take their place."

When Rick leaned in behind another punch, Wolpert twisted himself around as much as he could while tucking his head down good and tight. Although the lower section of the big man's fist scraped against his ear, most of the punch was absorbed by the back of the chair itself. Wolpert heard the distinct crack of splintering wood and tried to talk over it.

"I'm not trying to get lippy with you," Wolpert insisted. "I honestly don't know what's so special about those animals. It's a crime for anyone's horse to be stolen, but this is an awful lot of fuss just for a pair of them." Lifting his chin so he could point his swollen, bloodied face at George, he added, "Crooked or not, I'm still a lawman. Whatever those horses are, they must be awfully good for you to risk your neck doing all of this to a man wearing a badge."

"You mean that trinket you got pinned to your chest? Even if half of what I've heard is true, you've been taking enough bribes to make yourself rich. I could always just drop your body in a shallow hole and say it was left behind by some angry rustlers. Or I could dump it somewhere outside town and let someone else find it. You think anyone would doubt those stories?"

All of that sank in a bit too well for Wolpert's liking.

George started ticking his points off using sausage-like fingers. "I want to know where my horses are. I want to know who helped you take them and I want to know why you came back to Omaha. Let's start there and see if you give me a good enough reason to keep you alive."

Allowing his head to hang down and his jaw to droop, Wolpert tried to think of every angle possible where his current fix was concerned. Just when he thought he'd run out of time, Rick stepped forward to knock him around some more. The big man had switched his focus to the sheriff's chest and stomach. Despite the ropes absorbing some of the impact, enough got through to make it difficult for Wolpert to breathe. When he finally did manage to fill his lungs, he emptied his last meal onto the floor.

George got up and moved away from the puddle of sick faster than he'd moved when Wolpert's gun had been drawn. "I'll have someone wash you off and then we'll start again," he grunted. "You'll tell me what I want to know or you'll be coughing up blood to go along with all that other muck."

Wolpert had to get some of the dregs out of his mouth, so he made a statement while doing so and spat the sour juice onto George's shoes. He paid for that with another couple of thumping blows from Rick, but it was worth every last one. A few seconds later, he allowed himself to pass out.

Wolpert dreamed a hectic series of images, most of which involved him falling into a black, stinking pit. There was cold water at the bottom, which doused him from head to toe. He sputtered and choked on some of that water, which broke him from his dream and reminded him that the water was real. George stood in front of him with an empty bucket.

"Where's my horses?" he asked.

It took a few attempts for Wolpert to catch his breath, and when he did, he wasn't about to waste it by giving the businessman what he wanted. "Go to hell," the sheriff groaned.

A savage expression overtook George's face and he swung both arms around to knock the bucket against the side of Wolpert's head.

It hurt for a second.

Dizziness expanded out from the split section of Wolpert's scalp.

Darkness came, and then he dreamed of falling once again.

Instead of a splash of water, Wolpert was awakened the next time by an insistent slapping against his cheek. If he hadn't been tied to his chair, he would have lashed out with a good slap of his own to whoever was pestering him. When he tried to speak, Wolpert's mouth was quickly covered by a whole lot of toughened leather.

"Don't make so much noise," someone said. "You'll ruin this whole thing."

Wolpert forced himself to regain some of his fleeting consciousness until he could just make out Juan's face in the darkness. A bit of struggling confirmed that Juan was keeping him quiet by clamping his gloved hand over his mouth. When Wolpert growled to get the other man's attention, the leather glove was pressed even harder against the lower portion of his face.

Dropping his voice to a grating hiss, Juan said, "They knocked you around pretty bad. Do you recognize me?"

Wolpert nodded.

"Will you keep your voice down if I take my hand away?"

He nodded again.

"All right, then." As Juan moved one hand away from Wolpert's mouth, he raised the other one to show the gun he held at the ready. Judging by the look in his eyes, Juan was considering using it on the lawman as much as he considered using it on anyone else that might barge in on them.

"What the hell are you doing here?" Wolpert rasped.

"We waited for you to come out on your own, but it never happened."

"So you busted in here? I must have been out for a minute or two."

"No, we didn't bust in here," Juan replied. "We went to a saloon and had some drinks."

"Then you busted in?"

"No. Then we played some cards. You're real lucky we came for you at all, seeing as how many stupid cowboys there are in this town that don't mind throwing their money away on a pair of tens or less."

Wolpert squeezed his eyes shut, pulled in a deep breath and opened them again. After what he'd been through and all the punches he'd absorbed, he wouldn't have been surprised if this conversation was some sort of dream. But Juan was still there when he focused his eyes again. The lawman was still uncertain as to whether or not that was a good thing. "You went drinking and then gambling?" he asked.

"Yeah. We just figured you were in here negotiating or talking or whatever Burt sent you here to do."

"How long have I been here?"

"Five or six hours."

"Five or six *hours*?"

Juan pressed his hand against Wolpert's mouth, but pulled it away when it seemed the sheriff might actually bite it. "You told us to stay put, so that's what we did. You didn't tell us a damn thing about what you were doing or when you'd be done. How were we supposed to know if—"

"Do I honestly need to tell you to cut these ropes?"

And, like a wish come true, the ropes loosened. Wolpert shifted in the chair, which was enough for him to shrug out of the ropes completely. He turned and nearly jumped straight into the air when he caught sight of Cade behind him with a knife in his hand.

"Have you been there the whole time?" Wolpert yelped in a voice that he managed to soften before it echoed throughout the room.

Cade tucked the knife back into its scabbard on his boot and then stood up. "More or less. Whoever tied those knots sure knew his business."

"All right, then. So, where's Tom?"

"Outside," Juan replied. "Just give him another few minutes and he'll help us get out of here."

When he got up and rubbed some feeling back into his arms, a good portion of the room come into focus. It was the same room he'd been in since he'd been dragged out of George's office, but this time his view wasn't impeded by gunmen taking swings at him or waves of water being dumped onto his head. The only other things in there with him were a table and a few more chairs. Wolpert's attention was fixed on the table so much that he nearly overlooked the body crumpled on the floor beside it. "Is that George?" he asked.

Cade glanced toward the table and replied, "No. Just one of the men he hired to watch this place."

"Is he dead?"

"Don't know. I haven't checked since I stabbed him."

"Your gun was over there," Juan added. He took the belt that had been looped around his shoulder and handed it over.

Wolpert's eyesight was still uncertain enough for him to see the shape of the belt only after it was being handed to him. The moment it was in his hands, however, he recognized it as the genuine article.

"Can't believe you're still using that piece of junk," Juan scoffed. "How old is that gun anyways? Ten years?"

"A bit more," Wolpert replied while buckling the gun belt around his waist. He drew the Cavalry pistol and went through the motions of checking the cylinder. It was something he could have done blindfolded and in a windstorm.

"There are a lot better ones out there now," Juan said as though he were telling a child about the ways of the world. "Most men you face are gonna be carrying something a lot more impressive than that antique."

Wolpert snapped the mechanism shut and dropped the pistol back into its holster. "I know. I've faced them. Guess who didn't walk away."

"Say what you will. A good man with that old thing can still fall against an average man carrying a—"

Cade cut his partner off with a sharp hissing whisper. He'd taken position next to the room's only door without making a noise. As valuable as that kind of sneakiness could be, Wolpert was annoyed with himself for not having known the man was capable of such a skill.

Pressing one ear against the door, Cade said, "Something's happening out there. Get ready to move."

Now that he was up and moving, Wolpert was ready to run all the way back to Sedley. Before he took another step, however, he faced Juan and said, "I may have been out of sorts for longer than I thought, but I'm not about to do a damn thing before I know what's going on."

"We've been meaning to ask the same thing of you. From where we stood, you're the one that owes us an explanation as to where you got off to and what that tenderfoot in the cheap suit wants from you. You figure we should just strut out there and have another chat with 'em? Your first chat turned out well enough."

On the other side of the door, people were shouting to one another and moving like a herd toward the back of the building. Some of them even walked fairly close to the room where Wolpert and his two companions were huddled in the dark.

Cade placed one hand upon the door's handle and used the other to draw his gun. "Whatever you two are fussing about, we don't have the time for it. Are we going through with our plan or not?"

"What's the plan?" Wolpert asked.

Juan grinned as even more commotion sounded outside. "We walk out through the front door. Simple enough for ya?"

Chapter 9

"Yeeeee hawwwwww!"

The scream echoed through George's building like a battle cry from a tribe of rampaging savages. The moment he heard it, Cade chuckled and Juan shook his head. "That'd be our signal," Juan said. "The way Tom's going, we won't have to worry about getting him out of this town alive. Let's go."

Cade eased the door open and poked his nose outside. Wolpert was right behind him and had to remind himself that he was indeed looking at the same horse trader's stable that he'd entered earlier that day. All the basic structures of the stalls and walkways were still in place, but there was enough commotion to rival a saloon giving away free whiskey by the bottle. Men scrambled down aisles that were wide enough for a horse to walk with room to spare on either side. Some were running so quickly that the space barely seemed large enough to contain them. Overhead, a few others scurried along the boards stretched in between the roof beams, kicking dust and the occasional splinter down to the main floor.

When the first gunshot blasted through the air within the building, it sounded as if it had come from a cannon. Most of the men inside dropped or dove behind cover, while the others drew their guns and fired toward the other end of the structure.

"That's our signal," Cade said while opening the door the rest of the way.

Wolpert's first couple of steps were unsteady. As soon as a shot found its way to within a few yards of him, the jolt of blood rushing through his veins was more than enough to bring his senses all the way back. He dropped to one knee, brought his pistol up and thumbed the hammer back. The old firearm felt like a piece of him that had been missing. Now that it had been returned, all he needed was a target.

"Hey!" one of the gunmen said, as if answering the sheriff's unspoken request. "That law dog's getting away!"

Despite the continued ruckus from the other side of the building, several of George's hired guns shifted their attention to Wolpert and his unlikely escort. There were three of them in one group and the instant they spotted the escaping prisoner, they opened fire.

Cade was first to duck down and rush for the safety of the closest stall. When the gate didn't come open right away, he climbed over the partition and dropped heavily onto the bed of straw on the other side. Juan straightened up and put his back to a thick post that ran all the way to the ceiling. Wolpert, on the other hand, was tired of being knocked around. He crouched to present a smaller target, but extended his arm so he could take careful aim along the top of his pistol.

The gunmen in front of him might have been quicker to pull their triggers, but that didn't mean much when their shots either hissed through the air or drilled into any of the several wooden barriers between them and the battered sheriff.

A jabbing pain nagged the side of Wolpert's face that had been hit so many times that day. Because of that, he missed when he squeezed his trigger. His bullet blazed toward the lead gunman and dug a messy trench into the side of his neck, which was close enough to send that gunman to the floor in a panicked state and send the other gunmen in that vicinity scattering for cover.

Between the pain that had soaked into every inch of his body, the frantic beating of his heart and the excitement of the escape, Wolpert could see his surroundings with alarming clarity. Not only was he able to trace where each of the gunmen had dived for cover, but he picked out one of them who had tried to hide behind a sign that had been nailed to another one of the building's support posts. The sign showed a list of George's rates for buying, trading and renting horses, and it was barely as thick as the backrest of a flimsy chair. Wolpert thumbed back his hammer and fired a shot before that man had a chance to think better of his choice for sanctuary.

The Cavalry pistol bucked against the sheriff's palm, sending a nearby horse skittering to the opposite half of its stall. Its bullet punched straight through the cheap wooden sign, splitting it apart and dropping the man behind it.

"That all you got, you sorry bunch'a farmers?" someone yelled from the rear portion of the building.

Wolpert hurried to the stall where Cade had jumped. Along the way, he spotted Tom at the center of the commotion that had gotten the night's dance started. The big fellow stood outside with a gun in each hand. Even though most of his shots went toward the rafters, the look in his eyes was plenty wild enough to make any of the other men think twice about approaching him.

"I guess the owner of this rat hole don't care if I walk away with his stock!" Tom declared. "Maybe I'll come back later for a few more."

"Don't just stand there!" George said while shoving another one of his gunmen out from behind the barrels where they'd both been hiding. "I pay you men to guard, so guard!"

"You men go on," Wolpert said to Juan, who stood less than a dozen feet away.

Juan shifted to fire a few shots at the two gunmen who'd come after him and the escaping lawman. "We came here to get you out, so that's what we'll do."

"That's mighty loyal of you, but I've got other fish to fry."

"Loyal ain't a part of it. I don't wanna be the one to tell Burt that we left you behind when we weren't supposed to let you out of our sight."

Wolpert hunkered down and started moving toward the barrels stacked in a section that was roped off and marked with another sign. According to the painted words, those barrels contained a mix of grains and oat that was a specialty of Unger's Horse Trading. As he moved past Cade's stall, Wolpert heard another shot hiss toward him. Both Juan and Cade answered that with a barrage that sent one of the gunmen running and knocked the other flat on his back with a bloody hole in his chest.

When several more guards turned toward that eruption of gunfire, Tom shouted, "Fine by me! Bet I can make it all the way to Missouri before you catch me!"

The man whom George had shoved opened fire and screamed for the others to do the same. As soon as they had someone to follow, the workers didn't hesitate to carry out their boss's command. Tom turned and bolted out of sight, using speed that didn't fit a man of his size. As was surely the plan, all of the guards focused on him and allowed the rest of Tom's partners to slip away.

But Wolpert wasn't about to go quietly. He had a head full of questions and meant to have some of them answered. Also, he had a face covered in cuts and bruises that someone had to answer for. He couldn't think of anyone better for that particular reckoning than the portly man doing his best to blend in with the barrels of specially blended horse feed.

The lawman kept his eyes fixed upon his target as he hurried toward those barrels. Along the way, one of the guards stepped in front of him and gasped at the sight of the man who was supposed to be unconscious after being beaten to within an inch of his life. Wolpert's bloody face twisted into an angry mask as he put all of his momentum behind his left fist. His knuckles drove deeply into the other man's gut, doubling him over and putting him in prime position to be rammed headfirst into the side of an empty stall.

A pair of men crossed Wolpert's path on their way to

catch Tom, and one of them was too preoccupied to even notice anything else. Wolpert came at the second one with his shoulder down like a battering ram. Digging his boots into the floor, Wolpert charged ahead and drove the gunman's back into one of the posts surrounding the barrels of feed. He eased up for a second, allowed the gunman to suck in a surprised gulp of air and then rammed him once more into the post. The second impact knocked the air from the gunman's lungs and left him gasping. Wolpert placed an open hand upon the man's face and knocked his head against the post. He wasn't sure if this was one of the gunmen who'd beaten him earlier, but the notion added some fuel to Wolpert's fire.

After casting the bleeding gunman aside, Wolpert stalked toward the stout man who cowered in the futile, desperate hope that he might somehow be overlooked. "What's so special about those horses?" he snarled. When he didn't get an answer, Wolpert reached down to grab George's face. "Tell me about those horses that were stolen," he snarled while jamming the barrel of his gun against the other man's nose.

George's eyes snapped toward the fallen gunman. His worker stirred even after being introduced to the post, but was immediately overpowered by Juan. Then he snuck a quick glance toward the back of the building.

"I wouldn't worry about my friend," Wolpert told him. "Sounds like he's got a lot more steam than your boys."

Considering all the whooping and hollering Tom was doing and all the panicking the guards were doing, it was near impossible for anyone to dispute that statement.

"Each horse had a key," George said. "I don't know where they were hidden and I wasn't about to try and look for them. All I do know is that I was going to get the payday of a lifetime just for seeing those horses to their proper owner. They were dropped off here and supposed to be sold off at auction. I was to wait for a certain bid and then hand them off. That's it, I swear."

"Who arranged all of this?"

George's face twisted into a pained grimace. If he'd been smaller, his constant wriggling and squirming would have allowed him to burrow very nicely under the barrels and out of danger. As it was, he was just a nervous fat man in a cheap, dirty suit. Seeing the sheriff sight down the barrel of his gun with a steady eye was enough to push George the rest of the way.

"He was a man from Wells Fargo," George sputtered. "I don't know a name. I swear it!"

"Is he here in town?"

"Why would he be in town? The horses are gone. They didn't come back for the auction. He's got no reason to be here."

The shooting had eased up and most of the shouting had moved outside along with Tom's boisterous taunting. Several more voices joined the racket as the guards picked up some help from the locals. Before long, gunfire crackled through the night from nearly every direction.

"We should probably get outta here," Juan snarled from behind the lawman.

Wolpert had the portly man under his heel and squirming in fear. He practically launched George into the rafters when he grabbed him by the shirt and hauled him up.

George raised his hands as if they were thick enough to stop a bullet and squeaked, "I was only protecting my interests. You can't fault me for that. You're a lawman. I was within my rights."

Wolpert stared calmly at the fat man as hell raged outside. Cade and Juan were close, insisting they leave and threatening to go on their own if things didn't start moving quicker. But the sheriff wasn't concerned with any of that. He was used to being in hell and knew the other two weren't going to abandon him after coming this far. That just left him and George.

More than anything, Wolpert wanted to put a bullet through George's blubbery face. Predatory instincts honed through years of sniffing out the weak and making them pay screamed for him to put this sorry sack of lard down like the lame animal he was. Then he felt the weight of the neglected hunk of metal pinned to his chest. "This is your only warning," the lawman snarled. "You keep hiring killers and acting like an outlaw, you'll be shot like one. Understand?"

"Y-yes." It took a few seconds after he was released for George to realize he'd been pardoned. "I understand, Sheriff. I'll call my men off right away."

"And just one more thing." Wolpert balled up a fist that was as hard as a chunk of rock and then swung it at the businessman's jaw. The impact was sharp and very satisfying, culminating in George crumpling like a sack of dirty laundry. Looking down at George's unconscious form, Wolpert said, "I owed you that one."

Juan grabbed Wolpert's shoulder and spun him around. "If you're quite through, how about we get the hell out of here?"

The sheriff nodded and followed the others through

the building. Cade was already well ahead of them, waiting in the shadows against a row of stalls. Outside, the shooting had died down to a crackle of shots. Since Tom's voice and .45s were both silent, the men still shooting were pretty much spitting in the wind.

True to their initial plan, Juan, Cade and Wolpert walked out the front door and put Unger's Horse Trading behind them.

Chapter 10

Sedley, Nebraska

Wolpert's heart barely slowed down through the trip out of Omaha. Even when he rested his head against the window of the train's passenger car and took a snooze, he still felt as if he were galloping out of town with smoking gun in hand. Getting out hadn't been as difficult as he'd expected. Once Tom had quieted down, George's guards had been more than willing to let him go. Their salaries didn't quite cover risking their necks so far away from the company's main building.

After disembarking from the train, the lawman barely had the patience to climb onto the coach that would carry them the rest of the way into Sedley. By the time he arrived, Wolpert thought he would have been better off running to the saloon where Burt was supposed to be waiting for him. He stomped into the place, ignored the cordial greeting from the barkeep and asked, "Where is he?"

"Where's who, Sheriff?"

"Burt Sampil. Tell me where he is and don't say you don't know."

"He's in the back . . . with Dulcie. I wouldn't disturb them, though. They haven't been in there for long."

Wolpert stormed away from the bar and headed for the back wall of the saloon, which was filled with a row of evenly spaced doors and a neglected stage in the left corner. Since the customers were interested only in seeing girls lift their skirts, the owner of the place decided to cater to those appetites and employ a different sort of worker. One of those girls was Dulcie. Wolpert knew her room was closest to the stage, so that's the door he kicked in.

Dulcie was a short, curvy woman with a kind, round face and short brown hair. Jumping at Wolpert's entrance, she hopped off the edge of the bed wearing nothing but a faded white slip. Lazily pulling at the upper portion of the slip to cover herself, she asked, "Is there a problem, Sheriff?"

"Get out," Wolpert snapped.

Always the professional, Dulcie covered herself as best she could and got out. Judging by the amount of whistles and catcalls she received, she might have jumped onto the old stage as soon as Wolpert shut the door behind her.

Burt had been lying in the bed when the lawman came in, but he swung his legs over the side and drove his fingers through his hair. Wearing only a pair of stained britches left his partially sunken chest exposed, giving him the look of a man with a mild case of consumption. Either that or he was simply rotting from the inside out. "Couldn't have given me another few minutes before the interruption?"

"I'm sure you'll get what you paid for. She's understanding that way."

"So, how was Omaha?"

"I think you already know the answer to that," Wolpert replied. "In fact, it seems you knew the answer before I even got there."

"Ah, so the fat man talked? I only met him once, but he did strike me as a squealer."

"You told him I was the one who took those horses? What the hell would you do that for?"

"Toss me my shirt, will you?"

Burt's clothes were piled against the wall near the foot of the bed. As much as he would have preferred Burt being dressed for their conversation, he noticed the outlaw's holster hanging off the edge of the table on his side of the bed.

"Nice try, Burt," Wolpert said. "If you're so modest, wrap yourself up in a blanket."

The other man shrugged and started to stand up. Before he could get to his feet, he received a warning from the sheriff that convinced him to swing his legs over to the other side of the bed and climb down that way. "Can't blame a fellow for tryin'," Burt said.

"No, but I can blame you for trying to get me killed."

"Whatever do you mean?"

"Don't try to lead me around by the ear," Wolpert snapped. "I've had too long of a day for that. You sent word ahead of us that I was the one who stole those horses. What was the purpose of that?"

"You're the one tossing around the accusations. You tell me."

"If you wanted me dead, you could have shot me

yourself. Or if you were too yellow for that, you could have had your men do it. Instead, you send all four of us out to Omaha without telling anyone what we were getting into."

Burt raised his eyebrows and asked, "You're certain those other three didn't know?"

"Pretty much. They're the ones who cut me loose when that fat piece of trash took me prisoner."

Getting to his feet and walking over to his clothes, Burt looked genuinely baffled. "That horse salesman got over on you? Last time I talked to him, he barely had enough sand to hold a gun. You must be losing your touch."

"He had time to prepare thanks to the telegram he received. Hired a bunch of gunmen to watch the rest of his stock."

"Ahhh. That makes sense." After hiking on his pants, Burt scooped up his shirt and slid into it. The movements made his ribs slide beneath his skin like thin iron rods wrapped in wet sackcloth. His chest seemed even more sunken as he arched his back to get himself fully situated within the clothing. By the time he'd buttoned the shirt, a thin layer of sweat appeared on his face and neck. "You say my boys came and got you?"

Wolpert nodded. "Something tells me that wasn't on your orders."

"Why would you think that? Who even told you about the message I was supposed to have sent along? George Unger? What makes his word gospel?"

"He wasn't in any position to lie. You, on the other hand, don't know any other language."

Burt grinned like a kid who'd been caught trying to sneak up and give a fright to his ma. "It wouldn't have done any good to tell you everything that was going on when I sent you to Omaha. Also, it wouldn't have been half as fun. Sounds to me like you had an exciting trip."

"I'm getting sick of this. Answer my question."

"First off, I never expected you to get killed. I didn't even expect you to get captured. I did send that telegram, but it was for the same reason I sent you there in the first place. You were to throw the folks in Omaha off the trail."

"And you didn't think I'd do what I was supposed to do?" Wolpert asked.

"It's not that." Cocking his head, Burt sat upon the edge of the bed and looked at the lawman with something verging on pity. "I couldn't take the chance of you walking in there and drawing attention to our situation instead of defusing it," Burt continued.

"Then why send me at all?"

"Because if George Unger was absolutely certain he knew who'd taken his horses, he wouldn't have a reason to second-guess himself. I thought he might try to take a shot at you or possibly get some local law together to bring you in. You'd certainly be able to get out of a little mess like that and George would be so convinced what I told him was true that he wouldn't have any reason to stick his nose into our business any longer. So as you can see, it really wasn't that far off from what I originally told you."

"What did you tell your boys?" Wolpert asked.

"Pretty much the same thing. I'm sure they understood once you told them all about it."

Making his way to a little chair that seemed more like a spot for a man to set his clothes and personal items instead of his backside, Wolpert eased down until he felt certain the flimsy piece of furniture wouldn't collapse under his weight. The Cavalry pistol remained in his hand, but rested across the top of his knee where it was more or less pointed in Burt's direction. "I didn't tell them. At least, not everything that I suspected was true."

"Interesting."

It wasn't interesting in the slightest to Wolpert. The trip to Omaha, his talks with George, his capture, his escape, all of it had been pins on a map that led to a specific destination. He might not have known the route that was being traced while he'd been riding it, but now that a portion of the ride was over he could look back and see the trail just fine. He could even see that Burt was being mostly honest with him. Surely there were things the outlaw was keeping hidden, but the rest fell into place. Burt's reasoning had been sound from a killer's point of view. Even one unspoken part of his plan made complete sense. If Wolpert had been killed in Omaha for stealing those horses, the search for the real thief would have ended at the grave of a crooked lawman. Nice and neat.

Most men would have gotten their feathers ruffled a lot more after putting those pieces together because they would have been approaching the situation with too much personal interest in it. After all the years he'd spent living with his head down and doing the things he'd done, Wolpert was accustomed to detaching himself from things. It was like the clear, perfect quality of a winter morning. Everything was just clearer in the cold.

"Where are the horses now?"

"I sold 'em. They served their purpose, but there ain't no reason for me to squeeze just a little more profit out of them." Burt wasn't stupid enough to dive for his gun and wasn't quick enough to take the sheriff's weapon away from him, so he just sat.

Wolpert let the outlaw stew for a little while longer before relieving some of the tension. "You forgot to ask me an important question."

"Did I?" Burt asked. He rolled his eyes up into their sockets, gnawed on his bottom lip and then said, "I don't think so."

"You forgot to ask why George Unger didn't kill me."

That hit a nerve, but it was way down inside Burt's head. If he hadn't been watching so closely and if he hadn't known the outlaw so well, Wolpert might have missed the twitch.

"Why would I ask that?" Burt replied. "I know him well enough to think he couldn't get over on you."

"But he did."

"And here you are." Burt jumped to his feet and started pacing up and down the length of the bed. "You're the one who busted in here when I was trying to have a good time, which I paid for, by the way. Now you're upset because I didn't say the right thing when you wanted to hear it? If I wanted that kind of grief, I'd get a wife and not have to throw my money at Dulcie whenever I'm in town."

After pretending to find those comments amusing, Wolpert tightened his grip around his gun and asked, "Where were those horses headed, Burt? You might as well tell me because I'll only find out on my own soon enough."

"I won't know for certain until I have a word with a friend of mine." Regaining some of his composure, Burt curled one corner of his mouth into a grin and added, "He's another law dog for sale. Maybe you know him."

Wolpert's hand lifted only an inch, but it made all the difference in the world. Instead of being pointed mostly in the outlaw's direction, the Cavalry pistol was now aiming at a spot in the middle of Burt's head. "I want to know what's going on," he said in a voice that made it clear he wasn't about to tolerate another off-handed remark. "All of it."

"Or what? You're gonna shoot me if I don't? Why would you throw away all the money you're set to earn by doing something as stupid as all that?"

Burt was looking at him in a different way, so Wolpert knew he had to be seen more as a partner again instead of an enemy. Outlaws expected different things from their partners, and a little bit of heavy-handedness wasn't exactly viewed as a bad thing.

"Because what you're going to pay me has got to be a pittance compared to what you're set to earn," Wolpert growled. "I want in on the entire job and I want a real cut of the profits. I'll be doing enough to earn more than what you offered anyway."

"Is that so?" Burt asked with renewed interest.

"Yeah."

"Shooting me won't get you nowhere."

"Maybe," the lawman said without batting an eye, "but it won't lose me anything either. You were ready to pay me when I returned, so you must have the rest of my money around here somewhere. I shoot you, claim it was self-defense and get on with my life. Whatever you had planned won't get done and the world will keep spinning. Well, not for you, I suppose."

"Self-defense, huh? You think my boys will buy that one?"

"I don't care if they do or don't. When you're lying facedown with a messy hole through your skull, you won't care either. Seems like a mighty high price to pay just to deny yourself a valuable partner in your little endeavor."

Now it was Burt's turn to study the man in front of him. "You want in on the whole deal, do ya?"

"That's right," Wolpert said with a nod.

A crooked smile quickly drifted onto the outlaw's face. "And what about this business of what happened in Omaha? You gotta know I never thought you'd be caught by the likes of George Unger."

"Every now and then, the sun will even shine on a dog's ass."

"Lucky shot, huh?" Burt chuckled. "That must be it. Will that incident be put behind us or should I watch my back?"

"You should always watch your back, Burt. If I'd wanted you to bleed for what you did with that telegram, you'd be bleeding right now. I have jurisdiction in this whole county, but in this town, I could set this whole saloon on fire without having to answer to anyone. Instead, you'll repay me in cash."

Ignoring the pistol in Wolpert's hand, Burt strode up and clapped him on the shoulder. "To be honest, I never thought you had it in you to aim for the top of a deal like this. You always seemed content to collect your bribes and squirrel away the fines you collected."

"A man's got to think about his future. I figure a proper cut on something like this might just allow me to retire. I could even pass along my badge to someone I trust. Who knows?" Wolpert added. "Maybe that man would be someone you trust as well."

Burt's eyes widened with a flash of greed that hit him too hard and too fast for it to be covered up. "I could name the next county sheriff?"

"I do the naming, but I could most definitely draw from a batch of names proposed by an adviser. That is, if I have the means to retire. In the event that I'm killed in the line of duty or even if I happen to turn up missing while on a ride, I've made arrangements for another replacement. Let's just say he's a bright-eyed young man who's anxious to clean up Keith County and doesn't share my cooperative nature."

Already nodding enthusiastically, Burt was too eager to spot the bluff. "I get the picture. No bullets in the back of your head during the job or your replacement will hunt me down like a good little law dog."

"Something like that."

"All right, then. Let's do some talking, partner."

Lucy responded to the knock at her door with an angry scowl on her face and a thick piece of lumber in her hand. At that time of night, the only men to pay her a visit were either drunks or gamblers looking for her brothers. Either way, she didn't want to talk to them. Knowing those kinds of annoyances rarely went away on their own, she pulled the door open to speed the process along.

"What do you want?" she snapped. "It's too late to— Sheriff Wolpert?"

He stood leaning against the door frame as if he would fall over without it. "That's right," he said with a breath that was laden with the scent of whiskey. "If it's too late to call on you, I could go."

"No, of course not. Come in." After propping her makeshift weapon against the wall, she straightened the blankets that she'd wrapped around her shoulders. The skirt of her long nightgown made it past the blankets and fell to her feet, but she fretted as though she were barely half dressed. It made Dulcie's earlier walk through the saloon even more indecent in comparison. "I don't have any supper ready, but I'm sure I could scrounge up something."

"No need for that. I just stopped by for a quick word."

The more the lawman spoke, the thicker the stench of liquor became. Before long, it hung like a pungent cloud between them. "At least have some coffee," she pressed. "I insist."

Shutting his mouth and grinding his teeth as if chewing on the firewater he'd had after his talk with Burt, Wolpert nodded. "Yeah. That would be good."

"Come inside, then. You're letting all the warmth out."

Wolpert stepped inside and shut the brisk night out behind him.

The small front room was obviously hers and hers alone. Chairs were arranged just right and the few little tables were all topped by simple doilies and small picture frames. If either of her brothers was there very often, the place wouldn't be nearly as cozy. A small dining area and kitchen were at the back of the house, the latter of which emanated the warmth she'd been so anxious to hold on to.

"There's some coffee here from this morning," she

said from the kitchen. "If you like, I can make some more."

"I've drunk sludge made from river water and twice-used chicory, so your leftovers should be plenty good enough."

Lucy's face twisted into a disgusted grimace, which struck Wolpert as funny. She shook her head as if trying to knock his words loose from her ears and set about warming the coffee on her stove. "So, what brings you here, Sheriff? Are my brothers making fools of themselves again?"

"No," he replied while looking around the house for any trace of Matt or Dale. "It's not to do with them."

When she emerged from the kitchen, she wiped her hands on a cloth while looking at him with genuine concern on her face. Her black hair hung loosely on either side of her face, made her look pure and inviting. Without trying, she was more woman than any of the others Wolpert had ever known.

"So?" she prodded. "If my brothers aren't causing trouble somewhere, what brings you out on such a cold night?"

"I wanted to have a word with you. I'm heading out for a while and—"

"That's right. You mentioned that when I saw you last time. Or did you already come back from that?" She must have heard something in the kitchen, because Lucy turned on the balls of her feet and headed back there in a rush. "Things have been busy around the Thrown Shoe. A bunch of cowboys all got it in their heads to buy new saddles. Matt had a word with them and wouldn't you know, they've been pestering me ever since to match prices from John Lindsay's store at the other end of town."

Wolpert stayed in his spot just inside the front door, listening to the constant patter of her feet against the kitchen floor and waiting for her to come up for air. The more she talked, however, the longer she seemed willing to go without a pause.

"If any of those cowboys wind up buying anything more than a single stall for their horses," she said as she emerged from the kitchen carrying a cup of smoking coffee in her hands, "then my brother will have done some good. If all they do is waste my time and keep me running around to show them the saddles I have for sale, then I'll skin Matt and Dale and hang them both from the rafters." Shaking off that sentiment while also shrugging out of one of her blankets, she handed the cup over to him. "There you go, Sheriff. Why don't you have a seat?"

"No, thanks. I'd prefer to stand. If I get too comfortable, I'll want to stay the night."

Although that was meant in the friendliest manner possible, Wolpert couldn't help feeling uncomfortable by what he'd said. His brain was already working several steps ahead of his mouth and he could only hope Lucy wasn't right up there with it. Her smile faltered only a little, so she was either unaware of his thoughts or too polite to call him out because of them.

"All right, then," she said.

"I wanted to tell you I'd be leaving again."

"Does this have something to do with those stolen horses?"

"No. I'm leaving for a while again and I've got a

mighty big favor to ask of you. While I'm gone, I need you to be ready to get a message from me. When you get it, you'll have to act fast and possibly be ready to leave town yourself. Since you've always got horses available to you, I thought you'd be perfect for this."

"Shouldn't you have deputies for that?" she asked.

"I can trust you more'n anyone who'd agree to be my deputy. When I send word back here, I'll see to it that Dominick Moynihan is the one to get it. You know him?"

"The tailor at Fancy's? Sure. Everyone knows him."

"He'll get the message, but I'll have him pass it on to you. When you get it, you need to be ready to do what the message says and quickly. Understand?"

"I think so."

Wolpert took a sip of his coffee. It was good. That's about all he could concern himself with at the moment. There was just too much else going through his mind to enjoy something so simple.

"Are you all right, Sheriff?"

"Lucy, do you know who Burt Sampil is?"

She was obviously surprised to hear him say her name in such an offhanded manner, but she flinched as if she'd been struck when she heard the second name. "Yes, I know who he is."

"I'll be off doing a job with him," Wolpert declared. "That's where I'll be going."

She straightened up and crossed her arms. "Then I won't have any part in helping you. My brothers told me plenty about that one for me to know what kind of man Burt is."

Wolpert stepped closer to her. When she tried to move away from him, he grabbed her arm to keep her close.

"I won't be helping him. I'm going along because he's up to something that will lead to a lot of good men getting hurt or even killed. Whether I'm with him or not, he'll see his plan through. Even if I kill him, the others in his gang would be forced to move a lot quicker and that would just mean more people would get killed along the way. I aim to put a stop to it. No matter what you hear and no matter what anyone else might say, I need you to believe that."

As soon as she stopped resisting, Wolpert let her arm go. Once she was free, Lucy locked her eyes upon him. "You're the sheriff," she said. "Why do you need to go through all of this to do your job?"

"Because I've been letting my job slip for too long. If I start acting like a proper lawman now, this whole town will wonder what's gotten into me. It may be for the better, but Burt Sampil or any of the killers in his gang won't think so."

"It sounds like you expect to get hurt."

"It's bound to get bloody. I hate to even ask you to be a part of it in any way, but I'll see to it that none of that blood gets on you."

"Maybe if you arrest Burt and his men, make an example of them, the rest will just stay away."

Wolpert shook his head. "Greed don't work like that. I know all about it."

In the space of the last few seconds, Lucy had allowed herself to drift closer to him. Suddenly, she pulled away and steeled herself as if she were preparing to take a swing at his battered chin. "Do you take me for a fool? I do know all about you, Sheriff. You've done other jobs with Burt Sampil, haven't you? You've protected him for years."

"That's right."

"So why the change of heart now? Why should I believe you're not just trying to get me to do something that'll make it easier for you to rob some bank or do whatever else you're planning on doing?"

When he placed his hands upon her arms, Wolpert had intended only to hold her in place. The moment he felt the warmth of her body, it was all he could do to keep from pulling her closer. "Please, just trust me this once."

"Why me? Until those horses were almost stolen, you barely knew I was here."

"I knew you were here. Even if we never spoke, I always saw you."

Flushing in the cheeks, Lucy asked, "And why should I trust you?"

"Because nobody else will. Look, right now neither Burt nor any of his men know I'm here. The longer I stay, the bigger chance there is of that getting messed up. You were right in what you said before. It's high time for me to use this badge for something other than a license to steal. If this job that Burt had planned was just one big robbery, I could make sure it doesn't happen or even put Burt away before it does. But this job will open the door for lots of other jobs where the thieves will all have the upper hand. You ever hear of Little Big Horn?"

"Of course."

"That," Wolpert explained, "is what happens when the wrong kind of man gets too full of himself and thinks he got the upper hand. Even when he loses it, he fights harder to get it back. Usually, he and damn near anyone around him gets burned in that fire. This job will get some bad things rolling down a very steep hill."

She shook her head and pulled back. "I don't know about any of this. I just work in my livery and try to make ends meet."

"You don't need to be a miracle worker. Just be ready and trust that I'm working toward a proper end this time. Can you do that?"

When Lucy looked into the lawman's face, she saw enough for her to know that he was truly depending on what she would say next. More than that, she saw a strength that simply hadn't been there before. It lay beneath all the other bruised and beaten layers of his skin.

Arriving at an impasse, she let out the breath she'd been holding and let her instinct answer for her. "What do you need me to do?"

Chapter 11

Chimney Lake, Nebraska
Thirty miles southwest of Sedley

Just over half a day's ride across a whole lot of flat ground was a town called Chimney Lake. Compared to most towns, this one was a pit. Compared to Sedley, it was a thriving, sprawling community. In all fairness, however, it was still a pit.

Years ago, the town had been just another nameless stopover point for westward drivers. It grew as many towns did, populated mostly by folks who were too tired to ride any farther. Then, in the spring of '81, there came a storm that lasted the better part of two weeks. It rained so much that the prairie ground soaked up enough water for it to pool at the lowest point. Since more forethought went into planning some dinners than it went into planning this town, the lowest point just happened to be near the town's center, right along with its town hall. A sinkhole quickly developed, more rain fell, the hole grew and eventually a small lake was born.

All that could be seen of the town hall was a healthy section of its chimney. Folks were still too tired to move along, so they rebuilt around it and finally gave their home a name.

Wolpert always liked going to Chimney Lake. It was a town that could fend for itself. After having their center of government sink into the earth, the townspeople didn't have much choice. Their need for a sheriff was merely to haul away the few lawbreakers who hadn't been taken care of by vigilantes or to settle the occasional civil dispute. When Wolpert arrived, he was greeted with friendly waves and cordial nods from locals who were plenty aware of his reputation. Wolpert knew their friendliness would dry up if he looked over their shoulders for more than a day or two.

Civility in small doses.

Something about that frankness was comforting to the weary sheriff.

Wolpert would have been in town earlier, but he'd hung back for a few hours while Tom, Cade and Juan rode ahead. They were more than escorts this time around. They had a job to do, and judging by the panicked look on the face of the man approaching Wolpert now, the other three had done it beautifully.

"Hello, Sam. What's got you riled up?"

Sam Waterman owned a healthy portion of the land in and around Chimney Lake. He ran a dry goods store as well, which made him one of the prominent citizens in those parts. As such, he was always nervous and fidgety about the state of his precarious investments. He stood a bit taller than average height and wore his ample girth like a badge of honor declaring he had the wealth necessary to build such a round belly. All the suits he wore came from Fancy's shop in Sedley, which was a distinct difference between him and the other portly man Wolpert had met in Omaha.

"The bank's been robbed," Sam sputtered. "This morning, not long after it opened for business! Three men rode in and shot the place full of holes and rode out!"

"Is that so?"

"Yes, sir! Caught us with our pants down, you might say. Johnny and Mike fired back at them and are still out after them, but they probably won't catch 'em. They bolted out of here like their tail feathers were on fire."

"If I know Johnny and Mike, those robbers were lucky they weren't on fire."

Johnny and Mike were the most enthusiastic vigilantes Wolpert had ever met. They were decent trackers, but their strength was persistence. They weren't exactly early risers, however, which was why Wolpert had sent in the other three so they would arrive in the breaking moments of dawn. The First Bank of Chimney Lake had been cracked wide open right on schedule and Wolpert was supposed to be the man to see who'd swung the hammer.

"How much was taken?" he asked.

Sam walked alongside the tan gelding Wolpert had purchased from Lucy. It was a spirited animal that was better suited for several grueling days of galloping than his other horse. "I had a few investors come through here a few days ago and there was plenty in the safe then," Sam said. "Either those bandits didn't have their facts straight or they just got real unlucky, because they missed their chance to get that money. There couldn't have been too much in there. All the damage they did to the place is probably more costly than what they stole."

Wolpert rode around the next corner with Sam right beside him. If he hadn't known where the bank was already, all the lawman would have needed to do was look for the crowd of gawking locals. Close to a quarter of the town's population was gathered in the street in front of the bank, chatting and wildly gesturing toward the far end of the street. After dismounting and tying his horse to a post, Wolpert approached the crowd with Sam sticking to him like a very well-dressed deputy.

"I hear there was some commotion this morning," Wolpert said.

Everyone stopped talking, turned to look at him and then spoke in a stream of words that immediately blended into an indecipherable soup. Nodding at them without meeting the gaze of any one person in particular, Wolpert eased through the crowd and stepped up to the bank. Even before his boots touched the boardwalk, the acrid scent of burnt gunpowder filled his nostrils.

"Hold on, now," Wolpert said. "Just give me a moment to see what's left."

Sam stepped up and puffed out his chest in a stately manner. "The sheriff has just arrived in town, no doubt to see to this personally. Everyone step back and let him do his job."

Some of the people stayed behind and some drifted in behind Wolpert. None of them seemed affected in the slightest by what Sam said and they surely weren't listening to him as he continued to address the crowd.

Every step Wolpert took near or beyond the bank's

front door was marked by the crunch of boots upon shattered glass. The bank's wide front window had been shot to pieces. Studying the amount of broken glass on the floor and the small size of the shards that remained in the frame was enough to let him know the main intent of the gunfire had been to make a mess. Once inside, the sheriff looked around at splintered walls, chipped tables, busted chairs and a sagging crack in the counter in front of the tellers' windows that was roughly the size of a boot print. He shook his head while imagining Tom or Cade having a grand old time in there.

Wolpert walked through a narrow doorway that had obviously been forced open. It led around to the other side of the tellers' windows where a pair of small desks and a single closet-sized office were located. He could hear subdued voices in the office, but he took a moment to get a look at the area around the cash drawer and back by the safe. Despite all the bullet holes riddling the walls and desks, Wolpert spotted only a few small splashes of blood that led him back to the office.

Knocking on the office door, Wolpert's knuckles tapped the edge of a plaque that read Harold Meter— Bank President.

"Harry?" Wolpert said as a way to announce his presence. "You all right?"

Harold Meter was a barrel-chested man who seemed better suited to punching cattle than sitting cooped up in the little room. The jacket that matched his gray suit pants had been removed and thrown over the back of the chair in which he now sat. The cuffs of his sleeves were unfastened and his rumpled white shirt was smeared by blood that had been spattered on him like sauce from a particularly messy supper. When he saw the lawman step into his office, Harry stood up and lowered the handkerchief he'd been pressing against his nose.

"Good to see you, Zeke. What brings you here today?"

"I don't know," Wolpert chuckled. "Why don't you tell me?"

"Oh, we got robbed this morning. Didn't think you'd notice."

Along with the two men, there was also a slender woman with long, stringy red hair leaning against the wall beside Harry's desk. Her arms were folded across her chest as if she was using them as a shield. Her long, sour face was streaked with tears and the thick layers of clothing wrapped around her nearly doubled the amount of space she occupied. "Mr. Waterman's nose was broken by those vicious gunmen," she announced.

"It ain't so bad," Harry said while dabbing at his nose with the handkerchief. "One of them wanted me to open the safe. I refused, so he poked me in the nose. I've had worse."

"Why don't you start from the beginning and tell me the whole story?" Wolpert asked. "Then I can see about tracking those men down."

"Someone's already tracking them down," the redhead snapped. "Maybe they already found them."

"If you're talking about Johnny and Mike, I'm sure we would have heard the celebration if they'd found their men already. Besides, there's something to be said for getting all the facts and making a plan instead of pulling on your pants, jumping on the back of a horse and stampeding out of town like a pack of dogs. Come to think of it," Wolpert added, "there were a few times when Johnny forgot his pants, weren't there?"

Harold chuckled and then winced because of the pain that shot through his face, but the redhead wasn't amused. She barely sat still long enough to add her two cents to her employer's account of the robbery. The three robbers had thundered up to the bank, made a lot of noise, waved their guns around and demanded whatever money they could get. Going after the safe hadn't been in the plan when Wolpert and the other three had sat down to discuss it beforehand, but Harold said that "the big fella" insisted on trying to get his hands on the most money possible.

Wolpert gritted his teeth as he thought back to his earlier talk with Tom. He'd warned him from going after the safe because that would take too long and allow the town's vigilantes more time to catch them. Tom insisted on making a play for the safe, if only to make the robbery seem more authentic, and apparently had gotten his way.

"Was anyone else hurt?" Wolpert asked.

The redhead lurched away from the wall and stretched her arms out like a hawk swooping down to pick up a hapless mouse. "Take a look around you! Look at Mr. Meter's face!"

"Easy, Carla," Harry said. "The man's just doing his job. Tell him about the Mexican."

"One of the men was a Mexican. He stuck his gun in my face the whole time and threatened to kill me if I didn't do what he told me to do. He would have killed me. I know it."

If he had killed her or anyone else in that bank, Juan

was a dead man. Wolpert had made that perfectly clear the last time they'd spoken.

"So he didn't harm anyone other than Harry?" the lawman asked.

"Isn't that bad enough?" Carla said. "Lord only knows how many people they shot on their way out of town."

"Which way did they go?"

For the first time since Wolpert had arrived, the redhead's sour face brightened. "I heard one of them mention riding north. Probably the Dakota Territories if you ask me."

"You know something? I'll bet you're right. Thank you very much for that."

Since she had no way of knowing that bit of information had been dropped on purpose, Carla nodded proudly and fussed some more with Harry's busted nose.

"So, how much was taken?"

Without pause, Harry replied, "Two hundred sixty-three dollars and forty-two cents."

"I'll see what I can do to bring it back." Wolpert looked over to Carla and asked, "Anything else you want to tell me before I head out to pick up these bandits' tracks?"

"No, Sheriff. That's all I can think of."

"Good." After tipping his hat to them, Wolpert crunched some more glass under his feet and made his way to the front door. Once outside, he lowered his head and shoved past the crowd as if he were plowing a field with his shoulder. His horse seemed like a mile away and he knew he'd never make it there before Sam Waterman caught up to him.

"Did you see the bank, Sheriff? Did you see the

damage?" the portly man asked in a breathless rush. "Did you hear about the money that was stolen? Did you talk to Harold Meter?"

"No, Sam," Wolpert said in a dry tone. "I walked in, saw the broken glass and decided to make a withdrawal. Nobody came to the counter, so I left."

For a moment, it seemed that Sam might actually take the joke at face value. Then he hurried to get a few paces ahead of the sheriff and walked backward to stay in front of him. "Of course you did all you could, Sheriff. Where are you headed now?"

"To another bank. I said I needed to make a withdrawal, didn't I?" Since Sam appeared to be genuinely flummoxed, Wolpert strode to the post where his horse was tied and said, "My horse needs tending and a bit of water, so I'll see to that and be after those robbers. You know anyone else around here who saw what happened or might know which way those men went when they skinned out of here?"

Always eager to be in the thick of anything that seemed important, Sam nodded and nearly tripped over his feet while turning around so he could walk beside Wolpert instead of backpedaling in front of him. "I've been talking to folks all day. You know, to assuage their worries and what have you. It's my duty as the town's—"

"Point me in the direction of who knows the most and I'll have a word with them. Better yet," he added while taking the horse's reins and leading it down the street, "why don't you round them up and bring them to me? Would that be too much trouble?"

"Too much trouble? Why, of course not!"

Of course not. Wolpert had to fight to keep from

grinning at how easy it was to steer the other man in the proper direction. If he played his cards right, he'd probably be able to get Sam to buy him a steak dinner when he got back.

"Do your best and do it quick," Wolpert said. "I'll be at the Third Street Hotel."

Sam blinked a few times in quick succession. If he was a different gender, the motion might be considered a flutter of the eyelashes. "The Third Street Hotel?"

"That's right. Is that a problem?"

"Do you think they had something to do with the robbery?"

"Why? Do you?"

Sam looked toward Third Street and then quickly averted his eyes as if simply gazing toward the town's most widely known collection of working girls was a sin. "No, I never thought of that. It's just that those robbers are out there now. The longer they have to run—"

"The more tired they'll be," the sheriff snapped. Quickening his pace toward the corner, he explained, "There's a stable right next to the hotel and waiting there is just as good as waiting anywhere else. Besides, Emma can whip up some mighty fine eggs on short notice. You wouldn't want me tracking on an empty stomach, would you?"

Even though the sheriff had hastened toward the corner and was widening the gap every second, Sam muttered, "I . . . um . . . suppose not. I'll just send those folks over there to tell you their accounts of what happened."

Wolpert led his horse around the corner and down Third Street.

"Or I'll send word and you can meet them somewhere more appropriate," Sam continued to his audience of none.

Wolpert was almost out of sight, and if he heard any of that last sentence, he gave no indication.

Without a lawman's ear to bend, Sam hurried to the stores across from the bank, already anxious at the prospect of barging in and announcing he was there on official business.

Chapter 12

The instant she saw Sheriff Wolpert stepping through her door, Emma Brown ran for the tin of flour in her kitchen. Several other girls along the way were quick to hop out of her path. The men who weren't being entertained in one of the upstairs rooms watched her go as if they were observing a one-horse race. Emma was tall and gangly, with wavy hair that flowed behind her as she ran. Her long legs helped move her to the back of the hotel quickly while her slender body twisted and bent around the other people or pieces of furniture in her path.

Once in the kitchen, she grabbed the flour tin, rummaged inside and found what she was after. Removing her hand revealed very little flour on her smooth skin, but a whole lot of money gripped in a possessive fist. The tin was quickly replaced and her hand was stuffed into her pocket so it would be hidden during her return trip down the hall.

"Emma!" one of the younger girls shouted from the front room. "Zeke's here!"

"Send him up to my room," she shouted.

Without casting so much as a glance toward the door, Emma veered toward the staircase that led up to the second floor. She bounded up the stairs, made a left down the hall and went to the last door. Inside that room were her rolltop desk and several shelves that contained ledgers chronicling all of the business conducted in the Third Street Hotel, legal or otherwise. She grabbed a stumpy pencil, counted out the right number of bills from the money she'd collected, scribbled down the sum and put the remainder back into her pocket. Hearing the sound of distant footsteps, she looked up to find Wolpert already filling the doorway to her office.

"Good Lord!" she yelped. "How does a man your size walk so quietly? You scared the daylights out of me!"

"Sorry. Wasn't my intent."

"I've got most of your money right here. I know it's been a while, but I didn't forget. We were slow for a while, but a few cattle drives came up from Texas and those boys are always randy when they climb down from their saddles. Here you go."

Wolpert barely looked at the hand she extended. "Forget about that."

The smile on her face flickered like a candle that had been set too close to an open window. "Go on and take it."

"You heard me," he said in a level tone. "Keep it."

Some of the color drained from her face and she blinked several times in quick succession. "All right. I do have the rest," she said while digging into her pocket for the remainder of the money. "The only reason I held back was because winter's rolling in and it feels like it's gonna be a hard one, which means business will slow to a trickle. When that happens, we feel the pinch and if we feel too much of it, we may have to trim back on some things. If we trim back, I won't have the money to pay you the next bunch of times you come through town, and if that happens—"

Wolpert stepped forward and took both of her hands in his. "No need to be so flustered. I'm not here to collect any money."

"You're not?"

"No," he said while taking his hands away to leave every bit of cash in her possession. "I'm not."

"Then why are you here?"

"Didn't you hear about the bank robbery?"

"Of course, but nobody expects you to come running for every crime. The question is, how did you hear about it?"

He smirked and chuckled under his breath, amused by the fact that she was the first one to ask him that question. "Sam Waterman is gathering up some witnesses to tell me about what happened. I told him to bring them here. Is that all right?"

"Sure! Especially since some of them will probably stay for something to eat or maybe one of the other house specialties. Speaking of that, why don't you find your way to my room and we can work out something else to hold you over since you won't take my money?"

Reaching behind him, Wolpert made sure the office door was shut tight. "I didn't come for that either. I'm a married man, you know."

"You call taking the same woman's guff for way too long a marriage?"

"I suppose."

"Well, believe me, my girls and I see plenty of married men come through this hotel and their situation never causes them to miss a step on the way up those stairs." Emma's eyes narrowed and she looked him over carefully. "What's the matter with you, Zeke? You don't want any money. You don't want me. There's something different about you. What is it?"

"We've got some history, you and I," he told her. "Sometimes I figure you know me better than anyone. Better than Jane, even."

"Jane only knows how to spend whatever you put in her hand and she doesn't care how you get it. I may have only lived in Sedley for a year or two, but I knew her well enough to never drop any silver dollars where she could reach 'em. After you helped me set up shop out here, I half expected her to try and weasel her way in as a partner."

Wolpert nodded through all of that. Everything Emma said was true but didn't seem to matter any longer. He needed a moment to steel himself, but he was finally able to ask, "Are you afraid of me?"

"Afraid of you? No."

"A few moments ago, you sounded like you were bargaining for your life."

"Well, you normally don't like to hear your payments are late. Even if we're friends, I wouldn't want to try and step on you."

"What if I said I didn't want payments anymore?" Wolpert asked. "What if you just conduct your business the way it's supposed to be conducted?"

"Now I know something's wrong. What is it?"

"Something's always been wrong. I knew it, but never had the gumption to set it straight. Have you ever been buried so deep in something that it seems like there ain't no way out?"

"Do you know who you're asking?" she chuckled. "I'm the one that got so snowed under with debts to the men who used to be partners that they practically owned me, soul and all."

"What about the way you earn your living?"

"What, you mean being a whore?" Emma asked. "For your information, I do a lot more than what most people think. This is still a real hotel, you know. And as for my girls, it ain't easy running a business with so many employees no matter what they're doing to earn their pay."

"Did you ever want to get out?"

"I like what I do," she told him while pacing to the door and then back to her desk. "If this is about making an honest woman out of me, you should know I don't intend on giving up my hotel."

As Emma fluttered about the room like a panicked moth, Wolpert unbuttoned his coat, took a seat in a small padded chair against the wall, removed his hat and set it upon his knee. "I wouldn't dream of asking you to give up your hotel."

"Then what are you talking about?"

Rather than answer her, Wolpert continued fussing with his coat and getting situated on the frilly chair. He seemed more concerned with crossing one leg over the other than the growing tension pouring off the woman in the room with him.

Emma stepped right up to him, dropped to her knees so she could look him in the eyes and whispered, "Is this something to do with that bank robbery?" When

Wolpert looked at her evenly without seeming even vaguely surprised by the accusation, she drew in a quick breath. "You robbed the bank?"

"No, of course not."

"Then you arranged for it?"

"Well . . . there may be some truth to that."

"So those three men who shot the place up are with you? Did they threaten to kill you for your share? Do you need somewhere to hide for a while? Is that what you mean by getting in over your head?"

"No, Emma. What I mean is that I intend on bringing down Burt Sampil."

"I thought you and him were partners."

"I was on his payroll. I wasn't ever a partner. Not until recently."

"So, you took him as a partner and now you want to bring him in?" She straightened up and rubbed her temples. "I must have lost you somewhere."

Wolpert practically jumped to his feet. The little chair overturned behind him and he pulled off his coat as if he were angry at it more than anything else. Once he got it off, he placed his hands upon his hips and started pacing the room. "When I was in the cavalry, it wasn't so I could use my station to get rich. I had a duty and saw it through. I rode with good men who sometimes died out in the dirt without so much as a crooked stick to mark the spot where they fell. More than once, I thought I'd wind up beneath a few scoops of dirt, but the other men in my regiment saw to it that I came home.

"We did good work, Emma. We helped families survive attacks from the Sioux. I even defended a few forts. Some of them burned to the ground after I left, but one of them stands to this day. I was drummed out of my rank because of a couple stupid mistakes. When I signed on to ride on a posse with Sheriff Vincent, I felt the old rush of blood through my veins."

Emma sat upon the edge of her desk and gently reached out to hold on to one of his wrists as he paced by her. That loose grip was all it took to keep him from stomping a rut in the floor. "I never knew any of this, other than you used to wear an army uniform. I always thought you must have looked handsome in that."

Letting the compliment pass without the slightest acknowledgment, Wolpert said, "I met Burt Sampil on that posse."

"Burt was on a posse?"

"No, the posse was after him. I found him. He offered me a hundred dollars to look the other way so he could keep riding. It was easy money. I needed it. I looked the other way. When Burt showed up again after the dust settled, he said I could make even more without doing much more than I already had."

"So Burt's the reason you started . . ." Emma bit her tongue as if she'd almost called him a filthy name. "After that is when you decided to make your collections?"

"No. I took the money because I was lazy and because I thought that no matter what I did, the world would just keep turning like it always had. Men like him would always hurt folks. When I rode in the army, we'd help a group of wagons through some mess only to find those wagons upended and burning thirty miles down the same trail. Forts I'd defended burnt down anyway. Battles good men died to win were only fought again until they were lost. There just ain't no point to it."

Emma clasped his hand so his palm rested upon hers. She used her other hand to softly stroke the top of his hand, feeling muscles that were nearly taut enough to snap. "Soldiers see plenty of bad things. They see the worst of it sometimes. It takes a toll on any man."

"That doesn't give him the right to take the thing he's supposed to represent and make a joke out of it just so he can line his pockets." When he looked at her, Wolpert stared straight into her eyes with an intensity that was jarring. "What if I'd done that when I was wearing my army uniform?" he asked. "That would have made me a traitor! I would have been shot for it and rightfully so."

"That may be a bit much in your case. You didn't ever do anything traitorous while in uniform, did you?"

"No."

"As for using a badge for your own benefit, that's hardly anything new. In my line of work, I've seen more crooked lawmen than I can count. They're practically part of the natural order of things," Emma said. "In fact, I'd wager that there are just as many lawmen out there who bend the rules as there are those who enforce them."

"That don't make it right," Wolpert growled.

She smiled at him as if she were admiring the face of a young boy who'd gotten attached to her after paying for his first tussle under the sheets. "So after all these years, Sheriff Ezekiel Wolpert decides to polish off his badge and do right? I suppose after bringing Burt Sampil to justice, you'll make amends for all the money you stole or all the collections you've made to honest businesses like mine?"

Turning as if he'd entered into a whole other conversation, he grunted, "Honest businesses like yours?"

"More or less!"

"Because of me, this whole county is a haven for killers like Burt Sampil and his boys. Because of me, good folks are getting hurt. Don't you see that?"

Walking around her desk to sit in the larger of the two chairs, Emma took a cigarette from a pristine silver case and slid it between her full red lips. "I see, Zeke," she said while striking a match to light the cigarette. "I've always seen that your heart's in the right place. Just be sure it stays there."

"Are you my conscience now?"

"No, I mean make sure it stays in your chest. If you plan on crossing Burt Sampil, there's a real good chance that a lot of valuable parts of your body may wind up scattered to the four winds."

"You don't think I know that?" Wolpert snapped.

"I'm just giving you a friendly reminder," she replied. After studying him for a good, long time, Emma whispered, "You're really serious about this."

"Yeah. I am. I stopped by to ask you a favor. I know you've got a lot of friends from bounty hunters and lawmen all the way up to federals. If something happens to me or if you don't hear from me within the next few weeks, I want you to track me down. You'll probably need to start looking in Texas. No matter what becomes of me, you'll also need to go to my home in Sedley."

"You mean that old shack of yours?"

"That's the one. Pull up the floorboards underneath my cot and you'll find some money I've been squirreling away. If the banks hadn't gotten their money back by then, repay them using that money and you keep the rest for yourself."

"That's it?"

"Yeah."

"What makes you think I won't just keep it all no matter what?" she asked.

"Because I know you better than that. You wouldn't deny a man his last request."

She pulled in a deep breath and let it out along with a gust of smoke. "This request better not get me involved in the mess you got planned with Burt."

"There's no reason for it to, but I can't guarantee anything." Turning to face her head-on, he added, "But considering our history and that everyone knows I got a regular room at this hotel, I'd say Burt figures you'll always have some connection to me."

Emma sighed warily, took a pull from her cigarette and sent a plume of smoke into the air. "I'm surprised Jane hasn't found out about that room of ours and come here to set it on fire."

As the smoke curled around his head, Wolpert shifted his gaze toward the floor and muttered, "She knows. Just like I know about the men she's been keeping company throughout our farce of a marriage. We've been through with each other for a long time. Now I'm through with all them things that the boy in that old, clean cavalry uniform of mine wouldn't have been able to stomach."

"So what brought about this change?"

"I've been thinking of things differently since I met this . . . well, this livery owner."

"A woman?"

"I didn't say that."

Leaning to prop her elbows upon her desk and rest her chin upon her hands, Emma said, "You didn't have to. No man would talk about some smelly liveryman in that tone of voice unless . . ."

"Not unless," Wolpert said, "she's a woman."

"And not your wife," she pointed out with distinct amusement.

"No. Not my wife. The only thing Jane ever inspired me to do is go out to scrounge up some more money just to keep her satisfied."

"So this livery woman inspired you? She must be special." Raising her voice to a lyrical, singsong pitch, Emma said, "Like some angel that drifted from the heavens to set a poor wayward man onto the path of the straight and narrow."

"Even when I first met Jane and things were the best they ever were between us, I knew it wasn't anything miraculous. Meeting Lucy just once was different, though."

"Like a miracle?" Emma asked wistfully. "I've felt that once or twice."

Wolpert got up and went to the office's only window. Only after he'd pulled aside the curtains did the sound of an approaching bunch of people drift up from the street. One of the many voices down there belonged to Sam Waterman. The rest were chattering like a bunch of excited little birds. "It was something, but I don't know about all of that."

Realizing he wasn't going to say any more without being prodded a bit, Emma asked, "Did you gaze into her eyes? When you saw her lips, did you just want to plant a wet kiss on 'em?"

He looked over his shoulder to find Emma wearing a big, sloppy smile that was as bright as it was contagious. Turning back to the window, he replied, "Nothing so sappy."

"It had to have been like that." Feeling the slam of the front door as well as a parade of footsteps from the first floor, she tossed her pencil at the sheriff's back. "It sounds to me like you had a revelation after looking into a set of pretty eyes. It's all right for a big, rough lawman to get a taste of something sweet as that."

With the footsteps downstairs growing louder by the second and Sam's voice drifting closer to the stairs, Wolpert draped his coat over his arm and took a few steps toward the office door. Resting his hand upon the knob without turning it, he said, "It wasn't a revelation. It was just a moment that opened my eyes."

"If you're dead set on crossing a man like Burt Sampil, I'd think whatever happened to you was more along the lines of a miracle. Whatever it was, it must have been something big."

"Some of us don't bother looking for miracles or waiting for big revelations. We jump at little divine glimpses that other folks might allow to pass them by. For some of us," he said while pulling open the door, "it's all we deserve."

Chapter 13

Sam had worked a lot faster than Wolpert had expected, gathering several locals from stores near the bank or the street who'd witnessed the robbery. The entire group converged upon the Third Street Hotel like a mob and assaulted the sheriff with their accounts of the day's events. After hearing their frenzied reports, Wolpert could delay no longer. He pulled on his coat and hat, collected his horse from the small stable next to the hotel and rode out of town.

Every story but one said the robbers had headed west while making their getaway. The one account of the robbers riding north was either a mistake or a lie, because Wolpert had told Juan to lead the other two westward. A few of the more enterprising locals volunteered to ride along with him, but Wolpert refused on account of it being too dangerous. On his way out of town, he took several glances over his shoulder to make sure he wasn't being followed.

Fortunately, those volunteers weren't as tenacious as he'd feared.

If Juan led the others to the proper spot, Wolpert figured he should catch up to them in under an hour. Then again, judging by the gunshots that popped in the distance, he might catch up a lot quicker than he'd planned. Wolpert snapped his reins and leaned down low over his horse's back. The gelding tore across the landscape with a vengeance after having been cooped up in town. Even the staccato crackle of gunshots wasn't enough to slow him down.

Knowing the terrain well enough to navigate the uneven slopes, Wolpert rode beside a little creek that trickled toward Chimney Lake. His horse's steps thumped against the cold, packed dirt with more than enough force to send jagged cracks through the layers of ice on top of the water. When he caught sight of smoke hanging in the air like mud smeared upon a chilled windowpane, the sheriff steered his horse in that direction, cleared the creek in one jump and tapped his heels against the animal's sides.

In no time at all, he closed in on the source of the gunshots. There was a small cabin near a thin stream, its warped, neglected walls sagging beneath the weight of a partially collapsed roof. From a distance, Wolpert could see three horses clustered near the back of the cabin. As more shots were fired, he traced the puffs of smoke to two sources. The men were shooting at the cabin from different angles. One had sought refuge behind a stand of trees and the other was lying on his belly in the snow. As Wolpert drew closer, the man in the trees fired a shot over his head.

"Do that again, Mike, and I'll return fire!" Wolpert shouted.

The man on his belly rolled onto his side to get a better look at the approaching horse. "That you, Sheriff?"

"It is. Mind telling me what the hell you're shooting at?"

Mike was a tall, lean man in his late twenties with a face that was hardened by a combination of scar tissue and harsh prairie sun. Dressed in dark brown clothes and a tattered coat, he blended in nicely among the trees. His rifle was almost as skinny as he was and remained propped against his shoulder as he hollered, "Didn't you hear? The bank was robbed!"

"Of course I heard! How do you think I knew where to look for you two?"

"You're here to lend us a hand? Ain't that just perfect! You hear that, Johnny?"

The man on his belly looked like a bear that had been dropped by Mike's rifle. Short, thick legs were sprawled out behind him and his barrellike body had undoubtedly already made a trench in the ground. A floppy hat covered his head, but several clumps of wiry hair still managed to poke out from beneath it in several spots beneath the brim. He had a newer-model Winchester rifle in his hands as well as several shotguns lying on the ground within arm's reach. "You missed the fun, Sheriff," he said. "We chased these boys straight out of town. Saw they was cuttin' to the west, so we circled around to catch 'em before they crossed the old Cherokee trail."

Wolpert hadn't even known about that shortcut. Maybe the vigilantes weren't complete buffoons after all. "You got them cornered in that cabin, then?"

"Yep," Mike said. "Been shooting plenty of holes

through the walls. Thought we might check on 'em to see if we hadn't already done 'em in."

Just then, something rustled within the cabin and a muzzle flash lit up one of the small square windows. A bullet drilled through the tree a few paces away from Mike, causing the tall man to hold his rifle close and press his back against the tree he'd been using for cover. "Guess we need to make a few more holes, Johnny!"

Before Wolpert could say a word about that, both of the other men took aim and pulled their triggers. Between the two of them, they sent enough lead through the air to stop an elephant. Mike fired his rifle again and again, working the lever to chamber fresh rounds with impressive speed. Johnny lay on his belly, dug in like a tick and fired even faster. When his rifle ran dry, he grabbed the closest shotgun and sent two thundering blasts into the cabin.

"Will you two hold your fire?" Wolpert shouted. Since his words were drowned out by the echoing shots, he waited for a lull and tried again. "Hey! Lower those weapons!"

"What's the matter, Sheriff?" Johnny asked through a wide, sloppy grin. "Skin that pistol and join on in!"

Wolpert hurried over to the prone man and stepped on the shotgun so its barrel was flat against the ground and the stock wedged Johnny's hands in place. The vigilante let out a pained groan and squirmed like an earthworm that had been caught by a cat's paw. "Listen for a second, will you?"

"I am listening!"

"What do you think you're doing, Sheriff?" Mike asked from the trees.

Keeping his foot in place and his pistol pointed at

the cabin, Wolpert said, "I'm saving you men some ammunition. And I swear, Mike, if you're pointing that rifle at me, there's gonna be hell to pay!"

Like any vigilantes, these two were thirsty for blood. Mike snarled to himself and lowered his rifle as though he were going against nature herself. "I'm listening!" he said.

"Me too," Johnny grunted. "But I don't hear nothin'."

"That's just it. They're not even bothering to shoot back at you," Wolpert pointed out. "Could it be they're just inside waiting for the storm to pass?"

Looking up at him while still pinned to the ground, Johnny said, "Or it could be we hit the bastards. What do ya think of that?"

Wolpert didn't have to answer, because the men in the cabin did it for him. One of the last bits of glass in the windows was knocked out so a pistol could be propped against the sill and fired. The cabin's door creaked open just enough to allow another couple of gun barrels to poke out and spit fire at the vigilantes. Wolpert was also in that same line of fire, so he hopped off the gun barrel and dropped to lie in the dirt next to Johnny. The frozen ground was so hard it knocked a good portion of the wind from his lungs on impact.

The first few rounds had felt perilously close to hitting their target. After that, however, Wolpert could tell the men in the cabin were aiming too high to kill anything but a bird that had forgotten to fly south that winter.

Too excited to be upset about butting heads with the lawman just a few seconds ago, Johnny asked, "What do you think we should do, Sheriff? Go straight in or circle around and then go in?"

"I'm gonna get closer to that cabin and you two are staying behind." Raising his voice enough for it to carry over to the trees, he added, "You hear that, Mike? I'm going in!"

"That mean we're deputized?" Mike asked.

Suddenly, Johnny grinned like a kid with his nose pressed against the window of a candy shop. "Yeah! Does that make us deputies?"

Even in his most crooked days as a so-called peacekeeper, Wolpert wouldn't have made a mistake as big as deputizing the likes of those two. Doing his best not to let that show on his face, he replied, "That makes you members of a posse. I don't have time for the rest. Just keep firing and I'll see what I can do about flushing those three out of there."

"All three are in there? Did you see them?"

"Yeah," Wolpert lied. "Through the window. Now give me till the count of twenty and start firing some more." With that, the lawman patted Johnny's shoulder and pulled himself up to his feet. Hunkering down, he circled around to the left of the cabin in a wide arc. There was another door near the spot where the horses were tethered and Wolpert scurried toward that while putting on a show of trying to stay out of sight. The vigilantes were either fast counters or ignorant in their numbers, because they opened fire about five seconds too soon.

As much as he wanted to shove his way into the cabin, Wolpert wasn't of a mind to get himself shot full of holes by a bunch of jumpy outlaws. Instead, he crouched down next to the back door and rapped on it with his knuckles. After some rustling within the little structure, the door was pulled open and Tom glared out over the barrel of his Schofield.

"Where the blazes have you been?" the big man grunted. "We damn near got shot by those two crazy sons of—"

"Shut this door and tell the others I'm here," Wolpert cut in. "I'm making a lot of noise when I come through this door again, so I want plenty of noise in return. I don't want to get shot, though, you understand? Do. *Not*. Shoot. Me!"

"Yeah, yeah," Tom grumbled while kicking the door shut.

Wolpert took a few steps back and drew a breath. It wouldn't take much time for Tom to pass the warning along, but that didn't make him feel any better about charging in. Letting out something close to a howl, he threw himself at the door and smashed it open with his shoulder. Wolpert fired a shot into the ceiling, took a quick look around and then fired another through a wall where nobody was standing. As he'd figured, the three outlaws were low and behind the thickest portions of the house with some old furniture thrown against the front wall for good measure. They shouted something back at him and returned fire, but were careful to shoot everywhere but a spot that might hit anyone else in the cabin.

"Get to your horses and get out of here," Wolpert hissed. When they didn't move, he raised his voice and fired again to mask it. "Go!"

Tom and Cade were more than willing to head outside, but Juan stayed behind. No amount of gunfire from outside could distract him as he squared up to Wolpert and said, "We went to the spot you told us and those two pigs showed up instead. What happened?"

"I gave you a simple job to do and you couldn't get it done and get away before those two pigs caught up to you!" Wolpert shot back. "I'd like to know what happened myself."

"Those lunatics know this terrain so well they were ahead of us before we even know where we were going!"

"Well, I didn't see any horses out there, so now's your chance. Try not to linger or mess it up like you did at that bank."

Juan spat a few profanities at the sheriff as he moved past him. Since he wanted to make sure the exit was convincing, Wolpert kicked the outlaw in the backside on his way out. Sure enough, Juan turned and started firing at the cabin while shouting like an enraged wild man. Wolpert was sure to get out of the way and even ducked behind some of the cover the outlaws had already laid down. "I got 'em on the run!" he shouted.

The others were already in their saddles and turning their horses away from the cabin. Wolpert strode outside, motioned in the direction he wanted them to go and fired a few more shots in the air. Not only did the cabin provide excellent cover for their escape, but the shots acted better than a swat to each horse's rump.

"I'm coming around to fetch my horse," Wolpert announced. "Don't shoot!" He raised his hands and ran around the cabin to find both vigilantes on their feet.

"Did you kill 'em?" Johnny asked.

"I wounded a few of them, but they were ready for me."

Mike hurried over from the trees and said, "We was

gonna bust in there ourselves, but they held us off. I thought you had it that time, Sheriff!"

"So did I," Wolpert said while climbing into his saddle. "You men watch this spot in case they double back and I'll go after them."

"We didn't come this far to stand around and wait," Mike said. "We're comin' along with you!"

"By the time you get to your horses, they'll be long gone."

"Nonsense." With that, Mike let out a shrill whistle that cut through the air like a tomahawk. Before Wolpert's ears could stop ringing, a pair of horses stood up from the tall grass where they'd been hunkered down. He'd seen a few Indians and even fewer bounty hunters who'd taught their horses to lie down low like that, but he'd never expected the likes of Mike and Johnny to have such well-trained animals. Both horses shook the dirty snow from their coats and ambled toward their riders.

Trying to hide his reaction to that unwelcome surprise, Wolpert snapped his reins and said, "Well, these robbers have gotten a big enough head start already. If you can catch up, you're more than welcome to join the hunt."

"Don't worry about us, Sheriff!" Johnny shouted. "We can chase these boys all the way to Old Mex if we have ta!"

"Knowing my luck," Wolpert grumbled under his breath, "that's probably true."

He pushed his gelding as hard as he dared, riding as if he were the one with a posse gunning for him. Wolpert steered for a winding little trail that would allow him to catch up to the other three, but he didn't fool himself into thinking that would be enough to call the day a success. Within a few minutes of tearing across the tree-studded terrain at a full gallop, the three outlaws slowed their horses to a walk and waited for him to catch up.

"Don't stop!" Wolpert shouted as he frantically waved them forward. "Those vigilantes are right behind me! Keep going!"

"Go where?" Tom shouted. "This whole thing was your damn plan and you never mentioned a thing about no damn vigilantes!"

"Just get moving, will you?"

"Can we at least shoot them two?" Cade asked.

Wolpert's first instinct was to give a quick yes to that request. But, he reminded himself, those old instincts had brought him into the spot where he worked with known outlaws and killers on a regular basis. "Shoot *at* them," he said. "Don't kill them. The last thing we need is more men coming after us. That'd only punch holes through the plan we already got going."

Cade groused and the other two weren't any happier, but they all seemed ready to follow Wolpert's lead. That suited the lawman just fine. He did have a plan in motion, and having his partners be happy about it wasn't the most integral piece.

They followed the river west and then turned south. It wasn't long before Wolpert heard the sound of other hooves beating the ground behind him. He shifted in his saddle to get a look and found the vigilantes racing to catch up and then warned the outlaws by firing a shot that hissed through the air between Cade and Tom. When both men reflexively turned and pointed their guns at him, the sheriff waved and fired another shot that sailed well over Juan's head.

The outlaws weren't the only ones to take that as a cue. Both Mike and Johnny let out their own warbling war cries and started firing. Wolpert was pleased to see that Juan, Cade and Tom didn't need any more prompting to take appropriate action. They split up in three different directions while snapping their reins and urging every bit of speed they could from the horses. Every now and then, they turned and fired back. While their bullets were cutting through the cold winds in the general direction of their pursuers, their eyes were firmly fixed on Wolpert. That was enough for him to get a feel for what was surely going through their minds. They would play along with this for a little while, but weren't about to get killed just to spare a couple of loudmouthed vigilantes.

To be honest, Wolpert couldn't blame them. Being shot down by men like Johnny and Mike was as embarrassing a way to pass on as splitting your skull open after running into a brick wall on a dare. The only problem was that he couldn't think of another good way to get clear of the vigilantes without shooting them. They might not be the sharpest knives in the drawer, but they wouldn't give up any time soon. And then, Wolpert caught sight of something that was another one of Emma's little revelations.

He snapped his reins and let out a barking yelp that was too loud to be just incentive for his horse. Sure enough, Cade turned and looked back at him just in time to see Wolpert swing his arm toward the frozen section of stream that glittered in the sunlight. To keep up his appearances with the vigilantes, Wolpert fired a shot and waved again. The message was received and Cade led the other two outlaws toward the stream.

As Wolpert followed in the outlaws' wake, he knew the vigilantes weren't far behind. He also knew the next part of his plan was going to require a lot of good timing, some nimbleness and not a small amount of luck. The stream wasn't much more than a glittering hint of shallow water that had been turned into ice, but he eyed it as if it were the only thing in his world. With only one more bullet left in his gun, he slipped one foot from its stirrup and eased the other out so his toe was perched on the worn leather edge.

Cade, Juan and Tom rode straight at the stream and jumped over it without the slightest bit of difficulty.

Mike and Johnny were closing in on Wolpert even quicker than he'd anticipated, which made his idea seem worse and worse by the second.

A few more steps and Wolpert's gelding would be ready to make its jump over the crooked trail of frozen water. He could already feel the horse's muscles tensing in anticipation of the maneuver. Wolpert was all but convinced that he'd be a fool to even consider what he had in mind, but he knew he didn't have enough time to come up with something better. Once he tugged on the reins and eased one leg over his horse's back, it was too late to change his mind.

The instant his gelding's hooves touched down on the opposite side of the stream, Wolpert gave the reins another tug to slow it down and hopefully pull its head to one side. When the horse responded, the lawman pushed off using the toe that was still in its stirrup and dove to the ground. He hit the cold ground on his backside and rolled so his shoulder and leg knocked against the packed dirt. While he might have been fortunate not to have broken anything in his suicidal dive, Wolpert wasn't safe yet.

Mike and Johnny thundered closer to him. Their horses churned through the packed snow and cracked the frozen ground beneath it.

Wolpert tried to get up, but his leg was too banged up to support his weight so soon after the fall. Flopping around to lift himself onto all fours, he found the edge of the stream with one foot and slipped onto his face while sliding a few inches along the ice. He swore under his breath, closed his eyes and prepared as best he could to be trampled.

One of the oncoming hooves dropped so close to him that Wolpert could feel the ice flecks hitting his cheek. An animal spewed its heavy breath over him and the sun was completely blotted out by its massive torso. For one silent moment, Wolpert was certain he would feel the clubbing blow of a hoof or an iron shoe knock against his skull.

When the next set of steps thumped against the ground in front of him, Wolpert was afraid to open his eyes. If a hard death was still coming for him, he didn't want to see it. What he saw instead was the looming shape of Mike's horse landing on the other side of the stream. Johnny followed and spared only a quick glance over his shoulder to check on the sheriff's condition. Seeing Wolpert's shaky wave, the vigilante nodded and shouted even louder at the outlaws' backs.

No matter how much it hurt to do so, Wolpert pulled himself to his feet. His knees screamed for mercy and his entire left side felt as if it had been worked over with a shovel. Still, he committed himself to getting to his horse. Fortunately, the gelding had turned and was walking back to him. When he caught up to the animal, Wolpert took the rifle from the boot of the saddle, levered in a round and sighted along the top of the barrel.

"Come on," Wolpert sighed as he steadied his aim and figured the range to his target. "I don't care which of you does it, just *one* of you do it quick."

Wolpert trusted his ability with his Winchester, but wasn't so sure his aching arms could hold the rifle up for too much longer. Pain from his tumble seeped into his muscles and left them trembling with the strain of steadying the weapon. It reached up through his aching back, into his neck and squeezed the backs of his eyeballs like a pair of tiny fists.

Just as Wolpert's aim began to falter, one of the outlaws fired a shot at his pursuers. Wolpert squeezed his trigger, levered in another round and fired again. His first bullet sped through the air between the vigilantes and passed close enough to whisper into Johnny's ear. The second round went astray and cut a shallow groove through the flank of Mike's horse, which gave Wolpert an even bigger result than he'd hoped for.

The horse that had been grazed reared up a bit and peeled off its course while Mike tried desperately to steer it back. Johnny's horse was also spooked and followed the other animal's lead by shaking its head and digging its hooves into the dirt. It didn't slow to a stop, but it had lost all interest in the chase. Apparently, even their own animals were hesitant to let the overzealous vigilantes be the death of them.

Gritting his teeth, Wolpert forced himself to get back to his horse and place the rifle in the saddle boot. As much of a chore as that was, pulling himself back onto the gelding's back was even worse. Along the way, he took stock of the injuries he'd sustained in the fall. His legs were battered and bruised. His shoulder might have been knocked out of its socket and then shoved back in. His ribs ached and his neck punished him every time he so much as thought about turning his head. If not for the heavy coat and other layers of clothing he wore, Wolpert knew he would have been a lot worse off.

Once he was in his saddle, Wolpert flicked the reins and rode over to the vigilantes. Mike and Johnny had only just regained control of their horses and were checking on each other when he approached them and asked, "What happened? Either of you men hurt?"

"We ain't hurt, but those bastards tried to shoot my horse!" Mike replied. "What kind of scum-sucking rat does a thing like that?"

"The kind that don't live too long afterward," Wolpert replied. "I know where they're headed."

"You do?"

"Yeah. I had a word with a bunch of folks back in town and put their story together. Sounds to me like those men are part of a bunch that used to ride with Burt Sampil. They split off from Burt and struck out on their own and I know where they hole up."

"Then let's get 'em!" Johnny bellowed.

"That's just what they want," Wolpert protested. "What you two are going to do is rush back to town and round up some more men to go after them."

Both of the vigilantes nodded enthusiastically. "I know just the boys for the job," Mike said.

Wolpert knew about the same boys. They'd be the ones who rode with them when more than two sets of hands were needed for a hanging. The entire group of vigilantes worked well together, but they were bound to be disappointed when they followed the directions Wolpert quickly gave to Johnny and Mike.

"Maybe we should just tear after them before they get to where they're goin'," Johnny offered.

Wolpert shook his head. "They've got the whole trail scouted out and know exactly where to set an ambush. More than likely, the rest of their gang is waiting to pick off anyone who tries to come after them. You know who Jerry Treigle is?"

The vigilantes looked at each other and reluctantly admitted, "No."

Jerry Treigle was a smart-mouthed little skunk who'd pushed Wolpert around when they went to school together back in southern Kansas. Feeling the aches in his body reminded him of a time when Jerry had shoved him down the steps leading up to the schoolhouse. To the vigilantes, however, he explained, "Treigle is the reason I came to talk some sense into you boys before those robbers led you any farther. He's also one of the sharpest shooters I ever saw back in my army days and he's riding with those men now. If those robbers lead us any closer to the spot they got picked out, Treigle will knock us from our saddles like he was shooting bottles off a row of fence posts. You want to try dodging bullets on a skittish horse? Be my guest."

Mike calmed his horse down and pointed its nose toward Chimney Lake. Johnny did the same, but held off before flicking the reins. "So if we're all on this hunt together, does that make us official?" he asked.

Nodding solemnly, Wolpert said, "You do a good enough job and it'll make you deputies."

Both vigilantes raced to town, smelling their goal as if it were dangling two feet in front of them.

Wolpert still meant to turn away from his lying days, but didn't think of the incentive he'd given as a lie. If Johnny and Mike came up empty, they wouldn't expect an official title. And if they caught up with Wolpert and the outlaws again, a white lie would be the least of their problems.

Chapter 14

Wolpert rode until even his anxious gelding was running out of steam. Not long after that, he caught up with Juan, Cade and Tom at an old trading post run by an older German fellow who lived in the back of his own store. After watering the horses and collecting some supplies, all four men rode some more. They headed south mostly, splitting up every now and then to put down some confusing tracks, and met up a few miles later.

The sun drifted toward the horizon. The sky took on shades of purple and a few streaks of orange while the air grew teeth made of short gusts that gnawed straight through every rider's coat and raked against his bones. Wolpert's breath turned to steam as it left his mouth and was immediately captured by the wool scarf wrapped over his face before freezing. All too quickly, the stars appeared overhead and the dark became a treacherous thing that would cause an able horse to trip and spill its rider onto the ground.

And still, they rode.

Only when it became too treacherous to go on did

they find a spot to make camp. Wolpert wanted to press on, but decided he couldn't get much done if their horses tripped over or into something that blended in with the rest of the inky dark. Surviving one staged fall was lucky enough. Expecting to walk away from a real one was pushing his luck.

The fire they made was a sputtering flicker at best. When the wind howled, the bits of wood they'd been able to collect shielded the flame just enough for it to thrive. Cade and Tom sat close to the struggling source of warmth while Juan rubbed his hands together and paced like a caged animal.

"What was that mess back there?" Juan snarled. "You told us it would be an easy job!"

"It would have been if your idiot partner didn't try going after the safe when I specifically told you not to bother with it."

Tom shot an angry glance at Wolpert when he heard that, but he was too tired to do much else.

"You never said a thing about vigilantes," Juan continued. "And don't say you didn't know about them. I heard how you were talking to them back at that cabin. It was like you were old friends."

"Old friends is being awful generous," Wolpert said. Pulling a can of beans from the bottom of his saddlebag, he wandered over to the fire. "Found us some food. That is, if we can thaw it out."

"We could use a bigger fire," Cade said through chattering teeth.

"Sure," Wolpert grunted as he sat down and laid the can against one of the smoldering pieces of wood. "And those vigilantes can use our bigger fire to spot us from a mile away."

"I thought you sent them in another direction."

"I did, but those two are eager to prove themselves and they have good noses for hunting. That's a bad combination for us."

Juan stalked over to Wolpert. Keeping his arms crossed tightly over his chest, he kicked the sheriff in the back with the side of his boot. "I'm starting to think the bad combination is you working with us."

The pain he felt wasn't as much from the kick as from the impact that got his ribs and back aching again. He felt a jolt that was powerful enough to bring him to his feet, and that movement was enough to add even more pain to the mix. By the time he was up and facing Juan, Wolpert was ready to tear him apart with his bare hands. "You don't like this arrangement? How about you do something about it?"

Juan stared intently at the lawman. He didn't need to check to know the other two were watching him just as carefully. "You're the one who sent us into that storm. What's there for me to like about that?"

"We can go back and forth about this or we can sit and talk it over like civil men. One way will get your head cracked and the other involves getting closer to that fire. Right about now, I'm not favoring one choice over the other. How about you?"

A shrill wind raked over all of the men and nearly snuffed the fire for good. It also pushed Juan toward the possibility of warmth. As Juan picked his spot around the campfire, Wolpert collected a few more pieces of wood from the branches he'd collected earlier. After arranging the wood carefully, he stretched a tentative hand toward the can of beans. They were barely warm. "Why'd you go after the safe, Tom?"

"Because we were robbing a bank. What bank robber don't want the safe?"

"The kind that don't wanna get caught," Wolpert replied.

"Then maybe you should'a done it yourself."

"He's got a point there," Cade said. "Why don't you just tell us what the whole plan is before it bites us on the ass again? Or are you still just making it up as you go?"

"I'm not making it up," the lawman said while fighting to open the beans. "Well, not all of it." When he heard the rustle of iron against leather, he glanced over to find Cade aiming his gun at him. One by one, the other two outlaws followed suit. "You wanna use them things to open this can?" Wolpert asked. "It might go quicker that way."

"No. We'll use 'em to open you. Tell us what the hell we're out here for," Cade snarled. "I think we earned the right to know."

As he studied the other men, Wolpert barely took notice of the guns in their hands. What interested him more was the genuine look of concern etched onto all three of their faces. "You mean Burt didn't tell you?"

"He said we were to keep an eye on you while you broke them other boys outta some jailhouse in Kansas," Juan explained. "He said you used to live in them parts and knew the right men to approach and that we could walk in and out of there without a hitch. He also said to go along with what you wanted, so long as we wound up bringing them others out of jail in one piece. The rest has been you sending us into hell just so we could share a frozen can o' beans over a sorry excuse for a fire."

Just then, something about those men struck Wolpert as familiar. Seeing their angry, resentful glares took him back to many nights he'd spent wrapped up in army-issued wool, stretched out on hard ground when he would much rather have been in a warm bed. Back in his cavalry days, Wolpert hadn't always known why he was forced to brave the elements or weather hailstorms of hot lead. He wasn't about to mention these three outlaws in the same breath as the soldiers from his regiment who had died for a true cause, but he understood what was going through their minds. Like it or not, they all had their duties. They all had orders to carry out, but they just didn't get them from the same place.

"Do you know why we're going to free those men in the first place?" Wolpert asked.

None of the outlaws lowered their weapons, but Cade was the one to react to that question the most. "You sayin' you don't know?" he asked while his face pinched as if he'd just eaten something sour.

"I'm saying I don't buy what I was told. And since Burt was the one who did the telling," Wolpert added, "I think you can see where I may be concerned."

"It ain't gonna work," Juan snarled.

Shifting his eyes toward the other man, Wolpert asked, "What won't work?"

"You're telling us a whole bunch of nothing, trying to get us to believe you instead of Burt. Thing is, Burt's never tried to cheat us and he wouldn't never have made us put up with any guff from those vigilantes."

"What about sending men to get a job done when he knew they wouldn't come back?" Wolpert asked. "He ever do that to anyone you know? What about sending men to a horse trader in Omaha like a bunch of sacrificial lambs?"

After all the talking they'd been doing not so long ago, the silence that followed Wolpert's last question was striking. "You know he did that?" Tom asked.

"Didn't you have any suspicions?"

That struck a nerve in all of the other men. Reluctantly, Cade said, "Even if he did, he must've had his reasons."

"Maybe it was just to get rid of me." Chuckling at the surprise he saw on the outlaws' faces, Wolpert continued. "And since you men did such a good job of getting me out of there, I'm guessing he didn't let you in on that plan. If being in the army taught me anything, it was that the soldiers don't get to know much. In fact, maybe none of us knows the whole story of what's going on here. Do you know why we're going after these men who are locked up?"

"Sure," Tom replied. "So they can ride with us to the job in Texas."

"Do you know why he needs more men when he's already got the four of us?"

"Sure we do. We're after a lockbox loaded with gold or cash or something."

"And it takes more than five men to carry a lockbox? You fellas haven't wondered about all of this? Or are you just accustomed to blindly following Burt Sampil no matter what he's doing or where he wants to go?"

"That's some big talk," Cade grunted. "Especially from a man who's on a shorter length of rope than any of us."

"That may be true, but at least I know I'm tied to something," Wolpert pointed out. "If you men are putting your necks on the block for something that you don't even know about, then Burt must have you trained so well that he don't even need rope to keep you in line."

Hunching over and grabbing the can of beans that had been opened, Juan said, "It's cold and I wanna get to sleep. Say what you wanna say and be done with it."

It might have taken a bit of work, but Wolpert could tell he finally had the other men's undivided attention. "Maybe keeping us in the dark is a way to keep us from asking for our full cut of the profits."

"We're gettin' a percentage," Tom said.

"A percentage of what? Unless we all know what's going on, we'll just have to take whatever Burt gives us."

Tom's eyes narrowed into slits and his hand drifted back toward the gun he'd lowered just a few moments ago. "Are you proposing we cross Burt?"

"No. I'm proposing that we make sure Burt knows he's not dealing with a bunch of idiots," Wolpert told him. "Say what you want about how I make my money, but I've got plenty of experience in haggling over a fair price for services rendered. Undercutting another man's slice of your pie ain't cheating. It's doing business. Even sending word to that horse trader in Omaha was part of business."

Having listened to this without moving a muscle, Cade asked, "Why would Burt turn on us while we were in Omaha?"

"He didn't," Juan snapped. "He just didn't expect this crooked lawman to do what he was supposed to do."

"You know that for certain?" Wolpert asked.

"Yes."

Even if Burt had confided in one or two of his men, Wolpert still knew he had some room to work. "If I was being sacrificed alone, why didn't he send me on my own? Or maybe he told you men to go do some drinking and gambling while I was being captured?" Another shot in the dark hit its mark when all three outlaws shot each other quick, vaguely guilty looks. "He didn't. He just didn't know how capable his partners truly were . . . any of them."

The outlaws were more interested now than ever. A portion of truth mixed with a dash of flattery could do that. "Killing an incompetent partner to take his share of the profits ain't a new idea by any stretch," Wolpert said. "Working with smart partners on a level field, on the other hand, well, that's damn close to a pleasure."

"You think that's why he wants us to bring back all these old friends of his from Dog Creek Jail?" Tom asked.

Shrugging, Wolpert mused, "More men make for an easier job and if worse comes to worst, some fat can be trimmed without cutting too far into the steak."

The wind blew across the campfire as if purposely trying to reach down into the pile of twigs and pinch the flame out between a set of unseen fingers. The stars had become brilliant points of light, each one with only slightly less brightness than the sputtering flame. The can of beans had been passed around to the outlaws and was emptied in short order. Wolpert stood up and went to his saddlebags to hunt for some jerky and noticed that the others were no longer watching him like a hawk. They had other things to think about.

Finally, Juan asked the question that Wolpert had

been hoping to hear. "Do you know what's gonna be in that lockbox?"

The lawman shook his head. "Nope. And if none of you men know, I'd say that's a cause for concern. What I do know is that the lockbox is real important to Wells Fargo because it's got to do with a whole bunch of important shipments bound for Texas, New Mexico and California."

The outlaws were buying what was being said to them because they watched Wolpert the way a dog watched a piece of meat being dangled in front of its nose. When Cade spoke, he was practically drooling. "So it's a big payroll shipment that's bound to be divvied up and sent to other places?"

"Something like that," Wolpert said.

"Or maybe a bunch of gold?"

"I don't think it's gold. Do you know a man by the name of Eddie Vernon?"

Juan nodded. "Yeah. He's one of the men in that jailhouse we're going to. Got put in for busting open one too many safes for a gang of train robbers in Abilene."

"What about the gang?"

"Some got caught with Eddie and the rest scattered. Don't know what happened to 'em after that."

"Is Eddie good at his job?"

Bracing himself against a passing breeze that threatened to shred his coat with icy nails, Juan replied, "Real good. I hear the only reason he got caught is because that gang of his brought in too many safes for him to crack. Even hired him out for any other robbers to use his services. Word spread and the law came a-calling."

"So, if it ain't gold, what is in that box?" Tom asked.

"I don't know exactly," Wolpert said. "But I know

that once this job is over, there'll be plenty more on the horizon. That's why Burt will be glad to have partners he can trust."

"And what makes you such an expert about all of this?" Cade asked. "Why the hell should we listen to you?"

Wolpert was quick to explain, "Because I know what I'm talking about. Being any kind of lawman means you got to know how to take apart a gang of outlaws. Trust me when I tell you that a gang that trusts each other to the end is the toughest kind to crack. Any of you men ever been to Texas?"

"Sure," Juan said. "Plenty of times."

"Then you know those boys play by another set of rules. They're equal parts crazy and proud. Mix that up inside a man with a badge on his chest and it ain't a pretty sight for any outlaw that's in his sights. You fellows stepped up and got me out of a tight spot back in Omaha," Wolpert said earnestly. "For that, I owe you something more than just telling you where to go to get shot at again. Them vigilantes back there weren't supposed to get so close." Since that was the truth, Wolpert made sure the others could read it on his face. "I've dealt with Burt longer than you have and I'm telling you we could stand to earn some real money if we position ourselves as the part of this gang that ain't expendable."

Lowering his voice to a conspiratorial whisper, Juan asked, "What about the men that we intend on busting out of that jailhouse?"

"They got caught and tossed into a cage," Wolpert replied with a shrug. "We've kept out of messes like that. Which would you rather trust? As far as I'm concerned, I say keep them on the fringe, tell them only a little of what they need to know. When things get bad, have them prove their worth by stepping to the front line. If they don't come back . . . so be it."

There were nods all around the campfire before the outlaws stretched out to get some sleep. With that little bit of acceptance, Wolpert knew he'd taken one hell of a step. He might not be driving the gang, but the team had allowed him to take the reins for a spell. For a bunch of wild horses like these, that was saying a lot.

Chapter 15

The ride down into Kansas should have been an easy one. It was flat country where the biggest things working against any travelers were the wind and all the towering slopes it could create out of loose snow. That alone would have tacked some time onto the journey, but Wolpert and his new outlaw partners had more than the elements stacked against them. Three out of four of them were wanted men.

Under normal circumstances, Wolpert figured he could have covered the distance between the sputtering campfire where they'd started and the town of Lester in two days. Situated roughly thirty miles south of the Nebraska and Kansas border, Lester was built in a crooked stretch of Prairie Dog Creek. More important than the creek or even the town itself was the jailhouse sitting on its own like a brick that had landed after being dropped from on high. It was a solid chunk of rock and iron on a patch of land that was flat enough to deny any man a place to hide. Wolpert had been there only twice before, but that was enough to burn the picture of it in his mind along with a single sentiment: God have mercy on any poor soul unfortunate enough to be trapped in there.

But Wolpert didn't have the luxury of riding to the Dog Creek Jail as fast as his horse would carry him. He had other things to think about. Top among them was how quickly word would spread about the bank robbery in Chimney Lake. Folks had a tendency to gossip about any old thing, but something like that would spread like wildfire. Because of that, Wolpert couldn't spend any nights in a hotel room no matter how far away from civilization it was. Even the filthy town they'd spotted that was made up of canvas tents flapping around creaking wooden frames wouldn't suit their purposes. All four of them needed to stay out of sight while the rumors fermented and found their way to receptive ears.

After crossing into Kansas, he and the outlaws split up. Wolpert wanted to keep his head down for a while and encouraged the other three to do the same. He made sure to pass along just how many friends and cousins Johnny and Mike had in the neighboring states, and if those three wanted to take their chances with the vigilantes again, that would be their own foolish mistake. Considering the look of dread that crossed their faces at the slightest mention of Chimney Lake's self-proclaimed enforcers, none of the outlaws wanted to risk crossing their path again.

After five days of silently picking his way along broken trails and snowy fields, Wolpert caught sight of Lester. It was a decent-sized town, but the open desolation of the Kansas landscape made it seem much smaller. By this time, Wolpert had not only become accustomed

to the harshness of his journey but was embracing it.
Preachers often talked about serving penance for one's
sins, and the ride out of Nebraska was hard enough to
fit that bill. It was a start anyway, not to mention high
time he went through some hardship to make up for
what he'd done.

Looking into Lucy Myles's eyes as she'd called him
out had changed him. For some reason that he couldn't
quite guess, what she thought of him mattered and she
didn't think much.

Perhaps that had changed before he'd left town.

Perhaps that's why he'd paid her a visit before leaving. At the time, he'd simply wanted to get another
look at her. The more he thought about it, however, the
likelier it seemed that he'd tried to force her to change
her opinion by telling her what he intended to do. Either way, it had felt good seeing her that last time. It
had felt good hearing her voice and even seeing a smile
on her pretty face. Even if he'd imagined that smile, it
was a memory worth having. It was worth dying for.

Over the last few days, Wolpert had had a lot of
time to think. Now that Lester was in sight, even if the
ride had worn him down to the bone, it still didn't feel
like enough. It felt right that he should sit in the cold
for a while longer. He wanted to savor a few more days
of rolling up his sleeves and paying what he owed.
Then again, was a man supposed to enjoy his punishment?

That's where it all fell apart.

He never was too good at the philosophical matters.

Wolpert snapped his reins and steered his horse down
a narrow street that led to the town's main thorough-

fare. It was just before noon, which meant he was looking at a fairly good sample of Lester's busiest time of
the day. The town was more than triple the size of Sedley, but that wasn't saying much. Plenty of folks were
crowding the streets and tramping over the wobbly
slats that formed the boardwalk. Smells of several different kinds of food reached his nose with every breath,
tempting him more than the perfume of a warm and
willing woman. After having survived on the last of his
rations and a few bits of small game he'd shot along
the way, Wolpert nearly rode his horse directly into the
closest restaurant.

Instead, he rented a stall for the hearty animal and
made his way to a place recommended by the livery-
man for its tender steaks. The instant Wolpert got his
hands around a cup of hot coffee, he was a happy man.
The plan was to meet up with the others later that day.
For all he knew, Tom, Cade and Juan might already be
in town waiting for him to show up in the agreed-upon
saloon. Wolpert wouldn't know that until he had some
real food in his belly. Even if some flying pigs put on
a show outside, Wolpert wouldn't leave his seat until
he'd had his meal. Considering all the penance he'd paid,
he figured he'd earned it.

Just when he was feeling guilty for savoring the
quiet after insisting that the other three stay out of sight
and forsake all pleasantries along the way, Wolpert found
a better reason than the food to enjoy the warmth of the
little restaurant. Most of the front window was covered
by a curtain that had been faded from the sunlight. Even
with just a foot-tall strip of unimpeded glass through
which to see the street, Wolpert had no trouble making
out the bulky form of Marshal Luke Davis. And if he

did miss the sight, Wolpert would have needed to be blind to miss the small legion of deputies following him.

Marshal Davis was made up of large, simple angles that made him look as if he'd been quickly knocked out of a pattern etched onto a slab of solid oak. His hair was a light-colored scrub inching down from beneath the brim of a flat-topped hat where it turned into whiskers that added some texture to a chiseled jaw. The parade of lawmen blocked the view of the street for only a few seconds, but their heavy footsteps thumped against the boardwalk well before and long after they passed by. Even though Wolpert didn't think he'd been spotted, he kept his head angled downward and slightly away from the window.

Wolpert drank the last of his coffee and paid his bill as quickly as he could without giving the appearance of being rushed. Once outside, he didn't have any trouble catching up to the other lawmen. It would have been more difficult guessing which way a traveling circus had gone. All he needed to do was listen for the stomping and watch for the group of strutting deputies. Marshal Davis might have been a whole lot of things, but quiet wasn't one of them. Wolpert trailed behind the procession for several minutes. For the most part, the other men rarely broke their stride. When he spotted the marshal's office farther down the street and was certain the men were headed that way, Wolpert turned another direction. From there, he wound back across town, made his way to the entertainment district and picked out the Songbird Saloon.

As far as saloons went, the Songbird wasn't anything special. There was a bar on one end, facing the front doors. A few tables and chairs were scattered throughout the room, and several card tables were set up within sight of a few other games of chance. The air stank of burnt tobacco, cheap liquor and men who hadn't changed their clothes in recent memory. What made this saloon any different from most others was the narrow stage built at the back of the place. Plenty of saloons offered shows to attract customers. Not many of those shows were worth seeing, however, but the Songbird prided itself on its entertainment. As any of the partners who owned the place would proudly boast, the girls at the Songbird could do more than kick up their skirts.

At the moment, a sultry dark-skinned lady in a bloodred dress sang a slow song while seated with her legs dangling off the side of the stage. The crowd was thin at that time of day, making it easy for Wolpert to spot the faces he'd been looking for. No strangers to keeping out of sight, Juan and Cade drifted toward the bar and eventually closed in on the spot where Wolpert was standing. Tom needed a little more time since he had one of the songbirds on his lap. He stood up when he had a chance, gave her a swat on the backside and crossed the room to refill his beer mug. When a card table opened up, Wolpert headed over to claim it.

"What took you so long to get here?" Juan asked as he sat down in the seat next to Wolpert. "Did you cross paths with them vigilantes?"

The previous players had left two decks of cards on the table. Selecting the one with the least amount of water stains on the faces and a minimal amount of scorch marks along the edges, Wolpert started shuffling. "Didn't see a trace of them. What about you?"

"There were a few groups of armed men near the state border. Could have been them, I suppose."

Settling into the seat on Wolpert's other side, Cade said, "It was them. No hunters worth their salt would have been that noisy."

"Did they see you?"

"I think they might have picked up my trail," Juan replied. "But I didn't have any trouble shaking them. There's a bunch of Injuns that got a nice little surprise once I led those idiots straight to them."

"What about you, Cade? You sure they didn't spot you?"

"They may have spotted me, but they sure didn't follow me. I kept my head down just like you said. Made it tougher than it should have been to get here, but it was a quiet ride. I only just got here this morning."

"Then you did real good," Wolpert said. Turning toward Juan, he added, "You see what happens when you try to rush with a bunch of wild dogs nipping at your heels?"

It was plain to see that Juan wanted to fire back at that. Instead, he kept his mouth shut until he could pour some whiskey into it. After that, he didn't seem as upset.

Tom staggered up to the table, sat down across from Wolpert and slammed his mug down. "We playing cards or what?"

"Let me guess," Wolpert said, sneering. "You've been here the longest, just waiting for us to arrive."

"That's right! What took ya?"

Wolpert started dealing cards to each man. "Was your ride uneventful?"

"No. I found them vigilantes and gunned 'em all down. Then I rode into town and kicked my feet up." Laughing to himself, Tom added, "Of course it was uneventful. What'd you expect?"

After dealing the last card, Wolpert set the deck in front of him and locked his eyes on the big man sitting across from him. "Considering the spectacle you're making of yourself now, I'd expect the law to already have you in their sights."

Tom picked up his cards, fanned them and rearranged them. "You wanna know who sticks out like a sore thumb in a place like this? The men who aren't looking at the women or otherwise enjoying themselves. You fellas are like the dead fish floatin' around in a school of live ones."

The other two outlaws got a kick out of that, especially when they saw Wolpert was hard-pressed to refute it. Since they each had five cards in their hands, they all went through the motions of playing poker. That was just fine with Wolpert since he'd dealt himself three jacks. "Has the marshal noticed any of you since you arrived?" he asked.

"Which one was the marshal?" Tom asked.

Slapping two of his cards onto the table, Cade snapped, "The big fellow with the deputies following him like a pack of puppies. You really haven't stopped drinkin' since you got here, have you, Tom?"

"Nope, and I ain't about to start now. Stop, I mean. Start stopping. Aw, you know what I mean."

"Yeah," Wolpert sighed. "I'm afraid I do."

"I don't think the law knows we're here," Juan said. "At least the marshal doesn't know who we are. You think those vigilantes will be able to spread the word about us this far?"

"Hard to say," Wolpert replied while discarding his two extra cards and dealing out everyone's replacements. "They know enough folks to get the word spread all the way down to Oklahoma. Johnny has an uncle that's a stagecoach driver, so there's that. I'd say it's a fifty-fifty shot that anyone here knows that Chimney Lake even exists. Odds are even lower that someone knows the bank was robbed."

"Then why the hell did you want us to tiptoe all the way down here?" Tom growled.

"Because you boys already kicked up enough smoke already. Any more and this whole plan goes to hell."

"Well, we're here," the big man said with a grin. "And I'm feelin' lucky. I bet ten dollars."

"We're betting?" Cade groaned.

Smiling down at what had to be a peach of a hand, Juan told him, "Of course we're betting. It's poker. I call."

Wolpert nodded that he was in and all eyes shifted to Cade.

"Any of you fools play poker before?" he whined. "You can't just bet whenever you feel like it! There's a procedure to these things. There's an order, otherwise it's all one big mess!"

"Are you in or out?" Tom asked.

"Out."

"Fine, then shut up. Everyone else is in, but you won't be happy about it. Take a look at these beauts! Four kings!" When the big man laid his cards faceup on the table, all of the other three leaned forward to get a look at them.

"Are you kidding me?" Juan chuckled.

"Nope! Looks like I'm the lucky one out of all of you. Pay up."

"I'm not paying a damn thing," Wolpert said.

Tom's brow furrowed and he placed both hands upon

the table, tilting it toward him as he leaned in and asked, "What did you just say?"

"You're the drunkest out of all of us, I'll give you that much," Wolpert told him. "But the luckiest? Not hardly."

"Can you beat four kings?"

"No, and neither can you. Those are two kings, a queen and a jack. That makes you either drunk or blind."

"Or both," Cade chuckled.

Tom scooped up his cards and held them up so the brightly colored, water-smeared pictures were less than a foot in front of his face. Even after that, it took him a couple more seconds of close examination before he threw them back down and snarled, "Aw, to hell with all of ya."

"Three jacks," Wolpert announced.

The other two pitched their cards onto the pile of deadwood, admitting defeat but still laughing at their partner.

"I ain't paying a cent," Tom said. "These cards are too messed up to read."

"Keep it up," Wolpert said under his breath. "Almost there."

"Yeah, you're damn right!" Tom said as he jumped out of his chair. "If you think I'm honoring a bet made with these damn cards, you got another think comin'!"

Wolpert stood up, walked around the table and placed a hand on Tom's shoulder. A good portion of the saloon was looking over at their table, not fully interested just yet but waiting to see what kind of excitement might result from the argument.

"If it'll make you feel better, I'll let you boys settle the matter," Wolpert said calmly. "I'll abide by your decision and even buy a round of drinks. How's that grab you?"

Tom nodded and sat back down.

As he walked to the bar, Wolpert could already see the interest in his game had died down. Gamblers were getting back to their own games, other men had yet to take their eyes off the current songbird and others simply gazed down to the bottom of their beer. The barkeep was an older fellow with a head that was completely smooth on top and covered with shaggy growth on the bottom. It seemed as if someone had grabbed his beard and yanked until it drew the hair from his scalp all the way down through his chin.

"Four beers," Wolpert said.

As he filled the mugs, the barkeep said, "Looks like you might wanna keep an eye on that big one."

"Yeah. You recognize him?"

After squinting across the room at the side of Tom's face, the barkeep shook his head. "Can't say as I do."

"How long's he been here?"

"Better part of two days. The girls must know him pretty well by now. He's been working his way through a whole lot of them."

"Paying them?" Wolpert asked.

"You'd have to ask them that."

Although he knew exactly where Tom might get that kind of money, that was beside the point. The barkeep hadn't recognized Tom, which meant word of the bank robbery might not have gotten this far, or at least a proper description of the robbers hadn't. "Do you have any boys working for you to keep things under control?"

"Why? You think your game is gonna get out of

hand? If there's cheatin' going on, the manager will want to know about it."

"Just have some men ready to keep your customers out of my way." With that, Wolpert collected the beers and walked them over to his table. By the time he got back, another hand had been dealt and the three outlaws were discarding their unwanted cards. He set the mugs down and walked around to his seat.

"Here I thought you'd wiggle outta these too," Tom said. "I had a bet going that you'd be long gone before plunking down any money for drinks."

"Not hardly." When all three of the outlaws had their mugs in hand and were tasting the bitter, slightly gritty brew, Wolpert drew his pistol and thumbed the hammer back. "You boys use your left hands to toss your guns onto the floor without spilling one drop of that beer."

With their mugs held in their right hands, they let their cards drop and shifted in their seats to get to their pistols.

"What's the meaning of this?" Cade growled.

"What's it look like?" Wolpert replied as he flipped open the lapel of his coat to show his badge. "You've got to answer for a bank robbery."

Chapter 16

They might not have created much of a stir on their way into town, but Wolpert and the three outlaws sure kicked one up as they marched down the street to Marshal Davis's office. Tom, Cade and Juan had their wrists shackled and heads hung low. Two of their guns were tucked into Wolpert's holster or beneath his belt while the third was in his left hand to complement the Cavalry pistol in his right. It was a sight that the locals would be talking about for quite a while.

It was also the closest that Wolpert had felt to a real lawman in a month of summers.

The marshal's office was barely in sight when a group of armed deputies came out to meet the procession. One of them was a young man of average height with a face full of scars and a limp that forced him to favor his left leg. Reflexively aiming his .45 at Tom, he asked, "What's all this?"

"I want to talk to Luke," Wolpert said.

"You can talk to me."

When Luke Davis stepped forward, he parted the

group of deputies like a plow shoving aside stalks of wheat. Even as he grabbed the lead deputy's shoulder, he was quick to give it a rough pat as if consoling him for dropping a few rungs in the pecking order. "It's all right, Adam," Davis said. "I'll talk to him. What's on your mind, Zeke?"

The deputies looked at Wolpert in a different way now that they heard the marshal was on familiar terms with him.

"Hello, Luke," Wolpert said with a curt nod. "I found these skunks trying to hide out in your town."

Marshal Davis looked each of the three outlaws up and down. His hands remained propped on his hips near the double-rig holster strapped around his waist, but he didn't seem close to drawing either of the guns. A sneer crossed his face as though he'd just dislodged something rotten from one of his back teeth. "I recognize the Mexican from a few little spats up in your neck of the woods. He works for Burt Sampil, right?"

Juan's head hung low and his eyes were more or less pointed in the marshal's direction. The only acknowledgment he gave to the question was a halfhearted shrug of one shoulder.

"Yeah, he—"

Marshal Davis cut Wolpert off with a quickly raised hand as he took a few heavy steps forward. Even with his hands in the same spot, the fire in his eyes made it seem as if he was about to put his guns to work. He stopped when he stood toe-to-toe with the darker-skinned outlaw and glared at him as though he could see all the way through the building behind Juan's head. "I asked you a question, mister. Answer it."

Juan kept his silence out of pure stubbornness, but

even Wolpert could tell that wouldn't hold up for much longer.

"You're in my town now," Davis growled. "You're stepping on my soil. Sucking my air into your worthless lungs. You don't start showing proper respect, then I might take steps to knock a few holes in you so I can let that good, clean air out where it belongs."

Still silent, Juan let his eyes break away from Davis so they could fix upon a point near his own feet.

To the lawman, that was the same thing as a white flag fluttering in the breeze. "Good," he said. "Now answer the question. You work for Burt Sampil?"

"Used to," Juan grumbled.

"So that means these other men are Burt's as well?"

"We ain't nobody's men, law dog," Tom spat.

Wolpert rolled his eyes and waited for the repercussions of that statement. He had to wait about only a second before Davis reached past Juan to bury his fist into Tom's belly. The big man let out a gasp, but didn't buckle.

Davis fanned the hand he'd used to strike Tom in front of his nose. "I'll assume from the stench that that's the liquor talking. You're Burt's men, all right. They all get that same self-righteous air about them as if one man can protect them no matter where they are or what they do." Finally looking back to Wolpert, he asked, "So, what did they do?"

"Robbed a bank up in Chimney Lake, Nebraska. I'm surprised you haven't heard about it."

"I heard something about that from a salesman peddling fancy suits from the back of his wagon. That's in your jurisdiction," Davis added with a smug grin, "so I figured it was one of your jobs. You're good for that sort of thing, aren't you? Or is that a bit over your head?"

Choking back the urge to fire back with something worse, Wolpert said, "No. It's not my job. The vigilantes who chased them into Kansas are associates of mine, though."

"Someone's gotta do the real work, I suppose."

"Yeah. And someone else has to chase them into your state and deliver them to you with a bow on their heads. Seeing as how they probably weren't going to announce themselves, I guessed you may be too busy getting accolades from your deputies to bother with the likes of a few bank robbers."

Adam surged forward, but was promptly stopped by the marshal's outstretched arm. "It's fine," Davis said. "We're just flipping each other some grief." Davis's intentions were anything but clear as he reached out to grab Wolpert's collar. Odds seemed even as to whether he was going to shake or throttle him. He did the former with a wide smile. "That's what old friends do! So, how long are you gonna be in town?"

"As long as it takes to see to it these men are in the right hands."

Keeping one arm draped around Wolpert's shoulders, Davis used his other hand to point at the outlaws. The armed deputies already had their guns trained on the three shackled men and swarmed them when they saw the marshal's signal. "Done," Davis said.

"You'll be taking them into Dog Creek Jail?" Wolpert asked.

"First they go to my office. I got a few cages where they can cool their heels until I figure out where they go from there. You may do things however you please up in your little Nebraska corn kingdom, but I got procedure to stick to."

Davis laughed and Wolpert forced himself to laugh along with him. Although both men were roughly the same height, Davis made certain to press enough of his weight down upon his shoulder to shove Wolpert down an inch or two. That way, the marshal appeared to loom over the other man like an overbearing parent imposing his will upon a rambunctious child. The marshal nodded to his men, who pushed the outlaws toward the nearby office. Using his arm like a yoke on a mule's back, Davis moved Wolpert along in much the same manner.

"I'll want to stay to see the process all the way through," Wolpert said.

"Don't you have some more collections to make?"

Digging his heels into the street and pulling himself out from under Davis's arm, Wolpert lowered his voice to a snarl that could be heard by only the closest deputies. "I could just as easily have taken these men back to Keith County, but I brought them here because I respect how you run things."

"And because they'd probably only be shipped to Dog Creek anyhow if they was found guilty," Davis snapped.

"I suppose that all depends on which judge heard their trial. I doubt Judge Spencer has much good to say about you after that business in Wichita."

Once again, Davis propped his hands upon his hips. This time, he seemed more than capable of using both guns hanging there. Finally, he nodded and raised his eyebrows in a way that made him look slightly less perturbed. "Guess I earned that. It ain't fitting for men like us to butt heads this way."

"You're the one who started it."

"And you still have a gift for straight talking! I like that."

Judging by the cowed looks on the faces of most of the deputies, straight talk aimed at the marshal was pretty rare in that town. The one deputy who didn't appear to be even slightly intimidated was Adam. That meant he was a whole different kind of trouble.

Giving Adam a friendly slap on the back, Davis said, "See to it these boys get tucked away nice and neat. Do what you can to keep 'em apart. That is, after you've searched them." Turning to Wolpert, he added, "Not to imply you didn't search 'em."

"I know. Procedure."

"Right."

Wolpert followed the deputies as the outlaws were herded into the marshal's office. By this time, a sizable crowd of curious locals were gawking at the display of shackled men and chattering quietly to one another. Whenever Marshal Davis looked their way, the locals would stop talking and wave nervously at the lawman, who magnanimously tipped his hat in return. Although the locals didn't seem to be on neighborly terms with their marshal, at least they acknowledged him. Wolpert wasn't envious of such a thing, but it did grate on him. Where Luke Davis was concerned, it was harder for Wolpert to think of things that didn't grate on him.

The deputies did their job quickly and efficiently. They moved the outlaws along without once giving them enough room to so much as think about an escape attempt. When Cade stumbled and looked as though he was reaching for his boot, Adam was quick to straighten him up by the back of his collar and toss him into the office.

It had been a long time since Wolpert had seen the inside of Davis's office, but nothing much had changed. The old reward notices on the walls had been swapped out for fresh ones and some different coats were hanging on the hooks near the door, but it was still the same place. The marshal's desk was the easiest to spot, sitting like a bull amid a herd of calves. Two gun cabinets took up one of the rear corners of the room. In the other corner was a formidable door that opened to a short hallway and four cages fashioned from flattened strips of iron.

Once inside, the three outlaws were slammed face-first against the wall beside the coat hooks with enough force to rattle the door frame. Davis stepped inside, shut the door and walked straight over to Cade. After grabbing on to the back of Cade's neck, he drew one of his pistols and jammed the barrel against Cade's ribs so hard that he seemed intent on puncturing a lung. "See what this son of a bitch was trying to reach, Adam."

Adam moved to Cade's side and patted the outlaw down. When the search moved below Cade's belt, Adam dropped to one knee, continued patting and then stuck his hand into the outlaw's boots. "Found it," he declared.

Although he watched the deputy, Wolpert kept most of his focus on Cade. The outlaw had a fidgeting, unsettled look about him that was almost as good as a sign that read "guilty" hanging around his neck.

"What have we here?" Adam said as he pulled the

slim knife from inside Cade's boot. The blade was about six inches long, the handle was barely large enough to provide a decent grip and the entire weapon was small enough to slip by even if Wolpert had given the man a quick once-over.

As he charged at the outlaw, Wolpert didn't have to do any acting to look enraged. "Yeah," he snarled while snatching the knife from Adam's hand and sticking it under Cade's nose as if he were disciplining a dog. "What have we here? What did you mean to do with this?"

"Go to hell," Cade grunted. "All of you!"

Clenching his fist around the knife's handle, Wolpert caused every man in that office to choke on his next breath when he drove the little weapon into Cade's face. At the last second, Wolpert twisted his hand so only his knuckles made contact, but the edge of the blade got close enough to put a little cut onto the outlaw's cheek. Judging by his wide eyes and pale complexion, Cade was more surprised than anyone else.

"All right, that's enough," Davis said with an amused laugh. "Take these boys to their new accommodations and go over them real thorough. And before you shut the door on them," he added with a devilish smirk, "go over 'em again." Once the outlaws had been led away, he looked at Wolpert and said, "Them boys won't be walking straight for a while."

No matter what Cade intended to do with that knife, Wolpert couldn't help feeling a twitch of regret for putting all of them in that spot. And that twitch became a full kick in the guts when he considered the possibility that Cade really had just stumbled while the wrong people had been watching.

Standing in front of him as if he'd been waiting there for an hour, Davis asked, "So, do you need a place to sleep or will you be getting started on that ride back up to Nebraska?"

"I'll need somewhere to sleep," Wolpert replied. "And someplace I can get comfortable, since I intend on staying to see what happens to those men."

"What are you implying, Zeke?"

"Not a thing. That bank was in my jurisdiction. Those men tore through shooting up my streets. Even killed a few folks that were under my protection." The last part was a bit of spice added to the story, but Wolpert doubted the marshal would call him on it.

"So you think I'll do anything differently now than if you weren't looking over my shoulder?"

"Looking over your shoulder or watching from somewhere else, I want to see what happens to those men. If you'd chased them through this damned cold, I'd think you would want the same thing."

Davis glanced toward the window as a stray lick of wind caused it to tremble in its frame. "I can understand that much. Reminds me of the time we chased those skinny Kliner boys from one end of the state to the other. They only snatched some money from a few dry goods stores, but they gave us more grief than a proper gang."

"That was a rough couple of days," Wolpert mused. "I thought those Kliners would be the death of me."

Looking over to his deputies, Davis said, "And that's coming from two men who saw real combat in the army. But them redskins fought a whole different fight." After a few more seconds with his memories, he glanced back over to Wolpert. "You wanna stay with me while you're in town? I got an extra room and Marie would love to have someone else to cook for. Especially someone with your appetite."

"Thanks, but no. I wouldn't want to impose. Besides, I already rented a room."

"Fine. But you're coming over for supper. I won't hear anything more on the matter."

"So, what happens now with those robbers? I'm a little rusty on procedure."

Wolpert hated to play up to the marshal like that. Davis could be insufferable enough without thinking someone else had bared his neck to him that easily. More than that, it just went against Wolpert's grain to work to get on someone's good side. That sort of thing was best left to politicians. Whether his distaste showed or not, Wolpert's subtle bow to the marshal's authority had its desired effect.

"My boys will get them situated in their cages," Davis said in a more relaxed tone. "After they've been softened up a bit, we'll have a little chat with them about that bank robbery."

"You probably shouldn't soften them up too much."

"Why? You getting sentimental in your old age?"

"No. It's just that they've already been run from one state to another and are far away from Burt Sampil. Now they're looking at the inside of a cage with the prospect of a noose going around their necks. With all of that piled against you, would you care about another beating?"

"Maybe not," Davis admitted. "You got something better?"

"Let them sleep. Toss them some water and a scrap of food. Tomorrow, I'll go in and have a word with them.

You or your boys can be there, but we'll see about turning their heads before twisting them off'a their shoulders."

"Bribery, huh? Why don't that surprise me coming from you?"

"Not a bribe so much as incentive. Sometimes, if a man has something to live for, he can make a turnaround that'd surprise even you."

Davis grinned in a way that showed several sharp teeth. "We'll just have to see about that."

Chapter 17

Since he mentioned renting a room, Wolpert figured he should go ahead and do that before Marshal Davis checked up on him. And there was no doubt in his mind that Davis would be checking up on him. He settled on a nice little boardinghouse on Roswell Street. It was quiet, smelled of freshly baked bread and was a stone's throw from both the saloon district and the marshal's office without being too close to either one. The woman who ran the place had an old man helping keep it in shape. Neither of them must have heard of Sheriff Wolpert beforehand, because they greeted him as warmly as they would any upstanding keeper of the peace.

When he awoke the next morning, Wolpert was greeted with another scent that was even more pleasant than the one that had drawn him to the boardinghouse in the first place. Stumbling down the stairs while hitching his pants up, he pulled in a deep breath and asked, "Are those biscuits cooking?"

Henrietta was a short woman with wheat-colored hair

and a round face. When she smiled at him, her cheeks flushed a bit and became the shapes of small apples. "Close," she said. "They're muffins. Blueberry, from my own preserves. Care for one?"

"If I gotta stop at just one, you'd better hide the rest."

She giggled and waved off the compliment while leading the way to the little round table set up in the cramped room adjacent to her kitchen. "Did you sleep all right?"

"Just fine, thanks."

"So," she called from the next room, "are you in Lester on official business?"

"Yes, ma'am. I caught a bunch of bank robbers just the other day."

Emerging from the kitchen carrying a plate of steaming muffins that had already been neatly cut in half, she gazed at him with wide eyes. "I heard about that! Those men that were marched out of the Songbird!"

"I did the marching."

Henrietta could have been anywhere from her late twenties to midthirties. Although her face was definitely not one of a young girl, there was enough brightness in her features to shave off a few years no matter how old she truly was. "Oh my! How exciting," she said with genuine enthusiasm. "I heard there was quite a commotion."

"It could have been a lot worse, but I've had experience in that sort of thing."

"Yes, I imagine you would. Those men wouldn't be the same ones who robbed that bank up in Nebraska, would they?"

"Actually, yes. You've heard about that?"

"Only this morning. It seems one of my caretaker's

sisters lives in a town that straddles the border between Kansas and Nebraska. She heard lots of talk and told him all about it when she arrived for a visit." Seeing that he'd already helped himself to his breakfast and was almost done with the second half of his muffin by the time she took a breath, Henrietta said, "The short story is that yes. I've heard about it. Sorry for prattling on."

"Not at all. Sorry for eating like a pig."

"Would you like another?"

"As quickly as possible," Wolpert replied. When she picked the plate up and carried it to the kitchen, he said, "I delivered those robbers to your Marshal Davis."

"I wouldn't say he's mine, but go on."

"What can you tell me about him?"

She came back from the kitchen, this time carrying several whole muffins on the plate along with a healthy portion of butter to go along with them. After setting the plate down, she bustled back and forth to refill his coffee. "Not much, other than he seems to do a fine job. I don't think I've seen him enough to get more than a passing glance at him or his deputies. Things tend to be fairly quiet around this place."

"What about his deputies? Do you know any of them?"

"They seem like good boys, for the most part."

"Just for the most part?" Wolpert picked up on the subtle reluctance in her voice the way an experienced tracker could tell by a set of ruts if a wagon was listing more to one side instead of the other. "The reason I ask is that I want to make sure things go smoothly with the transfer from that office to the Dog Creek Jail. One little slip and things could get real messy. I'm sure you can imagine what I mean."

There was no reason why the owner of a boarding-house would know what he meant, but the key word he'd used was imagine. Since Henrietta's eyes wandered as she traced her fingers along the top of her table, it seemed she was definitely imagining something.

"I've only seen those deputies in passing," she said, "but you may want to keep your eye on Otto Berringer."

"Really? Why?"

"It could be nothing, but I've heard a thing or two about him. He's one of the newer deputies Marshal Davis has taken on, but he's lived in town all his life. I've been quilting with his mother for years and she would always go on about some sort of trouble that Otto got into."

"What sort of trouble?" Wolpert asked through a mouthful of hot, buttered muffin.

"Nothing serious. Mostly just sneaking into a saloon when he should have been at school. Some say he started a fire that burnt down a neighbor's shed. His mother sometimes thought he would be more likely to spend time in the jail instead of guarding it. But listen to me go on like this. None of this is very charitable talk. Otto should be just fine. He seems to be doing quite well for himself. He even helped his mother get into a new house."

And there it was. To some, those things might connect in a sloppy, haphazard way at best. For Wolpert, they were all too familiar. He hadn't gained his tarnished repu-tation by only taking a few bribes that were handed to him or looking the other way when the opportunity struck. He'd earned his dirty money by sniffing out opportunities that others would miss, as well as the people who were prime candidates to help him earn more. One very important part of that was being able to spot potentially bad seeds in the bunch. Perhaps it was a gift for finding like-minded souls that could be exploited. Whatever it was that drew him to the conclusion, he thought he could work with Otto Berringer.

"You're right," he said before more than a few seconds had ticked by. "It's probably nothing."

"Will you be staying for supper?"

"Most definitely. I suppose I'll be in town for a bit until that excitement you mentioned dies down enough for me to head home."

Henrietta didn't say much to that, but was obviously glad to hear it.

With a minimum of snooping, Wolpert was able to figure out where to find Otto Berringer. His mother worked at the town's only laundry and she was more than happy to talk about her boy. As for gleaning personal information about a man, there was no better source than his mother. No matter what the circumstances, they could always be convinced to tell stories or brag about their sons. Mrs. Berringer was a nice enough lady. So nice, in fact, that Wolpert felt bad for the ease with which he manipulated her into telling him what he'd wanted to know.

Apart from Otto being a stubborn child with a fondness for apple pie, he was making amends for the previous grief he'd given to his entire family by helping pay for a new home. While Mrs. Berringer was exceedingly proud of this, Wolpert saw it as confirmation that

Otto was indeed the young man he was after. No marshal's deputy should have been able to afford anything more than a rented room and the food it took to sustain him. When a deputy working for Marshal Davis was that prosperous, it meant either he was taking bribes to supplement his income or Luke had aged into a very generous employer. Wolpert's healthy mix of observational skills and cynicism steered him toward the former.

It wasn't quite noon when Wolpert made his way back to the marshal's office. Even before he could take a step inside, Adam rushed to the door to greet him.

"Did Marshal Davis tell you to meet him here?" the deputy asked.

"No," Wolpert replied. "I came to check on my prisoners."

Twitching at whose prisoners they were truly supposed to be, Adam replied, "They're doing just fine."

"Mind if I take a look?"

"You think we'd just cut them loose?"

"No," Wolpert replied as he stood there like a stump that was perfectly content to impede progress on a busy street.

"Fine," Adam grunted. "Otto's watching them now. Talk to him."

Of course Otto was watching them. Mrs. Berringer had told Wolpert as much during their little chat.

Adam was the only deputy in the front section of the office at the moment. He watched him so closely that Wolpert had to figure Davis had told him about the sheriff's smudged past.

The door to the back section of the office was shut tight. After he rapped his knuckles against it, another deputy opened it for him.

"Yeah?" asked the man who peered out at Wolpert. His eyes were dark and beady, situated at a height that would put their owner at about half a foot shorter than Wolpert.

"It's that sheriff from yesterday, Otto," Adam explained from behind his desk. "He wants to get a look at the prisoners."

Even through the crack of open space between the door and its frame, Wolpert could see part of a grin reflected in those beady eyes. The door was pulled open and a short, solidly built young man stepped aside. "Come on in," he said with the same hint of an Alabama accent that had colored his mother's voice. "I don't think they'll want to talk to you, though."

In the time it took for him to step into the room with the cells and the door to be shut behind him, Wolpert could tell the three outlaws weren't in a condition to talk to anyone. Juan was in the cell closest to the door. He lay on a cot that was just big enough to support his body while his legs hung off the end. His already dark complexion was marred by several bruises around his eyes and cheek. Tom was in the cell at the back of the room and sported several cuts on the sides of his mouth. His cot was the same as Juan's, but his larger frame made it look more like something that belonged in a dollhouse. Cade had them all beat. Most of his face was covered with a crust of dried blood and he held his left arm as if it were in a sling. Lying on his side on his cot, he pulled in a breath with a wheeze and let it out in a tired groan.

"What happened to them?" Wolpert asked.

Otto looked at each outlaw in turn. "Oh, they didn't

feel like talkin' to Marshal Davis. He didn't like that too much."

"I thought I was going to be here when they were questioned."

"Guess you thought wrong."

Wolpert fought to suppress the urge to knock Otto across the face. He allowed the outlaws to see the subtle, regretful shake of his head before turning a steely expression toward the deputy. "How'd they get so banged up?"

"Can't you figure it out for yerself?"

"I want you to tell me."

"Well, it's like I said. Marshal Davis come in to ask what happened with the bank bein' robbed and all. That one there," Otto said while flipping a lazy wave toward Cade, "he had a smart mouth on him, so the marshal told me to shut it. That big fella stepped in and took a mighty good load of a beating. Didn't seem to bother him much, though."

It didn't take astute senses to pick up on the changes that drifted across Otto's face. When he talked about Cade, the slightest reference to the punishment he'd been given brought a hungry glint to his eyes. The deputy was thinking back to the incident with such intensity that Wolpert could nearly hear the echo of punches cracking against flesh and bone. And when the deputy switched tracks to talk about Tom, the pleasure seeped out of him to be replaced with bitter resentment. Otto wasn't just disappointed that the big man hadn't caved. He felt cheated.

Wolpert had been party to a lot of terrible things, but he hadn't taken such pleasure in them. In Wolpert's sphere of influence, it was necessary to hold court with men who got a thrill from such disgusting pursuits. Fortunately, after Wolpert lowered himself to their level, they were easy to deal with.

Otto had been going on about some more of Davis's questioning techniques, but Wolpert didn't listen once he'd gotten a proper read on the deputy. He forced a grin onto his face, pointed to Cade and asked, "You know what's worse than that one's mouth?"

"What?"

"The fact that Eddie Vernon is still alive and kicking." Dropping his voice to a snarl, Wolpert asked, "You know how many women and children he's put through hell?"

Furrowing his brow, Otto replied, "Uhhhh . . . no."

"More than any shortsighted judge knows, that's for certain. If the law was put squarely into the hands of men who knew what to do with it, men like you and me, skunks like these three and filthy dogs like Eddie wouldn't live to see another sunrise."

Like any simple man who was too ignorant to know how simple he was, Otto nodded and agreed with what Wolpert said without thinking about it.

"It's fellows like us, who get our hands dirty every day out there in the muck, that know best about how to run things," Wolpert groused. If there was a quicker way to get on the good side of an ignorant wretch like Otto, he didn't know it. Bad-mouthing the higher ranks worked in the army and it worked in Lester, Kansas, just as well.

"You got that right," Otto replied.

"You know who Eddie Vernon is, right?"

"Sure. He's serving time in Dog Creek Jail."

Wolpert gave the deputy a nudge and asked, "Think you could get me in to pay him a visit?"

"Why would you wanna do that?"

"I happen to be friends with the father of one of the men Eddie gunned down. He's got a standing offer of a thousand dollars for Eddie's head, since there's not a judge around who'll charge him with a hanging offense. We go in there, ruin his day along with his good looks and split the money."

"Five hundred each?"

"If that's not enough, you can have six."

If Wolpert had any doubts about choosing Otto for his helper, they disappeared when the deputy asked, "And what do I have to do?"

"Just get Eddie alone in a room or out back somewhere so we can go to work."

"Marshal Davis will know if a prisoner winds up dead."

"Then we won't kill him. I'm sure the grieving family would be satisfied with some other bit of proof. Maybe an ear or a little finger. You think the marshal would notice if one of his prisoners got a little torn up in a scuffle?"

Otto chewed on that for all of three seconds before the nasty smile returned to his face. In fact, he got a look about him that most men got when they were thinking of much more pleasant things. "Yeah," he sighed. "I think that can be arranged. And you say we'd get paid for this?"

"Handsomely."

Blinking as if he'd just awakened from a dream, Otto grunted, "Why come to me with this?"

"Because I can tell you ain't like the rest. Surely not

like that fella in the next room who's got his nose buried up Davis's backside."

If Otto came to Adam's defense, he was just a little rat with no further aspirations. But if he showed contempt for those who did their jobs as best they could, then Otto Berringer truly was the sort of man Wolpert was looking for.

The sneer Otto wore when looking toward the front office spoke volumes. "What've you got in mind?" he asked.

"I'll be accompanying you men when we take these three into Dog Creek," Wolpert said. "That is, if they're headed in that direction."

"Oh, they sure are."

"Good. We'll drop off the trash and I'm sure you know someone who can arrange to pull Eddie Vernon out for a private conversation."

"Yeah. I think I know someone."

Of course he did. A rat could always sniff out more of its own kind. "Good. I'll let you work on that."

"Hey," Otto hissed. "Best if you didn't mention this to any of the others."

Since the deputy had beaten him to the punch with that request, Wolpert slapped him on the shoulder and said, "No need splitting that money any more than necessary, right?"

"That's right."

Chapter 18

By late afternoon the next day, the three outlaws were dragged into the back of a wagon to be transported to Dog Creek Jail like so many sacks of dirty laundry. Wolpert had heard about the move from Otto the previous night after the deputy bought himself and the sheriff a drink. Before leaving the saloon, Otto had also worked in a few not-so-subtle hints that he was looking for better work and willing to ride up to Nebraska for it. Wolpert accepted the drinks and promised him a prime spot once he weeded out some of his less ambitious deputies. The lie came easily enough and the liquor helped.

The following day, Wolpert rode alongside the wagon with Adam right beside him. Marshal Davis rode ahead of everyone like the tip of a spear aimed for one of the mangiest eyesores in the state. It was a short ride to Dog Creek, but the prisoners stooped over and hung their heads as if they'd been forced to walk every step of the way. The jail was situated near a bend in the creek, which amounted to only a crooked glimmer of ice beneath the castoff from a dirty snow drift. It was bigger than Wolpert remembered. Made of brick walls and iron bars, the jail was the one thing that didn't move in the slightest no matter how hard the wind blew.

"Here we are, gentlemen," Davis proudly announced. "Your new home until the judge figures out what to do with you. Even then, you'll be lucky to get this far outside the walls again. Soak up that clean air while you can."

Juan and Tom climbed down from the back of the wagon. Their wrists and ankles were shackled with a chain running through the lower set to connect all three prisoners together. Cade had a tough time stepping down without falling, but the other two held him up well enough.

"There ain't been a reward announced for these three, Zeke," Davis said. "That is, unless you know something I don't."

"I know plenty of things you don't, Luke. I intend on staying in town until we find out for certain whether or not someone's more grateful to have these men locked up."

"Do what you please."

"Mind if I see these men inside?"

Marshal Davis examined the sheriff carefully, but relaxed when he saw that the prisoners were having a hard time walking after the beatings they'd been given. Eventually, he shrugged and said, "You can follow along with my men if you want. I'll need to have a word with the man who runs this hellhole anyway."

With that, Davis climbed down from his saddle and handed his reins to one of the deputies. As the rest of the procession made its way to the front door, Davis veered toward the corner of the building where a smaller door reinforced with iron slats creaked open. Wolpert couldn't hear what was being said, but the man who greeted Davis had the look of someone who might be in charge. He was an older fellow with thinning gray hair and a rumpled suit. After exchanging a few enthusiastic slaps on the shoulder, both Davis and the other man disappeared inside.

"You coming or not?" Adam prodded.

Wolpert nodded and fell into step beside Cade. With Tom between them and Adam, the sheriff felt as if he could speak softly enough for his words to be marred by the shuffle of the big man's feet and the clanking of the chains.

"How you holding up?" Wolpert asked.

"How's it look?"

"Wasn't part of the plan."

"Doesn't matter."

Despite the clipped sentences and low voices, Wolpert still kept his eyes open for any trace that another deputy was getting too close. For the most part, the other lawmen were too busy waving at the guards in the jail and shouting a few instructions about who was coming in through the front gates.

"How long before you find our boys?" Wolpert asked.

"Shouldn't be long."

"What's that?" Adam snapped as he strode around Tom with his shotgun aimed at the prisoners. "What's he saying?"

"He's not saying much," Wolpert replied.

Looking to Cade, the deputy asked, "What's he saying to you?"

"He's asking where we hid the bank's money. Same

questions as the marshal was asking the other night. Ain't you law dogs got anything else to think about besides money?"

That earned him a short chopping blow from the butt of Adam's shotgun. It caught Cade squarely in the stomach and doubled him over, which was strictly for Adam's sake. Wolpert could recognize when a prisoner was playing possum just to avoid getting a follow-up blow to put him in line. The act was good enough to satisfy Adam for the time being.

Before Adam could issue another warning, Wolpert got in front of Cade, grabbed him by the collar and roughly stood him up straight. "You'd best think about keeping your mouth shut if you wanna stay alive." Turning to Juan, he added, "That goes double for you. What've you got to say to that?"

Deep down inside, Wolpert prayed the other man wouldn't let him down by breaking character. Just when it seemed Juan might choose the wrong time to reform, he grunted, "I say I'll live longer than you, law dog."

Without missing a beat, Wolpert stormed over to Juan and clamped a hand around the outlaw's throat. Pulling him in close, Wolpert gritted his teeth and snarled, "Find our men quick and prepare them quicker. I can have you out tonight if you're able." Raising his voice enough to be heard by the others, Wolpert added, "You understand me?"

"Yeah," Juan said.

"Good. And don't forget it." Acting every bit like someone who'd put a man in his place, Wolpert shoved Juan along and escorted the prisoners into the jail.

Two armed guards stood at the entrance, brandishing shotguns as if they were aching to use them. Large metal doors opened into a room with nothing in it besides the filth on the floor and hooks on the walls. Once inside, the prisoners were turned so they faced the wall and forced to raise their arms so the shackles between their wrists fit into the hooks. A large, burly man announced his presence by walking down the line and cracking each man in the small of the back with a thick wooden club. After that, the prisoners hung from their hooks like fish on a line.

"You better get used to that!" the burly one announced. "Because if'n you don't do what I tell you to do when I tell you to do it, that's gonna be the best you'll get."

As the man started rattling off the jail's rules and regulations, Otto tapped Wolpert on the shoulder and motioned for him to follow him into a small room stuffed full with a single desk and one old chair. Wolpert had no idea how the skinny fellow behind the desk got there without twisting himself into a knot.

"This is Chuck," Otto said. "He watches things when the warden's away."

Rising from his chair, but unable to stand up all the way, Chuck extended a hand across the top of his desk and said, "When the warden and both his seconds are gone, I watch things. Usually between midnight and five in the morning."

"Same difference," Otto said quickly. "We got a proposition for you, Chuck. You got a prisoner named Eddie Vernon?"

"Yes. Hasn't been here for long. Why?"

"He ran afoul of some rich folks before coming under your care and they're willin' to pay to see he gets his comeuppance."

"He's locked up in Dog Creek Jail," Chuck said. "What more comeuppance does a thief need? We ain't savages."

"Tell him," Otto demanded.

Wolpert stepped up and said, "He's a murderer. Just didn't get caught for it."

Chuck was out of his chair and on his feet fast enough to knock his desk forward an inch. "There ain't gonna be a lynching here. Not on my watch! Not after the last one."

"Wouldn't have to be," Wolpert assured him. "Just pull him out and let us have a few moments to show him the error of his ways."

When Chuck looked over to him, Otto said, "We'll hack an ear off. I'm thinking maybe a finger to go along with it. Send it to this rich fella and we'll get our money."

"How do you know you'll get anything?" Chuck asked. "This whole thing sounds ludicrous to me."

While Otto had been cruel and shortsighted enough to be convinced in short order, Chuck was proving to be more the thinking type. Of course, beating Otto in a thinking contest wasn't a particularly outstanding feat.

"No more ludicrous than the law putting a price on a man's head," Wolpert said. "This rich fellow had the law fail him, so maybe he's not thinking straight. The important thing is that his money's good and it's ours for the taking. Since you're the one on the job, how about we give you your cut first? How's fifty dollars strike you?"

"How about double?" Chuck asked.

"For escorting a chained prisoner into a room and leaving to get some fresh air, you'll get no more than sixty. I'd say that's awfully generous."

Despite the wariness in his eyes, Chuck still looked hungry. "You got the money?"

It was almost all the money left over from the bank robbery, but Wolpert took it from his pocket and counted it out as if it were nothing but paper to be burned for heat. "Yours when we get to meet our friend Eddie Vernon."

"Half now, the other half then."

Wolpert nodded. "Fair enough. Here you go. When can we have our meeting?"

"Come back tonight after one. Anyone else here will be busy making sure the new prisoners are settled in. You should have enough time to . . . whatever."

When he heard that, Wolpert allowed Chuck to take the money from him. "See you then."

He and Otto left Chuck to his paperwork and stepped out just in time to watch the prisoners shuffle through a door that led into a foul-smelling room. Instead of looking wounded and tired, the outlaws looked more like men who were trying to get out of work detail. They dragged their feet just a bit too much. Their heads were down, but their eyes were open and unblinking. They were taking in every sight and carefully studying their surroundings.

They were hurt, but not out of the fight just yet.

The room where they were headed echoed with other men's haggard voices, calling out to the fresh meat about to be tossed into the cage. Wolpert followed behind the prisoners and got a look into Dog Creek's main holding area. It looked more like a huge, poorly tended zoo. A large room roughly the size of a small house had thick iron bars running from floor to ceiling in a pattern that traced the outline of a path leading from one door to just past the middle of the room. At least two dozen men were behind the bars. Some were chained to the walls, while the rest roamed where they pleased.

Men clustered together, eyeing the bars and glaring at the new arrivals. A few of them kept to themselves. From his experience, Wolpert knew those would be either the very strong or the very crazy ones. Both kinds tended to stare out one of the few small windows cut up near the top of the walls. Thanks to the thick bars sealing those windows, only a sliver of light came in and just a small sampling of air made it through without putting a dent in the stench of filth and human waste coating every breath of air within that room.

"Is that it?" Wolpert asked.

One of the guards was a man about his age with the clipped and trimmed appearance of a military man. After a quick once-over, he must have pegged Wolpert as being cut from that same cloth, because he took an easy, relaxed demeanor with him when he replied, "What more did you want?"

"I thought there were more prisoners."

"There are. The really bad ones are kept in their own cells around the edge. Usually threatening to toss someone into one of those is enough to calm the rowdiest of them down."

"Ever have any escapes?"

"A few got out of the jail," the guard said with a shrug. "But they didn't make it much farther than that. I served as a sharpshooter for five years and the man who got out recently . . . I picked him off myself. Real good runner. Kind of like hunting rabbit."

"Sounds like our boys should be safe in here, then."

"Sure. They won't be happy," the guard chuckled. "But

they sure won't be goin' anywhere. You got a name, mister?"

"Zeke Wolpert."

Shaking Wolpert's hand, the guard looked down at the badge pinned to his chest.

"Sheriff Zeke Wolpert," he amended. "Friend of Luke's?"

"Acquaintance is more like it," Wolpert admitted. "Where did you serve?"

"Fort Randall."

"Ahhh," Wolpert said fondly. "Right up along the Missouri River. Must have been a nice post."

"It was. Sometimes." The guard studied Wolpert for a few seconds. He knew better than to ask for much else because it was plain to see that Wolpert didn't feel like talking. Since all men who'd worn a uniform through battle carried ghosts with them, they extended each other the courtesy of letting them rest. "You ever want to check on your boys here," the guard said, "be my guest."

"Thank you kindly. I may just take you up on that offer. Will you be around much more tonight?"

"Nope. I'm headed home to get some grub before too long. Won't be back until tomorrow morning."

"Glad to hear it," Wolpert said.

Chapter 19

Wolpert sat on the porch of Henrietta's boardinghouse, sipping tea that had been piping hot only a few minutes before being exposed to the chilly night air. He'd considered lighting one of the few cigars he carried with him just to have a little warmth, but he wasn't able to fetch it before Otto rode up the narrow path leading to the front door.

"Chuck's getting your friend right about now," the deputy said in a whisper that carried just as well as a normal speaking voice. "By the time we get to the jail, he'll be trussed up and ready."

Otto had the anxious look of a lonely man reaching out to open the door of a cathouse. Nodding and setting his teacup down where Henrietta could find it next to his chair, Wolpert turned around to slip into his coat. The cold kept him alert and ready to move, but he still needed a moment to keep Otto from seeing the contempt that bubbled up to his surface.

"Where's your horse?" the deputy asked. "Chuck won't wait all night."

"Right around back. Just keep your hat on."

The gelding was saddled and ready, so Wolpert mounted up and followed Otto out of town. It was half past midnight and all but the saloon district was bundled up for the night. Even the rowdier section of town wasn't about to stick its nose out into the cold without good reason, and two men riding past on horseback wasn't nearly good enough. They slipped away without being noticed and made the ride to Dog Creek Jail in about the same time it had taken the first time around. Although they didn't have to match the slower pace of a wagon, they needed to be careful since there was only a sliver of a moon to light their trail.

Chuck was outside waiting for them. At least, Wolpert assumed Chuck was the man who stood near the corner of the building waving his arms like a crazed goose. Otto slowed down and dismounted well before getting to the jail, so Wolpert followed his lead.

"Hitch them horses back with the others," Chuck said as he pointed to a shed near the back of the building. Two other horses were there, protected from the elements by thin walls and blankets that had been draped over their backs. Wolpert took his time situating his gelding, making absolutely sure the animal's back was covered.

In stark contrast, Otto barely seemed to care if his horse had water to drink or a hunk of ice to lick. "Come on, Zeke," he urged. "We won't have barely enough time as it is."

Wolpert twitched at the sound of his common name being spoken by the likes of Otto Berringer. What cut him even deeper was the ease with which Otto had accepted him as one of his own.

Chuck stood near the same door that Marshal Davis had used earlier that day. Just as Wolpert had suspected, it opened into a small office that obviously belonged to someone near the top of the jail's food chain. Framed pictures were on the walls. A nice rug covered a good portion of the floor. The desk was made from carved, polished wood and the chair behind it was well padded. Even so, the room wasn't a whole lot bigger than the space Chuck used for his office. Before either of the others could dawdle too much, Chuck shut the door and hurried through the room.

"Come on," he said. "I've got your man in one of the single cells. It's this way." When he caught Otto sniffing around a box of expensive cigars on the desk, he hissed, "This way!"

Wolpert shoved Otto toward the door and when Chuck was distracted by that, he snatched a few cigars from the case. By the time he crossed the office and strode down a narrow hall, the cigars were tucked safely into the sheriff's shirt pocket.

They walked along a narrow space beside the main cage. The walkway between the bars and wall was so cramped that Wolpert hadn't even seen it on his first visit. Most of the prisoners were asleep, scattered on the floor or using the bars to support their backs while lying on their sides. Cade and Tom were easy enough to spot since they were in the middle of the enclosed space, sitting back-to-back so they could support each other while keeping watch on the other prisoners in every direction. Juan huddled with another cluster of prisoners, engrossed in a whispered conversation.

Chuck opened the door at the end of the walkway and motioned the others through. Once inside, he locked it using a key from a ring he gripped tightly in one hand. "It's the door straight ahead," he said. "Don't kill him. I can't explain that away."

"Don't worry about that," Otto told him rather unconvincingly.

"And I want my money."

Wolpert stepped up to the door and peeked in through a slot that had been cut through it. Sure enough, there was a man sitting in a chair with his arms shackled behind him and his ankles tied to its wooden legs. Taking a wad of cash from his pocket that represented the last of what he'd brought with him, Wolpert said, "There's your money. Now go find somewhere else to be. We don't need an audience and you don't need to see what we're up to."

"Fine by me. You've got five minutes. Five. I'll be keeping track myself."

"Yeah, yeah," Otto said impatiently. "Five minutes. Now scat."

Twitching at Otto's command, Chuck took a step in the wrong direction before turning and rushing toward the door at the end of the hall. Once he was through it, he was more than happy to scurry down the hall and get back to his normal duties.

Otto pulled the slotted door open and walked inside. A wide, reptilian smile appeared on his face and grew even wider when he fished what looked like a short filleting knife from his pocket. Holding the knife out so the blade caught some of the paltry light being cast by the room's single lantern, he sneered, "I don't know who you ran afoul of, but you're about to be real sorry you did. See that?"

"Yeah," the man in the chair replied. "I ain't blind."

"Well, you're gonna get real acquainted with this here blade."

Wolpert stepped inside the room, which wasn't much bigger than a closet. Apart from the chair and the lantern, the three men were the only things inside that tight space.

The man in the chair let out a tired sigh. "Did that twitchy friend of yours wake me up so you could waggle that little knife in front of me or are you gonna do something?"

"Oh, I'll do something all right! How about this?"

Wolpert still had his back to the other two so he could make sure the hallway beyond the door was clear. Chuck had lingered for a few seconds as if he couldn't decide whether he wanted to keep an eye on what was going on or if he possibly wanted to stick around long enough to hear something. The guard finally left the hallway completely at about the same time Otto took a swing at the prisoner.

The knife flashed through the air, but was more of a flinch than a stab. Its edge bumped against the other man's face and drew about as much blood as might be found if he'd cut himself while shaving.

"That the best you got?" the man groaned. "Hope you don't mind if I go back to sleep."

"Sleep?" Otto said. "You wanna sleep? You'll be sleeping in hell by the time I'm done. No, wait. About halfway through when I'm done, you'll wish you were sleeping in hell! What've you got say to—"

Wolpert cut him short with a straight right cross that snapped Otto's head to one side. It seemed as if Otto might have had some fight in him, but he managed to stay upright for only a second before dropping. Rather than let the deputy hit the floor, Wolpert caught him by the shoulder of his jacket and held him up just long enough to lower him down quietly.

"Well now," the man in the chair said. "I wasn't expecting that."

"Are you Eddie Vernon?"

"Yeah."

"I hear you know your way around a Sharps rifle," Wolpert said as he rummaged through Otto's pockets. "Best shot in three states?"

Despite the spot he was in, the other man never seemed to fret. He even shrugged his shoulders and shifted a bit as though his shackles were simply a mild obstacle to his own comfort. "You got my name right, but that's about it. That is, unless you know of another Eddie Vernon."

Wolpert found what he was looking for and removed a set of small keys from Otto's pocket. Looking over to the chair, he asked as part two of his little test, "What about safes? Think you know your way around one of those?"

Eddie's face brightened in a way that let Wolpert know he had the right man. "Now, that's something I can do. I'll need my arms and legs free, though."

"Aren't you going to ask who sent me?"

"If it's not Bart Hankel, I'll be surprised."

"You mean Burt Sampil?"

"Yeah," Eddie replied with another grin. "That's the one."

It wasn't anything elaborate, but Wolpert knew he'd just passed a test himself.

"So I take it you're not here to give me a thrashing for something I done?"

"No," Wolpert said. "We're getting out of here."

Happiness flickered across Eddie's face for a fraction of a second, but was soon replaced by deep concern. "Where are we going? I didn't fight to stay alive in this pit just to get buried in a hole outside some ranch."

"Get on the wrong side of a rancher, did you?" Wolpert asked as he stepped around to unlock the shackles around Eddie's wrists. After that had time to stew, he stepped back around to where Eddie could see him. "I meant what I said about Burt." Backing up as Eddie brought his arms around front so he could rub some of the feeling back into his wrists, he tossed the keys so they landed flat upon the other man's stomach. "But if you don't get out of them leg irons soon enough, we won't be going anywhere."

"More like I'll be going back to my old spot on the floor in the next room and you'll be the fresh meat in the cage."

"Yeah. Something like that."

Wolpert stood with his eye to the slot in the door and his back to the chair. Thanks to Otto's glass chin, the deputy was going to be out for a while, but that didn't mean they had a lot of time. Wolpert needed to find something out as quickly as possible and he didn't think he'd have to wait.

While rummaging through Otto's pockets, he'd found the deputy's pocket watch and tucked it under the cylinder of Otto's holstered pistol. "How many guards are on duty?"

"Three."

Then came the clatter of the pocket watch hitting the floor. When Wolpert turned around, he drew his pistol and thumbed back the hammer in one smooth motion.

Eddie was crouched next to Otto with the deputy's gun in hand. He looked up at Wolpert and asked, "What do you plan on doing with that old six-shooter?"

"Depends on what you plan on doing with yours."

"Did you really expect me to go anywhere without a pistol? Why'd you leave it here for me, then?"

Wolpert couldn't fault the other man's logic. Also, Eddie wasn't aiming his pistol anywhere close to him. "You said three guards?" he asked. "Does that count the one that let us in here?"

"If you mean Chuck, then yeah," Eddie replied. "He likes to think he's cock of the walk so long as them other two are on duty. We only see them when they poke their noses out to make their rounds. Other than that, they're either playing cards or drinking whiskey."

"Hand over that pistol."

"What?"

"You heard me," Wolpert said as he stepped forward and extended his left hand. His gun was aimed at the floor for the moment, but was only a heartbeat away from changing that situation. "Hand it over. You want to waste time debating or should I carve a few holes through you right now?"

He wasn't happy about it, but Eddie flipped the gun around so the handle was pointed out toward Wolpert. As far as the sheriff was concerned, Eddie had passed the biggest test so far.

"What now?" Eddie asked.

"Now we see about getting you some company on the way out of here."

"Did Burt really send you to fetch me?"

"Yeah."

"Seems like he would have wanted me to be armed."

Wolpert tucked Otto's gun under his belt so it was tougher to snatch than if it was in his holster. After taking another glimpse into the hallway, he said, "Yeah, I'm sure he would have. But he's not the one doing this. I am. And I want to get out of here with a minimum of spilt blood."

"That could be difficult, you know."

"Yeah. I know. Where are those other guards?"

"They walked through the doors on the opposite side of the big cage," Eddie explained. "I don't know much about what's beyond them doors because the guards, warden and lawmen are the only ones who use 'em. Haven't you been here before?"

"Think you can wrap those shackles around your hands so it looks like they're still on?"

"I suppose. What about the leg irons?"

Nodding toward Otto, Wolpert said, "Put them on our friend down there."

All too happy to comply with that order, Eddie clamped one of the iron cuffs around Otto's ankle and the other around his wrist. When he looked back again, Wolpert saw that the deputy's chains had also been wrapped through the supports of the chair itself so it attached the piece of furniture to Otto's legs.

"Should slow him down a bit," Eddie said with a shrug.

"Fine. Stay here and wait for me to clear the way. If you come out before then, you'll take your chances with whatever is unleashed out there."

"Sounds ominous," Eddie said with an exaggerated shudder.

Chapter 20

Wolpert pulled the door open, stepped into the hall and eased it so it was all but completely shut behind him. The deserted hallway felt about three times as long as when he'd walked down it the first time. The door at the other end was open and he did his best to walk through it as if there weren't a thing wrong. The trick to that was in holding his head high and keeping a somewhat aggravated expression on his face as if he had every right to go where he was going and was in a rush to get there. Since there were only prisoners watching him from the large cage when he emerged from the hall, Wolpert motioned for Tom to come over to him.

He approached to the bars, shoving aside another prisoner who tugged on his sleeve while snarling, "You'd better be here to get us out."

"Or what? You'll rattle your cage at me? Just take a breath and tell me if you boys have managed to find the men we're after."

"Yeah," Tom said. "Two of them anyhow. They were

caught and tossed in here the same time as Eddie Vernon. Juan's been talking to 'em since we got here."

"Got acquainted pretty quickly, huh?"

"A few of these boys are friends of Burt's. Soon as they caught wind that something might be brewing, they been pestering us to be a part of it."

Looking around at the other sets of expectant eyes trained on him, Wolpert grunted, "We came for specific men. Not to empty this whole damn place."

"Don't worry about it," Tom assured him. "Burt won't want anything to do with these men anyways. They been caught so many times that they gotta be either stupid or cursed."

Wolpert stood up and looked toward the sound of an opening door. "You, Juan and Cade get the other men ready to go. And make sure you keep it down to those two. Anyone else will be shot and left here. Understood?"

Although a good portion of the prisoners were still asleep or too far away to hear much of the conversation, Tom took another look to make sure. He nodded and moved toward Cade, who sat nursing a wound that had been freshly reopened sometime during his stay. The fidgety ones who pestered Tom did so for only another few seconds before they were knocked onto their backsides by the big man.

As he made his way around the large cage, Wolpert was reminded even more of a large zoo exhibit. He hadn't been to many himself, but he'd seen a few pictures and heard several stories of folks who'd gone to throw bits of food at exotic critters and watch as they crawled around on rocks. Even if those were animals, they had to have lived in better conditions than those at Dog Creek Jail. There was another door on that side of the room that was marked GUARDS AND WARDEN ONLY. It looked solid and formidable enough, but Wolpert checked it before getting too worked up. The door was unlocked. More than likely, the guards that Eddie had mentioned were planning on making their rounds soon. Suddenly, the handle was jerked from his grasp and he quickly found himself standing face-to-face with Otto's friend.

"I thought I told you to stay put," Chuck said.

"No, you didn't."

"Well, I meant to. Where's Otto?"

"He told me to give you the rest of that payment." Reaching under his coat, Wolpert stopped and whispered, "Maybe it'd be better if these men out here didn't see."

Before those words were out of his mouth, Chuck stepped back through the door he'd just opened. He stood his ground and planted his feet so Wolpert couldn't go much farther than a step or two after closing the door behind him. The hallway was similar in shape and size to the opposite one, but the doors weren't reinforced and the rooms beyond them looked more like living quarters.

"Are there more single-man cells over here?" Wolpert asked.

"Yeah," Chuck replied. "Down that way."

When Chuck shifted to glance toward a door that was obviously more reinforced than the others, Wolpert made his move. He didn't care about where the trouble prisoners were kept and he didn't care about who might be

back there at the moment. All he did care about was that
Chuck had looked away from him long enough for the
sheriff to wrap his arms around his throat.

Hans Brueckner had been a sergeant when he'd
taught recruits how to take down another man without
making much of a sound. It had taken Wolpert several
lessons to learn the methods, which had extended his
cavalry training past the normal limit. But Hans had
taken a few young men under his wing and Ezekiel
Wolpert had been one of them. Hans was a stout fellow
who always reeked of pipe smoke and dark ale. Always ready for a fight, he had a more relaxed air about
him than most superior officers and would have done
his level best to knock some sense into Wolpert if he'd
caught him taking his first ill-gotten dollar. On the
other hand, he would have been proud of the way his
pupil brought Chuck to his knees.

The well-practiced move was swiftly applied and force-
fully maintained. One of Wolpert's arms slid around the
front of Chuck's throat while the other fell in behind to
shut the poor guard's neck in a makeshift vice. Chuck's
windpipe was neatly closed and all the struggling in
the world wasn't enough to get him loose. Within twenty
seconds, Chuck's body started going limp. A few seconds after that and he could no longer hold up his arms.

Wolpert hung on for just a bit longer to make sure
Chuck was completely out. As he lowered the other
man to the floor, he eased up on the pressure so as not
to choke the other man into an early grave. From the
time Chuck had uttered his last offhanded word to the
time when he was lying on the floor, no more than a
whisper of sound had been made. Yes, indeed, Hans
would have been proud.

"What the hell's going on?"

Whipping his head around, Wolpert spotted a pair of men walking down the far end of the hall. Without missing a beat, he replied, "I think Chuck slipped. Can one of you help me get him up?"

The other two men stomped down the hall like a pair of big brothers who had been asked to help pull their little sister out of the mud. They responded because they knew they had to, but made it clear that such an event wasn't new to them. Both wore long coats that hung open to show gun belts strapped around their waists and clubs dangling at their hip.

"What'd he trip over this time?" the first man asked.

"Hell if I know. He was giving me a tour and just dropped."

The second man kept his eyes on Wolpert while his partner squatted down to get a closer look at Chuck. "Ain't you one of those deputies that brung those new prisoners in earlier?"

"That's right," Wolpert said.

"What are you doing here so late?"

The first guard turned to see how Wolpert would respond, but certainly wasn't expecting to get shoved backward over his fallen partner. As he'd shoved him, Wolpert reached for the club hanging from the guard's belt and snagged it before its owner fell out of reach. By the time the guard hit the floor, the club was already on its way toward the second man's knee.

The second guard had sharper reflexes and quickly pivoted to keep from landing on the floor with the others. The club caught him more toward the back of the knee instead of the front where it would have sent a wave of pain all the way through his body. If the blow had landed on the side of the knee, he wouldn't have been able to stand no matter how much he'd wanted to. The impact of the club did cause his leg to buckle, which did put him off his balance for a moment.

Wolpert took advantage of that moment by rushing forward to swing the club again. This time, he anticipated the guard's next move by aiming for the man's gun hand. Sure enough, the guard started to draw his pistol but was cut short when the polished piece of wood rapped against his wrist. Even though Wolpert thought he'd heard a bone snap, he wasn't going to take any chances. He grabbed the guard's wrist and gave it a quick twist.

Not only did the guard let go of his gun, but his hand twisted almost completely around. Knowing that the broken wrist would preoccupy the guard for a while, Wolpert grabbed the other man's gun and tucked it under his belt where he had the start of a fairly decent collection.

When he looked at the first guard, he immediately spotted the shooting iron in that one's hand. It seemed the guard had collected himself just a bit quicker than Wolpert had guessed and was one finger twitch away from making the Nebraska lawman pay with his life. Rather than give the guard that pleasure, Wolpert dropped flat down onto his belly as the hammer of the guard's pistol dropped.

The shot blasted through Wolpert's ears as if the bullet itself had bored through his skull. Even as he kissed the floor, he tried to mash his face down harder against the gritty surface. He rolled onto his belly, unsure as to whether or not he would live long enough to look up at the ceiling again. Since being cautious would only slow him down, he kept going until something stopped him.

Wolpert made it onto his back as the guard's pistol barked at him again. That round punched into the floor even closer than the first, but he had enough to think about since he had only enough time to fire back once before the other man's aim improved. Setting his sights on the guard's face, Wolpert snapped his arm like a whip in that direction to send the club he'd taken from the other man into the guard's jaw.

Watching just long enough to see that man drop, Wolpert shifted his attention to the second guard. That one was still reeling in pain from his broken wrist even as he propped himself up and struggled to get to another weapon. It would have settled easier in Wolpert's conscience if the guard had simply stayed down, but he wasn't about to allow himself to be shot. "Sorry about this, mister," he said as he kicked the guard's arm out from under him. The guard reflexively tried to push himself back up again, only he mistakenly used the hand with the broken wrist. Wolpert felt as though he was doing the fellow a service when he placed his boot upon the side of the guard's head and knocked him out with a sharp tap of his foot. After collecting all the guns and keys he could find, the sheriff rushed back out to the main cage.

Juan stood near the bars directly in front of him. He was surrounded by his partners as well as two strangers.

"Those the men we're after?" Wolpert asked.

"Yes," Juan told him. "What about the guards?"

"Won't need to worry about them."

"Are they dead?" Since Wolpert didn't answer him, Juan shadowed him as best he could from his side of the bars. The prisoners who were awake either watched him or tried to follow until Tom pushed them away. A majority of the men were either asleep or curled up in the section of floor they'd claimed for themselves. "If they're dead, we should know about it!"

"Just shut up and get ready to move," Wolpert snarled.

He circled back around the cage in a series of quick strides and was back at the door leading to the spot where he'd left Otto and Eddie. When he opened the door, he found Eddie standing there waiting for him like a ghoul lurking in the shadows.

"What took you so long?" Eddie asked.

"Decided to stop and pick daisies," Wolpert said impatiently as he all but dragged Eddie with him to the cage's only door. "Keep an eye open to see if anyone comes in. Do you know which of these keys is the one for this door?"

"Sure," Eddie replied. "Start at the biggest one on the ring and it's the second one over. Should look newer than the rest on account of it's hardly used."

Despite his reservations as to the accuracy of such a detailed account, Wolpert followed the directions and tried the key he found. It fit within the lock and turned with just a little bit of work. "How the hell did you know that?"

Eddie chuckled and replied, "I been watching like a hawk every time a guard opens that door just in case a day like this would come. Now do I get a gun?"

"No," Wolpert said as the door shrieked open.

That sound had more of an effect on the prisoners than the rustle of slop to a sty full of starving hogs. Every man who'd been huddled in another part of the cage stalked toward the front. Anyone who'd been asleep snapped their heads up to get a look at why the door was being opened and pulled themselves to their feet.

"You sure you don't want us both to be heeled?" Eddie asked.

"Yeah. Move it, Cade."

Tom, Juan and the other two men were out the door in a rush, but Cade was having a bit more trouble. He hobbled along and gritted his teeth as one of his injuries flared up. "Just give me a second," he grunted. "I'm doin' my best."

"You might wanna do your best a little quicker," Eddie said. "Someone's coming."

Wolpert twisted around to look over his shoulder. The main door leading from the room was open and he could see all the way out to the dark reception area. "I don't see anyone."

"That's because they're still outside," Eddie explained. "We can all hear 'em. Why do you think these prisoners are so restless?"

Drawing his pistol while reaching out to grab Cade's arm and pull him out of the cage, Wolpert took aim at the closest prisoner who had been creeping up toward the entrance. "They're restless because they think they can fight their way out of here," he said to the prisoners as much as he did to Eddie. "What they're forgetting is that I only need to fire through one doorway to hold back that tide."

The prisoner at the head of the group was a wide-shouldered man with greasy blond hair and a thick beard. His mouth was pressed shut so tightly that it looked more like a line that had been sliced across the mound of flesh piled atop his shoulders.

Wolpert kept his aim fixed on a spot directly between the prisoner's eyes as he stepped back and shut the door to the cage. Some of the men rushed forward but weren't fast enough to get there before the key was turned in the lock. The clatter and clank of the tumblers set the prisoners off even more as they surged to the front of the cage to shake the bars all the way down to the building's foundation. One of them was eager enough to reach out between the bars and grab hold of Cade's other shoulder. Wolpert discouraged that behavior by dropping the grip of his pistol down on top of the other man's hand.

"Damn animals," Cade snarled as he wheeled around to kick the bars he'd just left behind.

"Forget about them," Eddie said. "We've got other concerns."

Wolpert stayed in step with Cade but urged him to move faster with a series of insistent nudges. "So you keep saying. I still don't see anyone and I don't hear anything."

As if to prove him wrong, the sound of hooves beating against the ground outside reached the sheriff's ears.

"Told ya," Eddie said.

"Probably just a few more guards coming to spell the boys that are already here," Juan offered. Looking over to Eddie, he asked, "Don't you think?"

Once they were all gathered in the reception area, Wolpert shut the door to the main room so he could hear himself think. He could also hear more horses along with the voices of the men riding them. "My horse and Otto's are around back. A few of you might have to double up, but we should be able to ride away from here."

One of the men Juan had brought along looked as if

he'd been locked up for most of his life. His face was sunken and his features were outlined in filth that was thick enough to form a crust. The cleanest parts of him were his eyeballs, which were on full display as he asked, "You didn't plan for us all to have horses? What if we're too heavy to outrun them lawmen?"

"Then we'll leave you behind and skin out of here," Wolpert snapped. "Any more worries? No? Then shut your mouth."

Eddie was already at the front door, pulling aside the shade to one of the few windows cut into the building. Wolpert stepped up to the window and looked outside. He counted half a dozen men on horseback and one on foot leading his horse by the reins. Marshal Davis walked toward the front of the building and flipped his reins around the post there. His hand was already on his gun as he approached the front door.

"Get out the side door," Wolpert said. "Best make it quick."

Chapter 21

"Funny how you can move so much better now," Wolpert pointed out as he hurried along behind Cade.

The outlaw hardly broke his stride as he raced down the narrow walkway between the wall and the cage. Desperate hands reached out for him every inch of the way. Some would scrape against his face or arm, while other clawing fingers snagged in his clothing or attempted to lock around him in any number of spots. "As long as it means getting the hell out of here, I'll find a way to run."

Juan was at the head of the line and when he got to the door, Wolpert told him, "Go on through and head straight back. There should be a door that leads outside." From there, he broke away from the group and started retracing his steps.

"Where are you going?" Cade asked.

"To see what the marshal wants. You men get outside, work your way around the back of the building and get to them horses. The first chance you get, ride away."

"Where do we go from there?" one of the other prisoners asked.

"My men know where we're meeting, so you'd better listen to what they have to say and make sure nothing happens to them. If they're not in good condition when I arrive at the meet-up point, I'll point the bounty hunters in the right direction."

The prisoner hadn't been hinting at a mutiny and he grumbled as much while the others prodded him along. Wolpert didn't stay to listen to the bellyaching because he was too busy working his way to the reception area. It wasn't until he was almost there that he realized he had someone acting as his shadow. "Are you deaf?" he asked Eddie. "I told you to get out of here."

"I'm coming with you."

"Wouldn't you rather be far away from those lawmen?"

"Sure," Eddie replied. "But if things go badly with you, none of us will get—"

A heavy hand knocked on the front door.

"You want to help?" Wolpert hissed. "Get out of my sight and stay with the others. If you're spotted now, I won't have a choice but to let these men toss you back into the cage with a bunch of angry prisoners who feel pretty damn slighted right about now."

"Say no more." Touching his forehead as though he had a hat to tip, Eddie backed away and through the doorway that led to Chuck's office. Since the knocking was growing more impatient with every thump, Wolpert removed the thick pieces of lumber barring the door. When he finally opened it, he found Marshal Davis standing there with his fist raised.

"What are you doing here?" Davis asked.

"I was just about to ask you the same thing," Wolpert said while forcing a tired grin onto his face. Since the grin wasn't winning anyone over, he dropped it and added, "Just having a word with my prisoners. Is there a rule against that?"

"There is if you don't have permission from me to do so. Step aside so we can have a look around."

"What are you looking for, exactly?"

"Just a quick head count."

Wolpert swore he felt the contents of his stomach drop through a trapdoor to empty into his feet. After all he'd been doing in the last hour, he doubted he had enough resolve in him to keep any of that from showing on his face.

Davis nodded and fixed him with a stare that let Wolpert know there wasn't a secret in the world that could be hidden from him. "I told you to step aside, Zeke."

Every second of delay only stoked the marshal's suspicions. He could have bought himself a few more minutes to think, but those would be purchased at much too high a cost. So Wolpert opened the door and stepped aside. "Whoever told you I was up to something has got it wrong," he assured the marshal. "I'm here at the behest of Otto Berringer. You must know him."

"Yeah, I know Otto," Davis said as he strode into the anteroom. "That's part of what brought me here. I went to Henrietta's boardinghouse to have a bite to eat. Aren't you supposed to be staying there?"

"I am staying there, but the last time I checked I wasn't supposed to be in at any certain time. Was Henrietta worried about me?"

"Not as such. She didn't know where you went to. I knew you weren't at a saloon or with my boys, so that meant you'd found some other bit of business to occupy your time."

"Is that a problem?" Wolpert asked.

"It is when the man who's rattling around in Lester has connections to Burt Sampil. It's men like you that make it so easy for him to live his life without spending a single night in jail. There's been rumblings about some mighty big irons Burt's got in the fire. Then you show up out of nowhere. It gets me to thinking." Davis followed Wolpert through the door leading to the space where Chuck's office was, looming like a specter over his shoulder.

Wolpert turned on the balls of his feet and doubled back. "What have you been thinking, Luke? Since you'll tell me anyhow, I figure I might as well ask."

"I'm thinking you're here to get some information out of one of these prisoners. Haven't some of these boys worked for Sampil in the past?"

"If you believe everything you hear on the matter, everyone's worked for Sampil. Ain't that why he never lands in a jail cell?"

"Partly," Davis replied. Before he could take more than two steps to catch up to the sheriff, Wolpert's hand thumped flat against his chest to knock him backward against a desk. While he flailed to regain his balance, the door to the office was slammed shut. Still struggling to right himself, Davis roared, "Stop that man!"

By the time those words hit the deputies' ears, Wolpert had already rushed past them, gone through the door that led to the main room and bolted it in place behind him. Some of the deputies must have gone to check on Davis, because there didn't seem to be many of them trying to come after him. That would most certainly change as soon as the marshal had a second or two to issue some more orders.

"Is that it?"

Wolpert turned toward the voice, expecting to find a smart-mouthed prisoner delighting in the hot water boiling at the feet of the man who'd left him in the jail to rot. But it wasn't a man inside the cage who'd asked that question. Instead, Eddie ambled along the side of the cage as if he were out for a stroll.

"Where are the others?" Wolpert asked.

Eddie had to get closer to be heard over the growing ruckus of the prisoners screaming obscenities at them and hitting the bars with whatever or whoever they could throw against them. Finally, he replied, "They got to the horses, but I don't think they'll have long before those lawmen get to them."

"If they know what's good for them, they'll get moving."

"I highly doubt they'll stay. Nobody's that loyal."

"Then why are you here?"

Shrugging, Eddie looked at the door that had started shaking as several deputized shoulders slammed against it. "I'm curious to see how this pans out and there's not a lot they can do to me besides toss me back in there."

"I'm sure they can come up with a few things," Wolpert chuckled. "How long will that door hold?"

Eddie looked at the door leading to the reception area as if it were an old friend. "It'll hold. The warden had it reinforced after some more of Burt's men tried to break some men out of here."

"The same ones we took with us tonight?"

"One of 'em. Not me, though."

After another wave of pounding upon the door let up, it was quiet. Wolpert closed his eyes and waited for what he knew was coming. He didn't have to wait for more than a couple of seconds before gunshots filled the next room. The prisoners must not have felt they had much more to lose, since the shots only riled them up.

"If you plan on making a last stand," Eddie said in a voice that was just loud enough to be heard over everything else. "You probably should give me one of those."

Wolpert followed the prisoner's line of sight straight down to the guns tucked under his belt. "This ain't a last stand," he told him.

"Well, maybe I should have one anyways."

"If that's really what you think, then go ahead and reach for one. See how far you get."

Eddie might have thought he was on the ragged edge, but apparently he wasn't far enough down the stretch for him to do anything as stupid as testing his luck against someone who'd gone even further. Once that opportunity was allowed to slip away, frustration showed in his pale blue eyes. "So, what in the hell do you propose we do? If you've got a plan, it's high time to get it rolling. If not, give me a gun and we'll bust outta here the hard way!"

"You want to do something to help?" When Eddie nodded anxiously, Wolpert told him, "Go open that door."

Eddie looked at the door that was being shaken on its hinges as if he was more unsettled by that than the prisoners who clawed, spat and screamed at him from inside the cage. "You mean *that* door?"

"That's the one. Go open it."

"Are you sure?"

The lawmen on the other side of the door fired at it repeatedly. Judging by the way the door shook in its frame, the damage was piling up but the sturdy barricade was holding.

"I'm sure," Wolpert told him. "You just be sure to get out of the way as soon as you open it."

"Any plan for afterward?" Eddie asked.

"Yep. Tear out of this place and run through that side door like the devil himself was nipping at your heels."

Eddie watched the sheriff for a few seconds to make sure he was serious. When Wolpert approached the door to the cage with keys in hand, Eddie pieced together what he needed to know and ran for the reinforced door that was the only thing holding Marshal Davis and his deputies at bay.

"All right," Wolpert said to the men behind the bars. "You fellas want out? You're about to get your wish. But I got to warn you you'll be facing armed men who'll have every reason in the world to cut you down before you get anywhere close to freedom."

Wolpert didn't expect to spark a rousing discourse. On the contrary, his words had as much impact as an election speech given to a bunch of rabid dogs trapped in a barn. Eddie was at the door, gingerly reaching for the handle as more shots continued to thump into the wood. When they let up, he unlocked it and ran away.

Waiting until the last possible moment, Wolpert turned the key in the lock and left the ring dangling there as he ran to catch up to Eddie. Behind him, the lawmen threw their weight against the door. Since there was significantly less resistance this time around, they stampeded through and spilled into the room at about the same time as the prisoners got the cage open.

Wolpert and Eddie ducked into the hallway where Chuck and his other two partners were lying as all hell broke loose behind them. The next room filled with noise. Shots were fired, men screamed, metal clanged against metal, knuckles cracked against faces, everything pretty much knocked against everything else. Near Wolpert's feet, Chuck lifted his head and groggily tried to speak.

Rather than stop to listen to the guard, Wolpert told him, "If you got any weapons stashed in this place, you'd best get to 'em. Seems like you've got a bit of a ruckus on your hands." While the guard figured the situation out, Wolpert dashed for the side door that the other two guards had used when they'd discovered him standing over Chuck earlier that night.

Cold air washed over his entire body and snow crunched under his boots. Those things were all as welcome as if he'd been locked in that cage himself for a number of years. His unsteady steps were even more welcome so long as they carried him away from that place. Eddie was several paces ahead of him, scrambling on his hands and knees after taking a spill on a patch of frozen mud. Wolpert reached down to pull him to his feet without breaking his stride.

"That was your plan?" Eddie shouted. "You let all of those men go!"

"I got the men I needed," Wolpert said. "The rest will just keep Davis and his boys occupied."

Both of them ran around the back of the building toward the shapes that had grouped together in the shadows. Tom, Cade, Juan and the other two prisoners they'd freed sat in their saddles. Wolpert picked out his gelding from the pack and quickened his pace to get there.

"What happened in there?" Cade asked. "Sounds like Armageddon."

"Just about," Eddie replied. "All the prisoners are loose."

While the three outlaws seemed surprised by that, the other two looked ready to jump out of their skins. "How did that happen?" one of the freed prisoners asked.

Wolpert pulled that man from his saddle since he happened to be on his gelding. "I set them loose. It was either that or test our luck with those lawmen." As soon as the prisoner's boots hit the ground, he hopped around as if he'd been tossed straight into the proverbial frying pan. Wolpert helped him climb back up and sit behind him.

The other prisoner allowed Eddie to climb up with him as he said, "There's real killers in that bunch. Setting 'em loose ain't the best idea. Lord only knows what they'll do when they get out."

"Ran afoul of some bad men, did you?" Tom said. "Maybe they'll be grateful Zeke set 'em free."

"I hardly set anyone free," Wolpert explained. "I opened a single door as a bunch of armed lawmen were charging straight in at them. No matter how desperate a man is, he'll think twice before testing his luck against those odds."

Smirking at the growing level of noise coming from the jail, Tom pointed out, "Sounds like plenty of 'em didn't need to think twice."

"And they're either gonna get themselves recaptured or killed," Wolpert told him. "If that many armed men can't defend against a bunch of wild dogs charging through a bottleneck as tight as that one back there, they shouldn't be carrying a gun in the first place. And if any man is crazy or desperate enough to run into that much hellfire, he was gonna get himself killed sooner rather than later anyhow."

As if to prove his point, the noise from within the jail died down. A few shots rang out, but the rumble of voices gave the impression that there were still plenty of men trading harsh words instead of bullets. In Wolpert's experience, death was much quieter than that.

It had been only a few seconds, but all of the men were taut as bowstrings. Looking at them in turn, Wolpert said, "Cade, you're still hurt, so you take Eddie to the spot we agreed upon. You recall where that was?"

"Yeah, yeah. I wasn't knocked in the head that hard," Cade grunted as he pointed his horse's nose away from the jail and snapped his reins. Eddie didn't need any incentive to follow along behind the outlaw.

"Tom, go with them. Juan and I will make sure these lawmen don't find you."

The big man got his horse facing the right direction, but paused before making another move. "Sure you don't need any more help? Sounds like you stirred up a mighty big hornet's nest."

"Just get out of here, will you!"

"Mind giving me and Cade a fighting chance in case we need to defend ourselves?"

Wolpert had nearly forgotten about all the pistols stuffed under his belt. Plucking two guns from his collection and tossing them through the air one at a time, Wolpert turned away from Tom and flicked his reins. This time, the bigger man was more than willing to ride away.

"We're splitting up to circle around this place from opposite sides," Wolpert told Juan as he tossed a gun to him. "Get some of them to follow, take a few shots if you must, but don't kill any lawmen. You do that, even on accident, and I'll see to it that you die here at this jail. I don't give a damn what your friends or Burt Sampil thinks about it."

The instant his gun was in his hand, Juan flipped open the cylinder to get a look at the rounds inside and then snapped it shut. "After all the sitting I've been doing, I'm ready for a good ride."

"All right, then. I'll race ya. First man to draw some deputies in the wrong direction wins a cigar."

Both men snapped their reins and rode in opposite directions. Wolpert circled around the side of the jail to pass by the spot where the horses had been tethered beneath a little shelter. His gelding wove between the shelter and the jail with ease, but the prisoner in the saddle behind Wolpert hung on and squealed as if he were hanging from the back of a runaway stagecoach.

"Almost forgot about you," Wolpert said over his shoulder.

The prisoner screeched something, but his words were lost amid the rumble of hooves and the sharply raised voices of the lawmen pouring out through the jail's front door. He didn't spot Marshal Davis among those men, but Wolpert wasn't taking a whole lot of time to look. Juan charged around the other side of the jailhouse, firing once into the air while shouting, "Any men who want their freedom follow me!"

There didn't seem to be any takers, but the lawmen didn't appreciate the offer very much. They fired back and rushed for the horses that were tied to the post at the front of the building. Before they could get into their saddles, Wolpert rode close enough to knock one of them in the shoulder with a well-placed boot. The kick thumped hard against his back and sent him staggering toward his partners. More shots crackled through the air, some of which hissed dangerously close to Wolpert's head. The prisoner behind him let out a pained grunt and clamped on to Wolpert's shoulder like a vise.

"You hit?" he asked.

The prisoner squirmed behind him before replying, "Caught me in the leg. Hurts!"

"We'll see to it later. Just keep your head down."

The only thing deadlier than a well-timed surprise was a surprise that was stretched out for too long. For the latter, the ones springing the surprise were in danger and Wolpert knew it wouldn't take long for this one to shift out of his favor. The deputies weren't firing wild any longer. They were getting their wits about them and figuring out the quickest way to end the fight. Before any of the lawmen steadied their aim or traded their pistols for something with longer range, Wolpert fired another burst of covering fire and then tapped his heels against the gelding's sides. The horse dug its hooves into the dirt to start building a head of steam.

Before too long, Juan was riding beside him and Dog Creek Jail was at their backs. Davis shouted at his men before they just raced off into the darkness without a plan. It was sound reasoning, but it also gave their quarry another minute or two to move along. Wolpert had organized enough posses to know that it never paid to just tear out after an escaping outlaw. The odds of stumbling into a world of hurt only got better when stumbling at night. Surely, Marshal Davis was using his knowledge of the terrain, the men he was after and the direction they'd gone to piece together a logical guess as to where they were headed.

All Wolpert had to do was use all of that against him. He led Juan to the main road so their tracks blended with those left behind by everyone else and then found a spot to lie low. Once the lawmen surged past them and charged into the night, they spent several cold hours praying they wouldn't double back.

Chapter 22

Kansas terrain was similar to Nebraska terrain, except flatter. Under normal circumstances, it would have been close to impossible for a man to find a hiding spot in the middle of all that flatness unless he'd scouted one out in advance. But Wolpert and his men weren't escaping under normal circumstances. In fact, the conditions surrounding their escape from Dog Creek were about as far from normal as they could want. The darkness was thicker than smoke. The cold was more unforgiving than steel. Without much of anything to break it up, the wind swept across it all like a massive, flailing set of arms intent on knocking down whoever defied it by staying upright.

Wolpert and Juan stayed still for several minutes after the lawmen had passed. The prisoner was happy enough to be sitting still for a spell and barely made a sound. Even after his eyes had acclimated to the shadows, Wolpert could hardly make out where the horizon ended and the sky began. A sparse bank of clouds marred the field of stars overhead as they slid from west to east, smearing everything into a dark gray mass. The three men sat for a little while longer and then walked their horses in the opposite direction that the lawmen had chosen.

The cold soaked into Wolpert's bones until every joint creaked when he moved. It wasn't just a sound that filled the inside of his head, but something he could feel like icy nails scraping along his aching tendons and the underside of his kneecaps. The more he rode, the less he moved his legs. By the time he and Juan arrived at the old cabin six miles away from the jail, Wolpert's body was numb from the waist down. The prisoner hung on to his back like a clump of leaves that had been stuck there by a splash of frozen water.

When he arrived, Wolpert could see a light flickering within the cabin. It was too old to be remembered by most folks in Lester and too stubborn to have fallen over in any storm. The horses were nowhere to be found, which didn't set well with the sheriff. Climbing down from his saddle, he drew his pistol and flipped his reins up to the prisoner who remained perched on the gelding's rump like so much baggage.

"Isn't this where we're supposed to meet the others?" Juan asked.

"Yeah, but there should be horses tied to one of those posts. Whistle if you see anyone trying to skin out the back."

Since he knew the piece of unkempt land so well, Wolpert was able to sneak up to the side of the cabin without making a sound. He stepped over pits in the ground left behind by rocks he'd pulled up himself and navigated patches he knew would be covered with dead grass or leaves. Avoiding the front door and larger window completely, he leaned against the wall next to a square side window that was only slightly larger than his head. Wolpert held his breath so as not to steam the glass as he got a look at who was inside.

The first thing to catch his eye was the fire. It wasn't burning in a stove or even a hearth, but in the middle of the floor where a portion of the boards had been pulled up to reveal packed dirt. Smoke rose from the flames and drifted straight up through a hole in the roof where a chimney had possibly been at one time or another. The horses were clustered at the edge of the room, but were such a sight that they caught Wolpert's attention before the men in there with them. He glanced at the faces of the men huddled near the fire and walked around to the back door. Knowing the latch didn't work properly, he pulled it open and stepped inside.

Both of the guns he'd divvied out earlier were pointed at him as the conversation around the campfire was brought to a sudden halt. Wolpert raised his hands and walked inside and across the room.

"Lord above, you gave us a fright," Cade said. "That's a real good way to get yourself shot."

"So is creating a nice, bright fire. The only way to draw more attention would be if you stumbled upon a lighthouse in the middle of this field."

"You picked the spot, Sheriff. Isn't it safe?"

Both of the prisoners straightened up, but one of them climbed to his feet and said, "Hold up, now. He's a sheriff?"

"Relax," Tom said. "He's a crooked sheriff and a friend of Burt's."

Wolpert wanted to hide the contempt he felt for being recognized that way, but did a bad job of it when he snarled, "And who the hell are you?"

"Oh, you can call me Malone," the prisoner replied cheerfully. "This here's Ben."

Ben was a skinny fellow who was easily the tallest man in the cabin. He had both gangly arms wrapped tightly around himself and nodded while scooting closer to the fire.

"Burt must be planning one hell of a big job, because he's gone through a lot of trouble to spring the best thieves there are from that jail," Malone proudly declared.

"It'd better be worth all that trouble," Tom grunted.

"Don't worry. It will be."

"So where are we headed anyway?" Eddie asked.

Wolpert, Cade, Tom and Juan all looked at him as though they didn't know whether they should laugh or shoot him through the head and be done with it.

"Where are we headed?" Wolpert snapped. "Aren't you the one that's supposed to tell us that?"

"Surely you men gotta have some notion of where we're goin'. Otherwise, you could just be tricking me into—"

"It's too cold to muck around with secret passwords and all that nonsense," Cade said while drawing his pistol and aiming it at him. "Here's your password. If it's not good enough for ya, I can give you another one that you're bound to like even less."

"We know we're headed into Texas," Wolpert said. "But that doesn't tell us what we truly need to know."

"All right," Eddie said in a voice that was calm, but not calm enough to keep from wavering a bit. "It's always a good idea to be safe. Surely you understand."

"We're a long ways past being safe," Wolpert told him. "Start talking so we can figure out the rest and get some sleep."

"The strongbox is headed into Dallas, but we need to catch it before it gets there. It's gonna be heavily guarded and impossible to just take with us. A friend of mine that works with the stagecoach company being contracted by Wells Fargo told me that the box will actually be bolted into the floor of the coach. If we just try to steal the coach, the Wells Fargo gunmen will be ready to burn us off of it if necessary. The strongbox is sturdy enough to be the only thing left standing even if that coach is blown to bits. The only way to get the strongbox is to get it out of that coach, and the only way to do that in a short amount of time is to unlock the brackets that'll be holding it in place. I ain't heard of a good way to do that, so that's on Burt's shoulders."

"How about getting the keys to unlock them?" Wolpert asked. "Think that would do?"

"He's got both keys?" When Wolpert nodded, Eddie grinned brightly enough to illuminate the sections of the cabin that remained untouched by the fire's glow. "Then all he needs are men tough enough to hold off the Wells Fargo boys and skilled enough to get out with the cargo intact."

"I can vouch for the first group," Tom said. "And before they spout off again, I figure they'll vouch for the second."

"I can vouch for them as well," Eddie said. "They can climb along the side of a moving train like a pair of monkeys and still keep their fingers moving deftly enough to pick a lock."

"If we're all friends now, maybe we should plan tomorrow's ride." Since Ben hadn't said much of anything since their introduction, everyone looked at him. A couple of the men seemed surprised that he could speak at all. Apparently used to that sort of reaction, Ben said, "The best spot to hit that Wells Fargo caravan is when it crosses the Red River."

"You know that for certain, do ya?" Tom asked.

"Yes, sir. That's why Eddie was certain I come along." Looking over to Eddie, he added, "I'm guessing it's time to lay our cards on the table now, right?"

"Yep," Eddie replied.

"I got a set of ears inside Wells Fargo. They're attached to the same man who told Burt about this deal to begin with. Sent word along when he struck out for Omaha with some horses."

Wolpert couldn't help smiling at the sound of that. There were plenty of times while he was in uniform when nothing he was ordered to do seemed to make any sense. For the most part, and especially when he was a soldier, Wolpert didn't get the pleasure of seeing how his piece of the puzzle fit in with all the others. Therefore, when he did get to see a few pieces come together, he made a point to enjoy it.

"The Wells Fargo men are starting somewhere up north of Texas," Ben continued. "I don't know where. What I do know is that they've already set out but shouldn't reach the Red River for at least another week. I think maybe they stopped somewhere along the way to get the coach properly outfitted and to pick up their cargo."

"So, what the hell is this cargo?" Cade asked. "We already got more lawmen on our tails than we know what to do with. Maybe this job ain't worth us stretching our necks out any further."

Since Juan and Tom looked as if they were getting ready to agree with their partner, Ben said, "Keys."

"Keys?" Tom grunted. "We know about the keys already."

"No. That's what's in the strongbox."

"So, what you're telling us is that there are more keys in that strongbox?" Tom asked.

"Yeah."

After twitching his eyes back and forth between all the other men, Cade felt frustration growing inside him like steam building within a piston. "Why are we gonna risk gettin' shot or hung for a bunch of keys?"

Wolpert leaned forward and dropped his voice. "Because those keys are probably the ones that open just about every other Wells Fargo strongbox that's being guarded like this one."

"Your crooked sheriff is pretty smart," Ben said. "Those keys will make it real easy for a gang of thieves to ride away with most of the biggest Wells Fargo shipments over the next year. Once we get a hold of those keys, Burt figures he and a small group of men can form a raiding party that will tear across the country, hit those fat shipments quick and easy and then disappear."

Cade's eyes grew wide. "We sure could. Without havin' to worry about cracking a safe or hauling one away to be broken later, we could hit them shipments fast enough to make the guards' heads spin."

"If the guards even know we're there at all," Ben added. "That's probably why Burt wanted men who knew what they were doing. Even with a key in hand, all it takes is one overanxious cowboy to spoil the whole thing. But a gang who knows their way around a locked strongbox will be able to do their job in a flicker."

"Like training to use a bayonet with a weighted rifle," Wolpert mused. "When the sergeant finally let us take the weights off, we could damn near stick that blade through a brick wall."

A few of the men seemed lost, but Ben could hardly contain himself. "That Burt's a smart one! And this whole thing will go even smoother with a lawman on our side."

Juan shook his head despairingly. "That badge was barely worth the price of melted tin before, but once word gets out about him breaking men out of Dog Creek, he'll be just another outlaw like the rest of us."

Ben looked at Wolpert with some of the most genuine admiration he'd ever had pointed his way since his early army career. "An outlaw, maybe, but one who knows how law dogs really think and where we can find other lawmen who'll be willing to take a few dollars to let us pass. Burt knew what he was doing in pulling this gang together. We're all gonna be rich."

Something tugged at Wolpert's chest, like a hook that he'd forgotten he'd swallowed until someone at the other end pulled it taut. It was the same thing that had pulled him into accepting his first bribe. The same thing that told him how any lawman who wanted to live comfortably couldn't do so in a clean house.

Chapter 23

Bear Grove, Oklahoma Territory
Six days later

Some might have called it a miracle to get to the little trading post at all. Wolpert had used or given away all but a few dollars of the money from the bank heist, and the other men had left just about everything they owned back at the Dog Creek Jail. According to Eddie, they were to meet Burt in a little section of hell carved out of some dangerous Indian country just north of the Texas border. After he got that bit of bad news, Wolpert followed the first telegraph lines he found to send a message to Fancy's Emporium in Sedley. It was a simple set of instructions that would be one of the most important messages Lucy Myles would ever receive. Wolpert could only pray that it got to her, because he didn't have time to wait for a reply.

Bear Grove was a small settlement at the end of their ride that had grown out of a trading post the way moss spread out from a moldy stump. The only marking on the trading post was a battered sign that read TRADIG POST. Either the owner didn't know how to spell or had lost a letter to all the lead that flew past his place of business. Additions stretching off the main building had been converted into a stable, a restaurant and several shacks that looked like homes. All of those were connected to the main body by crooked passageways that weren't much more than short, covered boardwalks.

Wolpert had never spent much time in the Oklahoma Territories, but had heard plenty about them from cavalry officers who'd visited his post back in his army days. As with most soldiers' stories, the ones that didn't involve lewd women were filled with blood. Very few of the stories from this neck of the woods had been about women. Even if the land wasn't breathtaking, however, it had its own sort of charm. A very wide, very flat charm. After less than two hours spent in Bear Creek, Wolpert was aching for the more familiar flatness of home. On a positive note, the winter conditions weren't as bad as they'd been up north, but were still harsh enough to set some teeth to chattering.

"Can't we go inside?" Malone asked once his jaw stopped trembling.

Wolpert shrugged and lifted his chin to catch a passing breeze. "And miss this delightful weather? This is the sort of thing that reminds a man he's alive."

"Alive and freezing his toes off."

"If you want to go back in to sit around that half-warm stove while listening to another sales pitch, go ahead. I'll take my chances with the cold."

Malone looked over his shoulder to a wide front window of the main structure. Inside, several men huddled around a potbellied stove that was surrounded by glass-topped counters. The fellow who ran the trading post and subsequently the entire settlement had been regaling all of the outlaws and escaped prisoners with the wonders of whatever it was he was selling. Even if he knew his audience was composed of killers and thieves, it was doubtful the salesman would be quiet. "You got a point there," Malone said as he shifted to once again face forward. "Maybe it isn't so bad out here."

One of the men inside stepped away from the group, was immediately singled out by the overzealous salesman and fought valiantly to break free. After several seconds of insistent arm waving and half-finished protests, the man finally turned his back to the group and walked out. When the front door opened, the salesman's last attempts to draw his audience back to its original size could be heard echoing out into the vast Oklahoma landscape.

"Jesus, Lord Almighty," Burt muttered as he stepped outside and shut the door behind him. "I don't think that man drew a breath the whole time he was talking."

"What's he goin' on about?" Malone asked.

Burt shook his head as if trying to distance himself from a bad memory. "I don't know. Some sort of tonic or shaving mirror. Could'a been new boots for all I know. I'm just glad to be away from there."

"What about them?" Wolpert asked while nodding at the window.

Gazing in at the rest of his gang, Burt waved and hissed, "They can fend for themselves."

"Hope you don't abandon us like that when we go after that stagecoach tomorrow."

"We'll all be in friendlier territory with Wells Fargo men shooting at us. Besides, if everything goes the way it should, it'll probably take longer for us to ride there and back than it will to get that strongbox."

Malone rubbed his arms vigorously and stared out at the desolate landscape as if he'd set his sights upon paradise itself. "And we'll be real busy after that," he said wistfully. "Hitting more stagecoaches from here to—"

Burt silenced him with a pat on the shoulder that was hard enough to rattle Malone down to his boots. Keeping his hand in place as though it was a friendly gesture, Burt said, "We all know what we're gonna do. No need to shout it to the Injuns out there."

"You think we'll get any trouble on that account?" Wolpert asked.

"From the redskins?" Burt scoffed. "Hardly. Wells Fargo don't send valuable shipments through hell just so they can get picked off by savages. They must have scouted a clear path or sent ahead some sharpshooters to blaze a trail."

"Or haggled with some of the tribal leaders to arrive at a good price for safe passage."

When Burt patted Wolpert on the shoulder, it wasn't nearly as harsh as when he'd knocked Malone around. "Leave it to a crooked lawman to think of the angles that require more cash than bullets. That's why I'm glad to have you along with us on this. We got all the angles figured. But if things do take a turn for the worse, we still got our own sharpshooters to do things the hard way."

"Yeah," Wolpert said as he looked through the window again. "You sure do."

Shoving Malone toward the front door of the trading post, Burt said, "Go on inside and warm yourself up. Me and Zeke need to have a word."

Malone wasn't anxious to be reintroduced to the salesman, but he was less anxious to go against Burt's wishes. Once Malone was gone and the door was shut, Burt lowered himself onto one of the old rocking chairs that were scattered across the post's front porch. The wood was warped from the elements and creaked loudly beneath him, but Burt settled into the chair with all the confidence in the world. "So, are you in or not?"

"Ain't it a bit too late to ask me that?" Wolpert mused.

"I know you were in this far, but there's a long ways to go. Once you come along past a certain point, you've gotta be in all the way. There'll be plenty of jobs after this one. Once the first few of them keys are put to use, there'll be more guards to contend with on every shipment. They'll be ready for us to hit 'em."

"That's why it'd be foolish to hit them all." Shrugging, Wolpert added, "It may even be foolish to think they'll use any of those strongboxes once the keys fall into our hands."

"You think I'm stupid? You think I'd steal all them keys and just assume Wells Fargo would keep using them boxes? There are a few master keys in the bunch that unlock more'n one strongbox, and Ben can figure out which ones they are. We'll leave the rest, along with a few I had made while you and the boys were in Lester." Burt reached into his jacket pocket and removed a ring of keys that all looked small enough to be teeth pulled from the jaws of a metallic animal. "These were made by a craftsman who swears they're close enough to the ones used by Wells Fargo."

"Close enough to fool men who make it their business to know the difference?"

"They'd better be. Otherwise, I got a serious bone to

pick with that craftsman I mentioned. Anyway," Burt added as he stuffed the keys back into his pocket, "it don't matter if it fools them for long. These keys will convince 'em to keep using them boxes for a while longer. I've got a line on three shipments passing through Texas alone that we can hit in the next week. From then on, I sell the keys off to other robbers lookin' to make names for themselves."

"That's not a bad idea," Wolpert admitted.

"Which is where you come in again. You think along the lines of who you can sweet-talk and who you can't. You gotta know some robbers who got more cash than brains. Maybe some of your law-dog friends could be interested. Between the two of us, we should be able to find a good amount of buyers who don't know Wells Fargo is wise to their keys bein' missing. I know plenty of outlaws myself, and most of 'em wouldn't even fig-ure it all out no matter what. Men like you and me, we can spot the weak and stupid folks. That's how we've stayed alive so long."

Once again, Wolpert was unable to counter a state-ment that insulted his very essence as a man. The truth of the matter was that he could pick out a weak or stu-pid member of a herd and he surely did know how to put that fool to work so it benefited him the most.

"We both put this gang together," Burt continued. "I'll see to it that we get them keys and use a few of the most valuable ones before it's too late. You'll help me unload the rest and we'll each make enough of a profit to buy us nice little haciendas south of the border. How's that sound?"

To Wolpert, it sounded like the very thing he'd been fearing since the moment he'd first heard about the plan.

It also sounded like a real good way to get a lot of Wells Fargo men killed as they were besieged by Burt and his gang. It could also be a way to send a lot of dim-witted outlaws to their graves when they bought the keys that became useless once Wells Fargo changed all their locks. That was a wrinkle that Wolpert hadn't foreseen. He'd actually thought Burt was foolish enough to believe he could be the one to put all those keys to use. But none of that mattered because Wolpert's own plan was already in motion. And if it wasn't, he'd be certain to muck up the works for Burt Sampil.

"Sounds fine," Wolpert said as everything else rushed through his head.

For a second, Burt didn't seem convinced. He eyed Wolpert suspiciously before shifting his gaze to the open expanse in front of him. "We'll just see for ourselves real soon, won't we?"

Chapter 24

Eight men rode toward the Red River, which stretched out before them beneath a crust of blown snow and dead weeds. The winter's teeth weren't as sharp this close to Texas, but they still did a good enough job of shredding through Wolpert's coat and raking against his tired body. That morning, Burt had gone to each man in turn, quietly discussing strategy and what was in store for them that day. No doubt, each man was told a different thing and promised a slice of the pie that was larger than what the others might expect. Since the outlaws surely had their own plans brewing, they nodded at some of what Burt told them and discarded the rest.

Breakfast had been a hearty stack of buckwheat griddle cakes served up at the restaurant connected to the Trading Post. As he'd eaten his meal, Wolpert sat with Tom, Cade and Juan to wait for their talk from Burt. When it was his turn to receive his whispered orders, Wolpert merely got a wink and a pat on the shoulder. Burt had already told him enough.

The sun was just a pale glow in the stark gray sky, framed by tattered clouds that seemed ready to fall onto the earth in cold wisps. Burt and his riders moved like a single beast. When he gave the signal, the men on either side of Burt passed it along so the procession could spread out to cover more ground. Not a word was said as the line of horses extended so the rider at one end could hardly make out the one at the other.

If Malone's information held up, the Wells Fargo wagons would be crossing the river sometime within the next day. Considering the hardships that accompanied any overland route across the Oklahoma Indian territories, those men would be lucky if Burt's men were the only ones to lay siege to their shipment. Indian attacks in this neck of the woods were expected, and if a Wells Fargo driver didn't take that into account, he deserved as bad as he got. Someone had struck a deal with the redskins. Wolpert was sure of that. Clearing a path using a more forceful method would create too many enemies among the tribes.

After the men approached the river, they found somewhere to keep out of sight and lie low. That wasn't an easy task given the flat terrain, but there was a fairly good rise north of the river that the Wells Fargo caravan would need to crest on their approach. Choosing a different route would only tack on another day or two as they found a spot to cross. Considering the coldness of the water, no driver would want to expose his horses to the torture of a long stroll across a river. For that matter, most drivers wouldn't want to venture so far this time of year unless it was absolutely necessary. Surely, that was supposed to be another factor acting to mask the shipment. There were plenty more factors in play and unfortunately, Wolpert had time to consider them all.

Finally, after hours of waiting and considering, he spotted a hint of movement to the north. Several stage-coaches headed toward the river at a quick pace and had yet to crest the rise in front of them. Wolpert went to his saddlebags and removed a set of field glasses to get a better look. While the other men sent signals up and down the line, he climbed into his saddle and rode to the spot where Burt was waiting.

"There's more men with them than we thought," Wolpert shouted as he approached Burt.

The gang's leader motioned for Wolpert to hide him-self, and when the lawman didn't budge, he hopped to his feet and snarled, "I don't care how many there are! We got surprise on our side and you'll ruin it if you parade up and down this river!"

"They're ready for an attack. They've got men flank-ing the coaches on either side. Take a look for yourself."

Burt caught the field glasses Wolpert tossed to him and took a gander through them. "Damn it," he grunted.

"Those men are ready for someone to come at them. If we do that, we'll just play into their hands and proba-bly won't live long enough to regret it."

"You got any ideas?"

"Sure do."

The coaches had disappeared behind the rise by the time Wolpert rode to Juan's spot. He lay on his belly with a rifle at his shoulder. When Wolpert was close enough to hear him, Juan asked, "What's got you so riled up?"

"Haven't you seen the men riding alongside those coaches?"

"Yeah."

"What about the men coming up behind us to the south?"

Juan rolled onto his side and took a look behind him. "I don't see any riders from the south."

"Well, they're there. Burt saw 'em too and he wants to go about this a different way."

Juan got to his knees so he could make himself more visible to the man at the middle of the line. Burt was already looking back at him and signaled that new orders were coming. It was a simple set of waves using both arms, but it was all Juan needed to see before shifting his focus back to Wolpert. "What's the new plan?"

"Remember how I got you fellas into Dog Creek Jail?"

"Aw, hell. Not that again!"

"Those men riding with the stagecoaches sure ain't there to keep the drivers company. They're armed and they've got position on us from two different directions."

"How the hell did that happen?" Juan snapped. "Did they know we'd be here?"

"We'll figure that out later. Right now, Burt and I want to finish this job without getting slaughtered in a cross fire. If we let that stage go, we won't get another chance."

"If they know we're here, how do we know the shipment wasn't moved to a different stage?"

"That's a good point," Wolpert said with exasperation tugging at the edges of his voice. "Why don't you go ask Burt what he thinks? Maybe we can hold a nice little committee. And if those armed guards get here before then, we can ask them what they think!"

"No need to get lippy. What would you have me do?"

"You got rope along with the rest of your gear?"

"Yes."

"I'll take that and you take these."

When Wolpert tossed him a pair of handcuffs, Juan looked at them with contempt. "What're those for?"

"They're for you. Put them on."

Any other time, and Wolpert wouldn't have expected an outlaw to entertain that idea unless he was being held at gunpoint. But after the ruse of being taken in to Dog Creek worked out well enough for them to retrieve Eddie and the other prisoners, the notion wasn't such a strange one. It fell along similar lines of army training. If you got a man used to peculiar circumstances, he was more apt to follow through with even more peculiar ones when asked again. Their time spent in Lester was a far cry from army training, but Wolpert hoped it had been enough to smooth the road for him now.

Juan picked up the handcuffs and cinched one of them around his wrist. It took some maneuvering, but he got the other one on as well. "What are you doing with the rope?"

"Tying up the rest of the men."

"So those Wells Fargo guards think you already caught us, eh?"

"Just like Dog Creek," Wolpert replied with a mischievous grin. "I'll even flag them down, show them my badge and convince them you men are all wrapped up prettier than Christmas morning. And once they let their guard down, we all spring a trap and take down the lot of them without a fuss."

"What happens when they disarm us?" Juan asked. "Is that when we jump?"

"No, because you'll already be disarmed," Wolpert said as he stepped up to take the pistol from Juan's holster. "Before you get your knickers in a twist, I'm going to bury the pistol five paces behind you." As Wolpert turned and walked the paces, he used the heel of his boot to loosen up some of the cold dirt, dropped the gun into it and pushed enough of the dirt back to cover the gun. He then turned around and walked back to Juan. "I'm tossing your rifle over in that same direction, but I doubt you'll need it. When Burt or I give the signal, those guards will be close enough for you to swat the backs of their heads."

"I don't like this," Juan said. "And neither will anyone else."

"Well, Burt doesn't like it that someone sent word ahead to Wells Fargo about us being here, but we all got our crosses to bear. Just do your best to get the job done, because if we don't come out of this with what we came for, those Wells Fargo men won't be the only ones bleeding."

Wolpert didn't need to bluff when he said that. Those words were painfully true and every last one of the outlaws knew it. After finishing up with Juan, Wolpert paid a visit to each member of the gang. He got a system down fairly quickly and once the men could see their partners had already agreed to act as prisoners one more time, it was easier to get the next fellow to fall in line. Once again, Wolpert was reminded of his army days where orders being passed along from higher up the chain were obeyed no matter how ridiculous they seemed. Those outlaws weren't fighting for their country or common man, but they were still soldiers taking orders. And, like any other soldier at the onset of a battle, they knew disobeying an order could get them shot quicker than if they charged a fortified position.

When the stagecoaches came over the rise, Wolpert had all but two men tied or shackled with their guns buried a few paces away from them. He'd just finished tying Ben's hands together when the riders approaching from the south quickened their pace to thunder directly at the outlaws.

"I'm taking your gun," Wolpert said in a rush.

Ben shook his head and struggled against the ropes. "The hell you are! I'll be defenseless."

"And you won't look like a proper prisoner if you're armed." Not waiting for permission, Wolpert reached out to grab the gun from Ben's holster. When the outlaw started to protest even harder, Wolpert cracked the side of the pistol against the side of Ben's head.

The outlaw dropped like a rock. Wolpert tucked the gun away and hurried over to where Burt was waiting. When he drew his horse to a stop, Wolpert stayed in his saddle and said, "They're not happy about it, but it's done."

"Why are they all just sitting there?" Burt asked anxiously. "Didn't you tell them to get their rifles ready and pick them guards off?"

"Nope. Different plan."

Burt's eyes narrowed. If he'd glared at Wolpert any harder, steam might have risen from his tear ducts. "Who said anything about a different plan? Those guards will be on us any second." As he spoke, Burt looked to the south where the riders had been approaching. While the silhouettes could still be seen, they weren't in the same spot as before. They'd spread out and weren't as close as he'd expected. "They're slowing down," he snarled.

"Probably because they know what they're up against."

"Do I have to ask how they'd know something like this?"

"Probably not."

"You son of a bitch. I knew I shouldn't have trusted you."

"Then why did you?" Wolpert asked. "Probably for the same reason that I took your blood money and looked the other way for so long where the law was concerned. Because it was the easiest method to put some money in our pockets."

"So you set this up?"

"Yeah."

"That's a long way to go just to get to me," Burt said through gritted teeth. His hand drifted to his holster and lingered within an inch of his .44.

Wolpert saw the movement but didn't react to it just yet. His Cavalry pistol was where it always was and he knew he could get to it at a moment's notice. "This isn't about you, Burt. And it's not about the rest of your gang either."

The stagecoaches were approaching at a steady pace that brought them over the rise and at the edge of rifle range. It would take a bit longer for the plodding wagons to get close enough to be hit by a bullet, and the horsemen accompanying them rode about only twenty yards ahead of the line.

"If this ain't about me, then why turn on men who trusted you?" Burt asked.

"Because it's something I should do."

"Says who?"

Without a word, Wolpert tapped the piece of tin hanging from his shirt.

"And what about them?" Burt asked while nodding toward the line of men extending on either side of him. "If you think you convinced them to turn on me, you're in for a nasty surprise."

"They're disarmed and tied up. Soon, they'll be in the hands of those men out there." Motioning to the south, Wolpert added, "They're Texas Rangers. Or possibly U.S. Marshals. Either way, they're higher law than me."

"This is a joke," Burt spat. "You're a joke. Or maybe you're just a fool. Better yet, I think you're just trying to wrest this gang away from me. Why the hell else would you risk your neck to break those men outta Dog Creek just so you could send 'em back again? I heard about what happened. There ain't no way to fake that sort of news."

"Exactly. And if I had tried, you would have gone into hiding and wouldn't be found again for a good, long while. You'd come up with some other plan and start this whole mess over again so I couldn't do a thing about it. If those men play their cards right and don't lose their heads, they'll serve their purpose by fattening up the goose I intend on bringing to market."

Burt started pacing as his hand dropped to his pistol. He didn't draw the gun, but gripped it as if he might crush the weapon within his grasp. "You're not making a lick of sense."

"I wouldn't expect you to understand even if I explained it to you."

"So what do you expect me to do? Just give myself up?"

"No," Wolpert replied. "That would be too easy. I would expect you to either try to shoot your way out of this or run. Since I'd only have one chance to do this properly, I needed you to commit yourself to the point where you couldn't run. There is the chance that you might do something I wouldn't expect, though. You could hand over your gun and take your punishment like a man."

"Just like you, huh? After all those years of takin' bribes, snappin' the law in half and doin' whatever you please, you think one good deed will set it all straight?"

"I'm not going anywhere. When this is over, I'll be judged like everyone else. The big difference between you and me is that I'll own up to what I've done. My guess is that, even if you were standing in front of your Maker, you'd still try to con your way through without admitting to all of your sins."

To Wolpert's surprise, a good portion of the anger in Burt's eyes faded away. He gazed wistfully at the stagecoaches, turned back to the men coming from the south and then looked at his gang. Some of them were struggling to get up, but most were crawling a few paces to dig in the dirt. "I suppose you're right about that, Zeke. When you know you're bound for hell, it never hurts to try and sneak a little glimpse at heaven."

"Trust me," Wolpert sighed. "It hurts."

"You really mucked this up good for me, huh?"

"Yeah."

Burt squared his shoulders to Wolpert and took a few cautious steps back. "I ain't gonna run and I sure ain't gonna hand myself over to some double-crossin' back-stabber like you."

"Didn't think so."

"Still, it's been good workin' with you."

Wolpert twitched at the earnestness in that remark. He hadn't seen it coming and didn't know what to say about it.

When Burt took his next step back, he dropped to one knee and drew his .44 in a smooth motion.

Wolpert reacted quickly, but shifted into a sideways stance that narrowed the target he presented to the other man. The Cavalry pistol was a comforting weight in his hand and he barely had to think about how to make the old companion sing. His thumb pulled back the hammer and his finger tightened around the trigger a fraction of a second before he felt the mechanism click into place. His ears barely took in the sound of Burt's gunshot, since his mind was entirely focused on his own actions. When the pistol went off, Wolpert felt it all the way down to his left foot.

No. That was something else.

Burt fired again, sending a round hissing past Wolpert's ear like an angry whisper.

Wolpert thumbed the hammer a second time and fired, punching a hole through Burt's rib cage. The kick of the bullet spun the outlaw around to show Wolpert a messy hole in his side. Despite being through-and-through, the wound was far enough out to one side that it barely cut through any meat. Burt snarled through the pain and fired again. He wasn't hitting his mark, but got close enough to send Wolpert to the ground.

Once he was down, the lawman rolled to his left and squeezed off another shot just to keep Burt from getting his confidence back. He saw his chance when Burt pulled himself laboriously to his feet. Just as the outlaw was regaining his posture, Wolpert aimed low and squeezed his trigger.

The bullet caught Burt in the shin and dropped him into a screaming pile. He thrashed about with such force that he nearly popped himself back onto both feet again. Instead, he fell over in the opposite direction and sat up to take proper aim. "I may not be getting what I want," he snarled, "but neither will you. I'll see to that, by God!"

Shots crackled on either side of Wolpert's head as a few of the gang members found holdout pistols that Wolpert had been too busy to take away. Their little guns didn't do anything but draw unwanted attention as the gunmen on either side returned fire.

"Give 'em hell, boys!" Burt shouted. "Zeke sold us out! Drop him along with the rest of 'em! *All of 'em!*"

Burt's voice was obscured by the gunshots echoing through the air. Their intent wasn't lost, however, as the gang members struggled to put up a fight against their restraints. Even if they could hold their arms in front of them, working a pistol correctly wouldn't be easy.

Pain seeped through Wolpert's lower half like water soaking through his clothes. A gust of wind brought the acrid scent of burnt powder to his nose, touching his leg with an icy hand that curled his toes within his boots. Sucking in a hard breath, Wolpert grabbed at a spot below his knee and found it to be soaked with the warm wetness of his own blood. One of Burt's shots had caught him in the shin and just keeping on his feet would be a trial he might not be able to win.

Burt himself was the one who saw him through the

pain. The outlaw screamed something at Wolpert and raised his gun for a shot that was most definitely going to be fatal. The range was too short for it to be anything else.

It wasn't the first time Wolpert had known he was about to be sent into oblivion. He'd faced similar moments when he rode with his old regiment or got on the bad side of a bad deal as a lawman. Things tended to get real quiet and real still, as though the world was giving him a moment to decide how he should proceed. Very sporting for such a wicked thing.

Wolpert took his moment to straighten his arm and let it do its duty. His hand steadied for the space of a heartbeat. His Cavalry pistol settled into its proper angle and he squeezed his trigger. He didn't recall thumbing back the hammer of the old single-action pistol, but he must have done it because the reliable weapon barked half a second before Burt's. The single bullet cut through the air between them, punched through Burt's head and knocked him back. Burt's gun went off as his eyes gazed upon the heavens with a longing that remained etched onto his face for his last few seconds.

Wolpert's senses came back to him in a rush, filling him with the chaos of his surroundings. The stagecoaches stayed behind as riders from north and south closed in to trap the outlaws in a pincer maneuver that was taught to every cadet in military school. Wolpert's instincts forced him onward despite the pain coursing through his leg. Bones scraped against bone, digging into muscle with every step, but he kept on.

He ran and stumbled as bullets ripped past him going in every direction. When he ran past Eddie, the former prisoner shouted and then took a shot at him.

One of the approaching riders fired at them both, but Eddie wasn't paying the others any mind. "You really killed us all? Coward!" He fired at Wolpert again, but soon had to contend with gunmen shouting for everyone to lay down their arms.

Wolpert made it to Juan, dropped to one knee and fell over. As soon as he heard the wet crunch fill his ears, he knew he wouldn't be getting up again on his own. "Here," he said as he tossed the keys to the shackles. "Take these and free yourself. You and Cade and Tom need to get out of here."

Juan was in the middle of digging up his gun when he scrambled for the keys. "Have a change of heart?" he said, sneering. "Or is this another trick?"

"No trick. I never intended for you three to be taken in." Wolpert closed his eyes and forced them open while he still could. The pain was ebbing and a heaviness settled upon him. It wasn't the first time he'd felt it. Unlike those other scrapes with death, he found it comforting. "All right. Maybe I did have a change of heart. You three saved my life. You're good partners and I can't . . . can't just let you get taken with them others."

Bound by shackles meant for a man's ankles, Juan struggled within the cumbersome restraints before getting the key to fit. "I ought to kill you right now."

"Go on and do it if you're inclined. Lord knows I deserve it."

The shackles came loose and fell heavily to the ground. Wolpert's eyes were open, but he could hear the world better than he could see it. Everything felt far away, but the sky seemed to squat down and stare him directly in the face. A rough hand closed around his chin and twisted his head around until he was looking at Juan.

"What're you . . . waiting for?"

"It's too late, you damned fool," Juan told him. "Them guards are swarming us all."

"The shooting stopped."

"Looks like Eddie's hurt. Ben's dead and Tom's wounded. What about Burt?"

"Gone."

Juan shook his head, let go of Wolpert and sat down with a resigned thump. "Is this your doing?"

"More or . . . less. I arranged for . . . the law to be notified. The real law."

"Great plan. You know they'll put you away too. If you think your name as a lawman holds any water with these fellas, you've got a real surprise coming."

"I ain't no lawman." Although Wolpert could move his arm, it felt more as if it were being swung on the end of a string. He grabbed his badge, tore it from his shirt and handed it over. "You are. The others . . . they'll let you go. Just say the other two are your deputies and you . . . arranged this whole thing."

"Arranged it? What—" Dropping his voice to a whisper as the riders approached, Juan hissed, "What am I supposed to say to convince them of that?"

"Just tell 'em how you brought everyone here for the big fall. Keep 'em occupied long enough to get to some horses and ride the hell away. That too complicated for you?"

Juan sighed. "You were playing up to this the whole time?"

"To tell the truth . . . I could'a set this whole thing up better. Maybe I should'a thought it through a bit more before I got started."

When Juan looked down at him, Wolpert could see

stark disbelief in the outlaw's face. The expression froze there for a few seconds until the only thing left for him to do was laugh as he pinned the badge to his shirt. "I'm gonna try to get you to a doctor."

"Don't bother with that. I can lie here and finally let it all go. No regrets." Wolpert's face twitched as if he'd been kicked in the messy wound in his leg. It hurt to move his eyelids, but he peeled them open anyway.

"Looks like you may still have a regret or two."

"Yeah. Just one."

"What's that?"

The beating of hooves rumbled through the ground under Wolpert's back. Men shouted down from their saddles, but all of that was dimming into an oddly comforting hum at the back of Wolpert's head.

"I should . . . should have had supper with Lucy."

Chapter 25

Fort Concho, Texas
Three months later

Wolpert didn't die.

That much was a pleasant surprise. The injury to his leg had been grievous and painful enough to make him think he was passing on, when in truth he was merely passing out. Then again, pleasant wouldn't have been his assessment of what happened after the combined forces of a Wells Fargo militia and Texas Rangers swept up the remains of Burt Sampil's gang.

For the days immediately following the short-lived gun battle, Wolpert was in and out of consciousness. He recalled being draped over the back of a horse and then bounced in the back of a wagon. He didn't know if he was riding along with Burt's prized box of keys or on a pile of potato sacks, but he was handed over to the Rangers with the rest of the survivors. Both of them. Malone screeched like a stuck pig and Eddie cursed Wolpert's name with such frequency that the foul words became part of his dreams as the doctor started working on his leg. There was talk of hacking it off below the knee, but that would have cost the doctor too much of his valuable time. It was still attached when Wolpert woke up again.

As soon as he was able to leave the doctor's care, Wolpert was handed over to a pair of uniformed soldiers and marched across a well-tended patch of grass in the middle of Fort Concho. He'd never been there before, but one stockade was pretty much like any other. When he was tossed inside this one, he was in the company of some Indians who were too tired to give him much trouble. One of them never stopped pacing at the back of his cell and the other put up a fuss until Wolpert was allowed to use a stick as a cane so he could walk on his own. White River was that one's name. He was taken from the cell a few weeks after that and Wolpert never saw him again.

Once that small bit of companionship was gone, all Wolpert could do was sit in a corner, watch the sunlight pass across his window, feel the pain move through his leg like a restless critter trapped under his skin and wait for the noose to be fitted around his neck.

Days passed.

Weeks slipped away.

The wind grew a bit warmer as it blew in between the bars and still no death sentence was handed down.

By the time someone came for him in what had to have been the first bit of spring, Wolpert was ready for whatever was coming.

"Get up," the guard told him. He was a thick man with a thicker mustache who kept a club hanging on a leather cord from a hook on his belt. The muscles on his arms were so prominent that he seemed more than capable of ripping the cell door from its hinges if the lock didn't give way. Still, he didn't take pleasure in kicking a gimp dog and always gave Wolpert a little extra time to move before becoming cross.

"What's the occasion? Supper's not for a few hours."

"You made me wait this long," replied a voice that was much sweeter than the guard's. "I suppose a few more hours won't hurt."

If Wolpert was able, he would have jumped up from his cot. Since he wasn't allowed to have his cane or anything else to support his weight while in his cell, he hobbled over to the bars as best he could. "It really is you, Lucy," he sighed. "Thought I was hearing things."

"I've heard plenty of things that I didn't believe," she said. "Until some of those outlandish promises were actually kept."

"So Dominick got my message to you? And you contacted Wells Fargo?"

"They doubled their guard, didn't they?"

"And then some," Wolpert chuckled.

"You were right about them being generous when it came to paying for good information. Within a week after I passed that word on to them about the ambush waiting for that shipment, a man came all the way out to Sedley to pay me a visit. He told me some of the robbers got away, but they got a man they'd been after for some time and it was all thanks to my guidance. Paid me enough to settle my brothers' debts and pull up stakes."

"You're not running the stable in Sedley anymore?"

"No," she said with a little shake of her head. "Got a

nice little spread in Missouri. Some hogs. A few head of cattle and plenty of horses."

"Sounds nice."

More than that, she looked nicer. Lucy's face was a bit rounder than before and showed signs of a more contented way of life. Her smile was brighter than he remembered. Not that he could ever forget a smile like that. Thinking he'd never set eyes on that beautiful sight again, Wolpert had done his best to put the thought of her deep down in a place where it could give him some brightness without torturing him with something he'd never have.

"Why are you here, Lucy?" he asked.

"A woman named Emma came all the way from Chimney Lake to see me. This was just after I'd been informed of how much money Wells Fargo was sending my way. She told me where you'd gone and who you'd gone there with. Between her resourcefulness and my funds, we uncovered quite a lot of stories about a jail getting cracked open, vigilantes and all sorts of excitement."

"Excitement is hardly the word I'd use."

"Well, I can't think of a better one. The Wells Fargo men told me a sheriff and his two deputies rode away while the smoke was still in the air after Burt Sampil was killed, and they were never heard from again. I figured that was you."

"Anyone heard from those lawmen?" Wolpert asked cautiously.

"Not that I know of."

"Good."

"When we didn't hear from you after so much time

had gone by, folks assumed you were killed. Jane declared herself a widow and caught Dominick's eye. When I left town, she was already strutting around like a peacock in a fancy new dress. No matter what anyone said, I knew you weren't one of those lawmen that ran away."

"Why?"

"Because," she said without pause, "you wanted to come back to me. I could see that much in your eyes before you left. For a while, I thought I may have just been playing it up in my head, but I wasn't. I can see that now." A bit of color flushed through her cheeks when she added, "At any rate, I kept pressing the matter with Wells Fargo and one of their guards told me that the prisoners were brought here. I arrived late last night. It took some doing to get a chance to see you and I prayed you were the one that was still here. The other two were shipped back to some other jail in Kansas."

"Dog Creek."

"That's the one." She cocked her head and looked at his bandaged leg. "I'm sorry you were hurt, but glad if that's what kept you here."

"And you came all the way down to Texas just to see me?"

"No. I came all the way down to Texas to get you out of here."

"I doubt that'll happen," Wolpert grunted.

"After the price I paid, it'll happen right quick or heads will roll." Seeing the suspicious glint in his eye, Lucy shrugged and told him, "Emma knew the names of a few men who might be receptive to some generous donations."

"You bribed someone?"

"It's only fitting, wouldn't you say?"

Wolpert shook his head and rested his head against the bars. "I can't be a part of that anymore. Not after all I already done."

"You're not a part of it, Zeke. It was my doing. Besides, the men here don't know what to do with you. Do you even know why you're being held in this cage? You were suspected of being part of Burt's gang, but all they got as proof was the word of them other prisoners. Those lawmen that got away spoke highly of you, but they're nowhere to be found. Seems that nobody else has mustered up enough proof to hang you for anything."

"There's got to be enough to keep me locked up."

"Sure," she said. "But there's also the word of some very insistent Texas Rangers who swear they saw you kill Burt Sampil single-handedly."

"How much were those men paid for that favor?" Wolpert asked.

"Not a cent. I wouldn't even try to hand a bribe to one of those men."

"Yeah, Texas Rangers don't like that too much."

"All it took was a little sweet talk and some incentive to grease the wheels," Lucy insisted. "You'll never convince anyone to pin another badge on you and that leg will give you troubles for the rest of your days. You may even have a price on your head thanks to that business Emma told me about, so I'd say you've paid your penance. How about you come back to Missouri so everyone can forget about you?"

"Will you cook me that supper you offered?"

"That one and a thousand more. Emma told me about the little revelation you had. It wasn't until you were gone for so long that I realized I'd had one too."

Wolpert looked over to the guard and found the big fellow nodding back at him. He unlocked the cell door and muttered, "If you're leavin', the sergeant says it better be quick. The captain's due back within the hour."

At that moment, the guard reminded him of Tom. Despite the circumstances of their introduction and the purpose for them becoming partners, those three outlaws would be remembered as friends. It didn't even matter what they thought of him at the end. He couldn't bring himself to sacrifice those three for his own gain and he couldn't dredge it up in him to do the same for this one. "What are you going to tell the captain when he finds out I'm gone?"

"I'll think of something," the guard said with enough confidence to let Wolpert know it wouldn't be the first time he'd covered similar tracks out of that stockade. "Would you rather stay here?"

"No," Wolpert said as he reached out to touch the face he'd been dreaming about through the duration of that long, harsh winter. "I sure wouldn't."

Don't miss another exciting Western adventure
in the *USA Today* bestselling series!

THE BURNING RANGE

A Ralph Compton Novel by Joseph A. West
coming from Signet in December 2010.

When a gambler is trying to outrun a losing streak, he sometimes forgets the rules. That night Chauncey Drake misplaced two of them: He was playing poker under a blood moon, always unlucky for him, and he'd stubbed his toe on a dead man.

In more prosperous times he'd have sat out the unlucky night in his hotel room with a bottle and a couple of whores who were a credit to their profession.

But these were not thriving days for Chauncey Drake.

And he suspected that harder times were coming down.

"The game," Peter J. Grapples said, "is poker."

The eyes peering over the top of the banker's glasses nudged Drake gently. A man doesn't push a known and named gunfighter too much.

"I'm studying on it," Drake said, staring at his cards.

"It's not difficult, Mr. Drake," Grapples said. "I raised you ten."

"Man's got the right to take his time," Ed Winslow said.

"But not all night," Grapples said.

Winslow nodded. "No, not all night. Truer words were never spoken."

Drake studied his cards. Aces and eights, a dead man's hand.

Nothing about the damned night boded well.

Grapples wasn't pushing him hard and Drake understood why.

But what the banker didn't know was that Drake's blue Colt currently reposed in Sy Goldberg's Pawn and Mercantile on Second Street, tagged, bagged and pigeonholed.

In return for the revolver, Drake had received, from Sy's own hand, as befitted a regular customer, a ticket and ten dollars.

The ten dollars now sat in front of him and there was not another thin dime in his poke.

Ed Winslow's eyes moved to the saloon window. "Blackest night I've seen in a spell," he said. He cocked his head, listening into the darkness. "Coyotes are hunting close."

"There's blood on the moon," Grapples said.

"Unlucky for some," Winslow said.

"Maybe for you, Mr. Drake," Grapples said, smiling. "Or me."

The banker's smile faded and he sighed. "The game is poker," he said for a second time.

Drake made up his mind.

He pushed his ten into the pot. "I call." He spread his cards. "Got me a dead man."

"Too little and way too late," Grapples said. He tossed his hand onto the table. "Three ladies."

"Unlucky for some," Winslow said.

Grapples gathered up the deck. "Shall I deal?"

Drake shook his head. "I'm done."

He rose to his feet, a slim man of medium height, dressed in patched and faded gambler's finery.

"Another time, perhaps," Grapples said.

Drake nodded. "Yes, another time."

He walked to the door and stepped outside.

The blood moon was rising, but for the moment it had spiked itself on a pine at the edge of town. The night gathered close, and along First Street, kerosene lamps glowed red in the darkness and smoked like the cinders of fallen stars.

Drake found a ragged cigar stub in the pocket of his frock coat, then took a seat in one of the rockers scattered along the saloon porch.

Across the street, outside the marshal's office, the dead man was propped up in a pine coffin, illuminated by the railroad lantern on the boardwalk in front of him.

The man's face was as blue as marble, his eye sockets pooled in shadow and he showed his teeth in a death grimace.

The reason for the grotesque display was that when Marshal Dub Halloran killed a man in the line of duty, justice had to be seen, by the whole town, to be done.

The dead man had been a small-time thief and all-round nuisance by the name of Bates or Baxter—nobody knew for sure.

He'd stolen a side of bacon from a farmer's smokehouse and Halloran had tracked the man to a box canyon north of the farm. Bates or Baxter had promptly surrendered, but, for convenience' sake, the marshal had gunned him where he stood and dragged the body back to town behind his horse.

Nobody much cared, Sy Goldberg pretty much summing up the town's attitude when he declared that the man's death was a case of "good riddance to bad rubbish."

Drake didn't have much sympathy for Bates or Baxter either.

On his way to the saloon, he'd tripped over the man's coffin, and everybody knew how unlucky that was.

Drake took a last draw on his cigar and ground it out under his shoe.

He was busted. Broke. Destitute. Penniless. And it hurt.

He'd sold his horse a while back, then his watch, then his diamond stickpin, then his emerald ring. Sy Goldberg had his Colt and the shoulder holster that went with it.

Farther down the street he saw the lights of the Bon-Ton Hotel. He couldn't go back there until the manager left for the night. The man was pressing Drake for money and had threatened to padlock his room if the eighty dollars he owed was not paid "instanter or even sooner."

A six-month losing streak had exacted its toll, and that night Drake knew he had scraped the bottom of his last barrel.

He rose to his feet and stepped to the edge of the boardwalk.

A cowboy walked past, leading his horse, looking neither left nor right. Then one of the respectable matrons of the town followed behind him. Drake touched his hat to the woman, but she lifted her nose and ignored him.

Despite his gloom, Drake smiled. Could people sense

poverty? Or did they not care to look at a man who was wrapped up in his own gloomy shadow?

Round as a coin, the moon had broken free of the pines and was riding high in the sky, spawning crouching shadows all over town. Out in the darkness coyotes yipped, their fur rippled by a rising wind.

Drake was seized by the urge to flee, to steal a horse and outrun the tiger. But flee to where? To yet another hick town in the middle of nowhere where no one would be glad at his coming or sad at his leaving?

From the frying pan into the fire.

"Evening, Chauncey. Still prospering, I see, huh?"

Drake turned. Savannah Swan stood on the boardwalk, a smile on her scarlet lips.

"That obvious?"

"I'd say. You've mended them britches you're wearing so many times, they look like Grandma's patchwork quilt."

Drake said nothing and Savannah said: "Still trying to buck a losing deck?"

"That sums it up."

"Let me buy you a drink."

"I'll pass." That sounded harsh and Drake sweetened it with a smile. "How's business?"

The woman shrugged. "Tuesday night. It's slow. All the married ones are to home with their skinny wives and the drovers don't get paid till Friday."

"Things are tough all over," Drake said.

Savannah ignored that and said: "Why don't you talk to Loretta?"

Drake shook his head. "Loretta ain't exactly a whore with a heart of gold. She stung me on my ring."

"She likes you, Chauncey. And I know she's holding. Got a big roll."

"Smooth that out for me."

"Like I said, she's holding. Ask her for a grubstake."

"I've got no, what they call, collateral. Loretta has my ring and Sy Goldberg has my gun."

"So? You ain't going anyplace, are you?"

"Loretta is holding, you say?"

"Big roll."

"I'll study on it."

Savannah smiled. "Don't study on it too long. She's leaving town tomorrow to visit a sick aunt—be gone for a week."

"She's home right now?"

"Washing her hair. She's had no gentlemen callers and isn't expecting any."

"Maybe I'll go talk to her."

Savannah smiled, looking over Drake's shabby clothes and down-at-heel shoes. "Maybe you should."

She gathered her shawl around her naked shoulders. "I got to get down to the Alamo. There will be no customers, but Hank Bowman expects me to be there on the chance that somebody gets horny."

The woman glanced at the sky and shivered as she walked away. "Blood on the moon, Chauncey," she said over her shoulder.

"Yeah, I noticed that," Drake said.